Dropp

forward.

"Peter!"

In slow motion he turned toward her. With one fluid movement, she shoved Peter out of the way and deflected the card out of his hands. Unbalanced, he sprawled to the floor. A small explosion ravaged the quiet of the office. Something sharp slashed the skin of her cheek.

Adria turned to Peter. "Are you all right?"

He stood and brushed shards of cardboard from his perfectly pressed pants. His cheek twitched. His stony gaze moved slowly to her face. "Who are you?"

"Adria Caskey."

He crossed his arms over his chest. "*What* are you? Because you sure as hell aren't just a secretary."

Dear Reader,

Silhouette Bombshell is dedicated to bringing you the best in savvy heroines, fast action, high stakes and chilling suspense. We're raising the bar on action adventure to create an exhilarating reading experience that you'll remember long after the final pages!

Take some personal time with *Personal Enemy* by Sylvie Kurtz. An executive bodyguard plans the perfect revenge against the man who helped to destroy her family—but when they're both attacked, she's forced to work *for* him before she can work against him!

Don't miss *Contact* by Evelyn Vaughn, the latest adventure in the ATHENA FORCE continuity series. Faith Corbett uses her extrasenory skills to help the police solve crimes, but she's always contacted them anonymously. Until a serial killer begins hunting psychics, and Faith must reveal herself to one disbelieving detective....

Meet the remarkable women of author Cindy Dees's *The Medusa Project*. These Special Forces officers-in-training are set up to fail, but for team leader Vanessa Blake, quitting is not an option—especially when both international security and their tough-as-nails trainer's life is at stake!

And provocative twists abound in *The Spy Wore Red* by Wendy Rosnau. Agent Nadja Stefn is hand-picked for a mission to terminate an assassin—but getting her man means working with a partner from whom she must hide a dangerous personal agenda....

Please send your comments to me c/o Silhouette Books, 233 Broadway, Suite 1001, New York, NY 10279.

Best wishes,

Natashya Wilson
Associate Senior Editor, Silhouette Bombshell

Please address questions and book requests to:
Silhouette Reader Service
U.S.: 3010 Walden Ave., P.O. Box 1325, Buffalo, NY 14269
Canadian: P.O. Box 609, Fort Erie, Ont. L2A 5X3

PERSONAL ENEMY

SYLVIE KURTZ

Silhouette®

BOMBSHELL™

Published by Silhouette Books

America's Publisher of Contemporary Romance

SILHOUETTE BOOKS

ISBN 0-373-51343-7

PERSONAL ENEMY

Copyright © 2005 by Sylvie Kurtz

This edition published by arrangement with Harlequin Books S.A.

® and TM are trademarks of Harlequin Books S.A., used under license. Trademarks indicated with ® are registered in the United States Patent and Trademark Office, the Canadian Trade Marks Office and in other countries.

Visit Silhouette Books at www.eHarlequin.com

Printed in U.S.A.

SYLVIE KURTZ

While flying eight-hours solo cross-country in a Piper Arrow with only the airplane's crackling radio and a large bag of M&M's for company, Sylvie Kurtz realized a pilot's life wasn't for her. The stories zooming in and out of her mind proved more entertaining than the flight itself. Not a quitter, she finished her pilot's course and earned her commercial license and instrument rating.

Since then, she has traded in her wings for a keyboard at which she lets her imagination soar to create fictional adventures that explore the power of love and the thrill of suspense. When not writing, she enjoys being outdoors with her husband and two children, quilt-making, photography and reading whatever catches her interest.

You can write to Sylvie at P.O. Box 702, Milford, NH 03055 and visit her Web site at www.sylviekurtz.com

For Chuck—for the hours of online
research to keep things real.
And for Axel—for the help with brainstorming
action scenes. Watching all those movies
had to pay off someday.
☺

Writing this book has made me realize how
technologically challenged I am. Thank you to everyone
who helped me understand the details.

Francis Langlois and Kerry Fosher
for their automotive help

Jean Kurtz and the NHRWA loop
for their hospital and nursing help

Ed Lecius of the Nashua Police Department
and Lawrence Pickett, firefighter

Prologue

Oahu, Hawaii

Lightning cracked the black of night and made the rain look like dragon tongues licking at the bedroom window. Daddy said the rain couldn't hurt her; she was safe inside the house. But Adria Kaholo didn't like it, especially when the bangers came. And bangers always came after lightning. She brought her pink blankie up to her mouth and sucked on the satin corner.

The thunder came, low and growling, like an angry beast. She squeezed her eyes tight, but inside her lids, the black dragon still spit fire. She tried to shut her ears, but couldn't. The thunder came again, closer this time.

I'm a big girl now. I'm six. I'm not afraid.

The bangs came closer. Deeper. Louder.

Then lightning ripped the sky and thunder rocked

the house. She scrambled from beneath the covers and raced into her parents' room, dragging her blankie behind.

"Ma-ma, I'm sca-red!"

Without a word, her mother lifted the sheet, inviting her daughter in. Adria snuggled close to her mother's warmth. The song of Mama's heart against her back lulled her. The sweet flower smell of Mama's skin made the monsters go away. The thunder lost its growl, the lightning its power.

Safe in her mother's arms, on the edge of sleep, Adria thought nothing of the crash until her mother's body stiffened.

"What was that, Lance?" her mother whispered quick like a knife chopping veggies.

"Probably just the storm," her father said. "Stay here. I'll go check."

As her father's weight eased off the bed with a squeak, her mother drew her closer. Adria wrapped her blankie's frayed edge around her thumb and stuck it in her mouth.

She waited. Daddy told her he was her knight. Nothing could happen to her while he was around. He'd fight dragons and slay giants. He was Sir Lancelot and she was his princess. The blanket eased out of her mouth. Daddy would make it all right.

Two pops burst from the living room, echoing like thunder in their small house. Then slow, sneaky footsteps on crushed glass.

"Lance?" Her mother's voice shook. She gathered Adria in her arms and slipped out the far edge of the bed.

Silence, except for the eerie whistling of wet wind through broken glass. Silence, heavy like being buried in the sand, except this was no fun.

"No, oh, no!" Mama tightened her hold on Adria and ran toward the window.

Her mother's heart beat hard and fast against Adria's back. The tight arms around her chest made it hard to breathe. Mama threw open the glass and dropped her into the dark rainy night.

"Mama!" Adria whimpered, lifting her arms to her frightened mother.

"Shh, quiet, *keiki*. Run to Grandpa's. Hurry. It's a race. See if you can beat me there."

Mama's mouth smiled, but her eyes didn't.

"Ma-ma!"

"*Awiwi, keiki.* Hurry!"

Her mother gave her a shove in the direction of Grandpa's house down the beach. But Adria couldn't run. Her legs froze like icicles. Why didn't Mama come with her? Mama knew she didn't like the night.

The thunder rumbled in the distance and everything was wet. Hot tears slid down her cheeks. *Mama said quiet.* Adria stuffed more blanket into her mouth.

On the beach, the waves crashed high and loud, the palm trees whipped about like mad monsters in the wind and shadows swirled all around waiting to swallow her whole. She took shaky steps forward. *Mama! Daddy!* She wanted Mama and Daddy to come with her. She didn't want to race alone in the dark.

Mama screamed. Adria spun toward the window, her heart stopping, then booming inside her. Mama's terrified shriek echoed in the night. Then she cried.

No, no, Mama, no! Don't cry!

Adria ran back to the window. Holding on to the edge, she peered over the sill into the room. One man dragged Mama to the middle of the room. Another man and a boy waited by the door.

"Kill her," the fat one said. The one holding Mama raised a gun to her head.

"Please, no, please…" Mama fought. But the man put the gun snug against her long brown hair.

Pop.

Mama fell back, limp like the rag doll on the dresser in Adria's room.

The blankie, still in her mouth, muffled Adria's shrill of terror.

Mama, Mama, Mama!

Her icy fingers gripped the window, her toes scuffed on the wall's rough surface, but she couldn't climb, the ledge was too high. The man with the gun shoved Mama back onto the bed and left.

The boy's rounded eyes stared at Mama. The fat man grabbed the boy and pulled him along toward the bed.

"Why?" the boy mumbled.

The fat man paused and smiled as he looked at Mama. "This is power, son. These people defied my power. They thought they didn't need my protection. Now they'll serve as an example to the other merchants on the strip. I wanted you to see my power firsthand. Power is everything. Life, nothing. Do you understand?"

The boy nodded, then put a hand over his mouth and gagged. The fat man shook his head in disgust. "Good God, what did I ever do to deserve a gutless brat like you?"

The boy ran toward her. Adria let go of the window's edge and crouched in the nearby hibiscus bush. Rain-heavy leaves soaked her nightgown. She shivered. The boy poked his head through the open window and threw up. When he was finished, their gazes met through the black of the night.

Would he tell the fat man? Would she get popped and fall like Mama?

She waited, shivering. The boy stared.

"I'm sorry," he said finally. She wasn't sure if he was talking to her or the fat man. He wiped his mouth with the back of his hand and disappeared.

She waited still and silent for a long, long time, cold and wet in the noisy dark, afraid they would come back for her. She rocked back and forth in the bush with the hot-pink flowers. Sobs racked her chest. As the sun peeked like peach fire over the ocean, she stirred. When she stood, her legs wobbled. Everything looked hazy through the shimmer of tears.

"Mama! Daddy!" Even when the blankie fell from her mouth, her parents didn't answer.

On bare feet she padded through the wet grass. As she walked through the smashed lanai door, broken glass cut into her soles. Daddy lay in the middle of the living room floor. She knelt beside him and shook his shoulder.

"Daddy, Daddy, wake up!"

But her knight didn't move.

She continued to her parents' room and climbed into bed beside Mama. Mama was so cold. Adria lay down next to her anyway and wrapped her wet blankie around them both. She snuggled into Mama's curves. So cold. She tried to fill her nostrils with Mama's sweet scent, but all she could smell was something yucky in the air. When she put her hand over Mama's heart, it was still.

As Adria closed her eyes and tried to pretend everything was all right, she knew she would never again feel good.

Chapter 1

Stamford, Connecticut

Adria Caskey slid out from the front seat of the aging brown Chevy onto the sidewalk in front of the Dragon, Inc. building. The glass structure glittered under its slick coat of rain—one of a hundred such jewels in this town of glitzy corporate headquarters. But even the gray sky, low clouds and drizzle couldn't quite hide the grim neighborhoods surrounding Stamford; they reflected onto the shiny skyscrapers like carbon flaws in a diamond.

As she swiveled to shut the door, fractious butterflies fluttered in her stomach. Being irresolute wasn't like her. She'd worked hard for her self-confidence. She always got the job done and had a file folder full of letters to prove it. But she wasn't sure honor and revenge mixed well.

Caleb Stuart, her grandfather's friend and a sociology professor on sabbatical from Yale, leaned over from the driver's seat and stared up at her through the open passenger's side window. He was in as dire a need of a good grooming as Norm, the golden retriever sitting in the back seat. Both sets of big, brown eyes were worry personified. "Are you all right?"

Misting rain dewed her hair, her face, her coat, chilling her already-cold insides. How could anything be all right now that her grandfather was gone? "I'm fine."

"You don't have to do this."

"I do." Her well-being depended on it, depended on her confronting the man whose father had killed her parents, destroyed her family and stolen her sense of security. He'd built his empire on blood money and he would soon find out that blood made weak underpinnings.

"Your grandfather would want you to continue his work." Caleb's words panted out in overeager puffs as if he were Norm wanting to play ball.

"It hurts too much."

Caleb's bearded cheek twitched as if he understood the dichotomy of the situation. "But a secretary, Adria?"

"I need a change."

He grabbed her raincoat's sleeve and jostled her hand playfully from side to side. "Then help me finish your grandfather's book."

"Writing is not my best skill." Adria pulled her sleeve free from Caleb's grasp.

He shook his head, flapping the loose skin of his neck. "I'm doing the writing. I need you to help me understand your grandfather's notes."

"I can't. Not now."

He turned his gaze out toward the street. The beard beneath the generous nose was as grizzled as Norm's muzzle. Cars honked up and down the busy avenue. A bus rolled to a screeching stop at the corner, belching diesel fumes when the light turned green once more. "At least keep the business open for a while longer. In case you change your mind."

"No, I have to do this." She leaned in and reached through the window for her soft-sided briefcase. Norm rewarded her with a wet kiss on the hand and a worried whine. "Julie's wrapping things up. She should be done in a week or so. She can help you with your book when she's done."

Caleb's eyebrows rose in an arc. "I really hate to see you do this. Your skills—"

"Are easily replaced."

"No, not the way your grandfather taught you. There's more there. There's—"

"Thank you, Caleb. For all you've done for me. I don't know how I would have gotten through the funeral, these past few months, without you. But this…" Her shoulders hiked up to her ears and she shook her head, digging past the rawness of her grief for words Caleb would hear. "This is something I have to do."

Caleb snuffled a dissent. "He was so proud of you, of the way you'd carry on his legacy. Please, Adria, reconsider."

She didn't answer. What could she say? Caleb saw only one side of her grandfather. He saw the man of honor, the philosophy of being still and moving like a great river, the art of using ounces to deflect pounds. He saw old ways exercised in a modern setting and found it all fascinating. What he didn't see was the deep scar the death of Adria's mother had caused, how her grandfather had wanted to excise the pain, but couldn't get close enough to find the soft underbelly. How could Caleb know when even she hadn't recognized the depth of her grandfather's torment until he'd wrenched his deathbed promise?

"Some day," she said, tamping the painful memories back into a dark corner of her mind, "I'll tell you a story and you'll understand."

With a sigh, Caleb slid back to the driver's seat and rammed the cranky transmission into gear. Norm hopped into the front seat Adria had occupied and hung his head over the window's edge, his pink tongue lolling. "If you change your mind, I'm here for you."

She scratched Norm's ear. "Thank you."

"I have some banking business to take care of. I'll be back to pick you up in an hour."

Holding her briefcase in front of her, she nodded. As the Chevy nosed its way into the traffic, she turned toward the building. The menacing growl of thunder, like a beast ready to pounce, rumbled in the distance. She shrugged away the shiver of fear. *This is a job like any other. You've been tasked with finding Peter Dragon's weakness and bringing down his empire. You can do this.*

A cottony cloud of memory sponged at her mind, floating her back in time to her grandfather's training sessions.

"What do you hear, keiki?" Her grandfather's gentle voice filled her mind. The Hawaiian word for child he'd used as an endearment fluttered against her raw heart.

Adria saw herself at ten, sitting in a chair in the middle of an otherwise-empty room with her eyes closed.

"I hear the sea, Grandpa. And the children on the beach. And the wind in the trees."

"What else?"

"You, breathing." She giggled.

"Adria! You must be serious."

"Sorry, Grandpa."

"What else?"

"Nothing."

"Relax, concentrate, suspend yourself more. What do you hear?"

Adria did as she was told. She wanted Grandpa to smile at her, tell her she was a good girl. His smiles and his hugs made her feel warm and it seemed she was always so cold. She concentrated her entire body and mind, feeling the force of her energy flowing through her. *"I hear tiny footsteps."*

"Open your eyes, keiki."

When she did, a small bamboo cage stood on the wood floor and, inside, a cricket walked its boundaries. And when she looked up, the bright beam of her grandfather's pride shone down on her.

Adria juggled her briefcase into one hand and searched her sodden coat pocket for a tissue. Finding none, she used the back of her hand to wipe away tears she'd promised herself she wouldn't shed. She missed her grandfather so much—missed his wisdom, his strength, his love. Would this painful hole in her heart ever heal?

She closed her eyes once more. *Grandpa?*

What do you hear, keiki?

I hear the rain, Grandpa.

What else?

Adria breathed in deeply, bringing in an intense awareness of her surroundings. *I hear a telephone ringing. I hear an elevator's door opening. I hear footsteps, Grandpa. Dragon feet.*

In her mind's eye, she could see her grandfather's boat of a smile. *You've learned well,* keiki.

You've taught me well.

Warmth seeped back into her icy limbs. He was still with her.

She squared her shoulders and stepped toward the main doors.

Peter Dragon had chosen the building's location well, but after that, he seemed to have left security up to luck. He'd made maximum use of glass. At least it was tinted. Anyone could walk through the front door—again glass—that swung outward, instead of in, and was protected only by a tape-type alarm that looked worn. No security camera monitored the ins-and-outs of people. The plush reception area with its soft lighting, its overstuffed furniture and jungle of potted plants offered a multitude of hiding spots—for people and bombs.

Her grandfather had taught her all about dragons—the western medieval kind with their poisonous skins and flesh-eating habits, and the gentle eastern ones with their wise and generous natures. Had he known this day would come? Had that been his way of preparing her even then for her honor-bound duty?

She shook the thought away and concentrated instead on her goal.

She stopped in front of the honey-blond receptionist partially enclosed in a half-moon-shaped desk of warm oak. The name on the placard read Tiffany Banks. Although dressed in a business suit and styled like a *Vogue* model, the woman came across like a squeaky-clean teenaged cheerleader at a pep rally.

"Excuse me," Adria said, "could you tell me where I might find Mr. Peter Dragon?"

Tiffany's red lips parted to reveal a set of perfect white teeth. Her orthodontist must be proud. "Do you have an appointment?"

"Yes."

Without verifying her claim, Tiffany turned a palm up, à la Vanna White, and fanned it toward the elevator bank. "Tenth floor, to your right."

For a financial wizard who'd fought his way ruthlessly to the top, Mr. Dragon seemed to take security much too lightly. That he wasn't worried about payback said a world about him. Arrogance. Sheer arrogance. And that arrogance would cause his downfall.

Adria pushed the elevator's up button and the brass doors swished open. Soft, piped-in music made the ride pleasant enough even though her skin itched with anxiety. A muted *bing* announced she'd arrived at her destination. Her stomach took a dive. The tenth floor appeared deserted. No one sat at the lone desk in the reception area. Warm browns, rich creams, leafy greens and antiqued brass accents provided a comfortable décor. From her left came the hushed sounds of ringing telephones, the clacking of computer keys and the rise and fall of muffled laughter.

No one challenged her presence. She smiled.

Was Peter Dragon really as formidable as her Yale business professor had made him out to be? Was he really as commanding as the profile in the latest issue of *Business, Inc.* described him? Would he prove as ruthless as his father if he found out who she was and what she wanted from him?

She already had enough ammunition to arrange for his physical demise—if she so chose. But even her grandfather wouldn't sanction cold-blooded murder. That wouldn't be revenge; that would simply be falling to the enemy's level. No, what she needed was something more painful, and for that, she had to have access to his most sensitive data.

She rounded the secretarial desk and examined the agenda opened to today's date. Didn't he realize that with just a glance anyone could know where he'd be at any time of the day?

The elevator door sighed open, revealing a pert brunette. Flushed, she juggled an umbrella, a large Tyvek envelope and a purse that looked like a leather backpack. "Excuse me. I've got an appointment with Mr. Dragon about the secretarial job?"

"You're late—" Adria looked pointedly at the agenda "—Miss Murray."

"I know. I'm really sorry. But the bus was late and—"

With a hand, Adria cut her off. She didn't want to feel her heart softening at this girl's plight. "The position's been filled."

The brightness of Miss Murray's smile faded even as she held on to its shape. "But I didn't get to interview."

A twinge of guilt nipped at Adria's conscience. It couldn't be helped. To get to Peter Dragon, to find his weakness, she had to stay close to him. "With a face like yours, you'll have a job before the week's out."

What was left of the brunette's smile collapsed under the weight of her disappointment and curled back into a grimace. "Thanks anyway."

As Miss Murray retreated, a voice boomed from behind the closed double doors of the office. Enough like thunder to rattle down Adria's spine. "Janine, is that you?"

Razor-edged agony cut through the greasy knot in her stomach. Drawing in a breath, she took off her raincoat and draped it over the back of the secretarial chair. She squared her shoulders and strode to the Dragon's lair.

Showtime.

Adria rapped on the heavy wooden door and pushed it open. The reception area might have been set up for comfort, but this office was furnished to exude power. A massive glass-and-gray-granite desk stood in the middle of the room and a thronelike black leather chair dwarfed the two overstuffed gray visitors' chairs in front of the desk. Everything from carpet to curtains shaded the room in degrees of black and white. Even the splashes of paint on canvas that passed for art.

The dark-haired man bent over his work possessed every inch of space of his territory. He glanced up for a fraction of a moment, then returned to his paperwork. "Who are you?"

"Adria Caskey. Your nine o'clock appointment for the secretarial position."

Distractedly, he lifted his agenda from below a neat stack of papers, checked the entry and frowned.

She attempted to relax and took in the man beneath the air of utter confidence—the charcoal-gray suit molding his athletic body to perfection, the tie's red knot in precise position between the starched points of his shirt collar, the manicured hairstyle that left not one straight brown hair out of place. She searched his lean face for something to hate and found herself fascinated by the sheer power in the set of his long, straight nose, the reflection of light on his prominent cheekbones, the dark slashes of eyebrows above his dusty-green eyes.

Definitely a western dragon. An unexpected twin thrill of excitement and fear ran through her. Peter

Dragon would make her task a challenge. He would defy her at every turn. He would question her judgment. He would oppose her suggestions. She could see why hanging on to a secretary might prove a problem. A man like him didn't believe in second chances. And the provocation of his unspoken defiance spurred her contrary nature into overdrive.

You can't do it, keiki.

Oh, yes, I can, Grandpa. Watch me!

So it had gone throughout her training in her grandfather's secret art of self-defense. When she thought she'd gone as far as she could, he'd challenged her and catapulted her to new achievements despite the underlying ripple of anxiety. That's why she'd taken on the risky jobs. They gave her purpose—a barrier to climb, an obstacle to overcome, a way to transcend the constant wash of terror lying just beneath her skin.

Peter Dragon would be her ultimate test.

But she was ready.

She held his gaze as he looked up. She'd seen those eyes before on a stormy night twenty-one years ago, staring down at her from her parents' bedroom window. They'd looked innocent then. Now they were tinged with something ruthless and fierce. Steady strength peered at her through the shield of his glasses and, for an instant, she feared he could see right through her.

Not what she'd expected, this palpable power. It disturbed her enough that her mind couldn't soften her gaze to read his aura as her grandfather had taught her to do. Not good.

Would he recognize her after all this time? Not likely. That night held no meaning for him. He'd probably forgotten. Would he see his childhood in the Polynesian features she'd inherited from her father? Or would he choose to see only the pale skin she'd received from the mixed bag of her mother's European heritage? How much of his past had he managed to erase from his mind?

Pain rolled through her in a tsunami-size wave. She fisted her hand with joint-crunching force to keep herself from letting it surge over her and crash into him in a breaker of anger.

Use mind, not external force, keiki.

Grandpa was right, of course. If she wanted the job, she would have to feign admiration and interest. Her brittle smile hurt her cheeks. "You're looking for a secretary."

"I have a capable assistant."

"It's my understanding she left the position. Mr. Russell Dragon arranged for the interview."

Not a muscle moved on his face, as if losing an employee happened every day.

"Do you have a résumé?" His voice reported across the room in an imperial decree. The degradation of interviewing his own assistant seemed to grate on his nerves.

She boldly ate the space between them. Resting her briefcase on the seat of a chair, she plucked a single sheet of paper from its depth. She reached over his desk and handed it to him.

He didn't invite her to sit so she remained standing. This way they stood on equal footing. She had no doubt the people-swallowing chairs were chosen on purpose. Was it for power or security? Power, definitely power. He'd shown too much disregard for security to care that the throne chair, the dominating desk and deep visitors' chairs all hindered attack.

He leaned back on his throne, perusing her revised life's work with serious intent. *If you only knew!*

"I can't help notice that you're overqualified for the job, Ms. Caskey." Arching an eyebrow, he dared her to prove him wrong. He dropped her résumé on his desk and propped his elbows on his throne's arms, tenting his fingers under his chin. "Why would you want to work as a secretary when you could easily get an entry-level managerial position elsewhere?"

"My education is extensive." Perspiration prickled her armpits in spite of the cool air blowing against her face from an overhead duct. The pins holding her chignon bit into her scalp. *When the opponent is hard, you must remain soft,* keiki. *Calm your mind.* "But my real-life business experience is limited. I earned my MBA at Yale a year ago."

At the time, she'd sat through those classes guarding a foreign dignitary's daughter. The girl hadn't made her job easy, but when it counted, Adria was there and had saved the girl's life. Lorna at the registrar's office owed her a favor. She would back up her story of being a student and neglect to mention her other duty, should Mr. Dragon bother to check out her reference.

"I've been taking care of my dying grandfather since then."

Peter listened carefully, not showing the slightest hint of reaction. More than anything his stillness fanned her anxiety. Did he hear the half-truths beneath her story?

"He died two months ago." At least that much was true.

"I'm sorry for your loss, but I still don't understand why you'd want this position."

Her fingers itched to twist themselves with her rain-

coat's belt. She forced her hands to lie unmoving along
the seams of her skirt. An undercurrent of heat radiated
from him, wafting the faint scent of leather and spice
toward her. He waited for her answer with unnerving
stillness, emphasizing his quiet power.

"The economy being what it is, openings are rare
these days. I'm older than most graduates and have less
experience." A little flattery never hurt. "One of my
business professors used your rise to success as an example of impeccable business ethics." How had Peter
managed to hide the source of his start-up capital?
How many people besides her mother and father had
died to make his empire possible?

"I've done some research. You have a lot of growth
potential. That's the kind of company I want to work
for. I'd like to learn the business from the ground up.
Grow with it." *Find its weakness. Destroy it.* "I'm not
planning on being a secretary forever."

No, her future beyond this obligation was a blank
canvas she had no idea how she would paint. But before she could think about her future, she had to put her
family's past to rest.

"I see." The unexpected display of dimples surprised Adria with its swell of warmth. "You understand I can't pay you what your degree could get you
elsewhere."

Of course not. Worth didn't enter the equation. Had
it ever with him? She leaned the heels of both hands
onto the glass edge of his desk, her gaze a bull's-eye
into the black of his pupils. "I can understand your
hesitation, but my business background is an asset in
a secretary. I'll get the experience I need. We both
win."

She let the words sink in for half a moment, then

moved in for the kill. "Since your secretary isn't in today, try me out for the rest of the day. Then make your decision. What have you got to lose?"

How could someone concerned only with the bottom line refuse such an offer?

Something about the gleam in his eyes unraveled the edge of her poise. No, not sexual, but interest. He viewed her as an enigma, and Peter Dragon had a reputation for liking puzzles. She'd won. He would keep her around until she stopped intriguing him.

"How well do you know our computer system?" he asked, butting against the invisible line she'd drawn.

"Intimately." She breathed the word suggestively and silently gloated at the renewed spark of curiosity in his eyes. Knowledge would give her power and he was handing it to her on an electronic network.

"All right, Ms. Caskey." His voice was like rich velvet over rocks. "I accept your offer."

He rose and reached across the desk to shake her hand. His firm grip tingled the sensitive skin of her palms. But he stood only an inch taller than her own five foot ten. Just a man after all, not a mythic creature with magical powers.

She withdrew her hand from his, careful not to jerk it from his heated grasp and telegraph the spark her disdain had ignited.

"I'm getting ready for a very important presentation in ten days." He settled back into his throne. "I have a lot to do and not much time to spare for explanations."

He thinks I can't do this. The trace of a smile curled the corners of her mouth. *You don't know it, Peter Dragon, but you've met your match.* "I'll keep up."

Without another word, she took the stack of files he handed her to the desk outside his office, stripped off the jacket of her black business suit and, with adrenaline pumping through her system, she plunged right into the job.

She had entered the dragon's domain.

Phase One was over.

Peter Dragon disturbed her. She couldn't trust him. He was the enemy. Never again would another family suffer because of his greed. He would know what it was like to lose everything he cared for, to feel small, alone and helpless.

She would make herself invaluable to him. Then she would cut him off at the knees.

Chapter 2

"See me," read the note scrawled in a bold handwriting.

With a weighty sigh, Adria plucked the summons propped against her keyboard and headed toward Peter's office. *Figures.* She'd left her desk for five minutes to meet Caleb downstairs and let him know she wouldn't need a ride home.

She raised her hand to knock on the closed wooden door, then paused when she heard voices. Peter had a visitor. Friend or foe? She cracked the door open to assess the threat level.

The man sitting in the visitor's chair in front of Peter's desk gave her a start. For a second, she was once again six, standing on her tiptoes, straining to see inside her parents' bedroom, staring at the fat man who had ordered her mother's execution. The wild gestures of hand, the dark, curly hair, the corpulent figure...the anger that threw a neon-bright red aura around him so big it nearly filled the room and stopped her cold.

"How does it feel to know you'll be dead within two weeks?" a voice she didn't recognize said. "How does it feel to know you'll die in shame? I know your secret, and soon the whole world will, too." Paper rustled. "You can't get more to the point than that, Peter."

"The letter means nothing, Russell. File it. Call the police, make a report and get back to work."

Russell. The brother. Four years younger. Her background search had shown a man who seemed to abhor work and spent most of his time on his boat at the yacht club.

Russell launched the letter at the desk. It landed in Peter's hands. His fingers cupped the sheet as if he wanted to ball it up. She winced at his and Russell's disregard for any possible forensic evidence that could lead to the anonymous letter writer. Even from the door she could make out the cutout magazine letters glued onto photocopy paper. Could be anyone. Yet the words were so personal, so vicious. Was Peter's bloodstained past finally coming back to haunt him? Who else knew his secret?

A pleased smirk greased Russell's lips. "It's not the first."

Peter peered over his glasses at his brother. "Why wasn't I informed of this before?"

"I've been trying to reach you for a couple of days now. If you ever returned your calls, you'd know. You've had several of these love letters in the past week."

Peter glanced at his watch. "I've been here since five. Where have you been? And how come I had to interview a secretary this morning? What happened to Janine?"

Russell sank deeper into the chair and smug satisfaction grooved the chubby cheeks of his baby face. "Janine quit. You're always telling me to take initiative. So I placed an ad for a new secretary."

"She quit? She wouldn't quit without giving notice. Besides, she likes working here."

"She did. But that was before you came down on her lover like a ton of bricks. They eloped two days ago."

"Her lover?" Irritation spiked Peter's clear blue aura.

"Jeez, Pete, what planet do you live on? The whole building's buzzing about it. Didn't you notice your chief financial officer's not in his office, either? Terry Atwell quit because you questioned his judgment."

Peter ground his teeth as if to keep his rising temper in check. A transparent red ball of anger bounced out from his chest only to rebound back as if he'd caught the flying emotion and turned it inward. *Control. Interesting.* He pivoted his chair to the ebony credenza behind his desk and pulled open a drawer. "I've been out of town for a week."

"You've been in your office for almost five hours. How could you have *not* heard about Janine and Terry? How could you *not* have seen the other letters? I left them on your desk."

Peter flipped through the file folder tabs in the drawer. "Unlike some people around here, I actually work."

"Unlike some people around here, I don't have my head stuck up my a—"

"That's enough, Russ." Peter glared at his brother over his folder.

"I told you this would happen." Russell hoisted himself out of the chair and paced, swirling the red of his aura into a small tornado around him. "Terry wasn't doing anything wrong and you had to go lord it over him like he was a kid fresh out of college."

"We've been over this. It had nothing to do with Terry. It has to do with his procedures." Tiredness seemed to catch up with Peter and sag his jaw and shoulders. "I've worked too hard to get where I am to have my name tarnished by the appearance of impropriety."

Adria sneered. As if building an empire on blood money was snow-pure.

Russell slammed both hands onto the glass desktop. The heat of his anger steamed the glass beneath his palms. "Everything was legal and above board."

"I have my standards." Peter ground the words as if they were gravel. "Terry knew that coming in. He fiddled with the numbers to make Mystic Pleasure Crafts look better than they were."

"But they—"

"The company's had problems with environmental violations in the past. Deliberate violations they tried to hide from E.P.A. investigators."

"In the past." Russell smacked a fist onto the glass desktop. "That's over now."

"There's no evidence. The same management team heads the company."

Russell shook his head and jutted out his lower lip like a kid denied candy. "Ah, jeez, Pete. Can't you let me have anything?"

"The foundation's set up to maintain certain standards. We help companies who offer worthy services to the community—"

"Yeah, yeah, I know all that. What's wrong with relaxation? That offers a benefit, too."

"Not when it harms the environment. Their standards are not—"

"What the Dragon Foundation stands for. I know. But I *could* raise the standards. I *could* set the change of management as a condition for funding."

Peter rolled his shoulders as if he were trying to dislodge a too-heavy burden. "Controlling interest is owned by the family. And it's not just one thing. It's the way they run the whole operation, from the paint they use on their hulls, to the engines they employ, to the environmental safeguards they ignore for getting rid of the toxic waste they produce. They've shown a blatant disregard for laws and regulations. I don't want to reward that kind of behavior."

Russell leaned forward over the desk, as if the force of his will could bore through Peter's resistance. "I can do this, Peter. I can turn that company around. Mystic Pleasure Crafts has great potential."

"I don't want to get involved with the inevitable environmental clean-up bills that are going to start piling up."

Money. Adria shook her head. It always came down to money.

"You think I'm a screw-up. You can't see that I'm not fourteen anymore." Russell's flying hands punctuated every sentence. "Drugs—gone. Cons—gone. Debts—paid back. I buckled down. I did what you wanted. I've changed. I can do more than shuffle papers that aren't even an important part of this company."

"I feel the foundation is the most important part of this company. You're my right-hand man. I depend on you."

Russell snorted and plunked his ample bottom on

the corner of the desk, glaring down at Peter, who was still searching through the file folders. "You sure could've fooled me. I have to run everything by you. You question my judgment. You disregard my suggestions. And when I ask for one damned project to guide by myself, you tell me I'm an idiot."

"Russell, I don't have time for this right now. Until Mystic Pleasure Crafts can prove they've cleaned up their environmental mess and settled the claims against them, I don't want to tie Dragon, Inc.'s reputation with theirs."

Russell grabbed a pewter dragon from the top of Peter's desk and tossed it up repeatedly as if he were testing the heft of a baseball he wanted to aim at his brother's head. "Yeah, well, if you followed that reasoning, nobody would get any of your precious foundation's grants."

"Tell that to this year's recipients."

"Pete—"

"Russell. No."

"No second chance with you, is there?" Russell tumbled the dragon back to the desk. It landed sideways, but he didn't stand it up on its base.

Rubbing his temples with the palms of his hands, Peter closed his eyes. "Russ—"

"Forget it." Russell threw his hands up in defeat. "The great and mighty Peter says no, so the answer's no. I get it."

Russell leaned one forearm on the wrinkled pants of his blue suit, and with the other plucked a folder from beneath a stack of papers, toppling the pile. "Here are the other letters."

"Did you call the police?" Peter asked, frowning as if he were trying to squeeze out a headache.

"No, didn't know how you wanted to handle it." Russell shrugged, passing the blame. Adria had had the guilt card played against her often enough by clients to recognize it. "Couldn't reach you."

Peter pulled out a file, then jammed it back into its slot. "How about Ben Crumb in the mailroom? Did you check with him?"

"For all the good that'd do." Russell chuffed, twirling a finger near one temple. "The man's a little slow in case you hadn't noticed."

"He runs a tight ship down there."

"If you say so."

"Do you know where Janine filed my notes on credit card debt?"

"How should I know? I have enough stuff to keep track of without adding your paperwork to the list."

Sibling rivalry. She'd forgotten its power. Siblings often knew how to push each other's buttons to cause maximum aggravation and pain and she was witnessing a prime example of parry-and-thrust. Interesting, too, that Peter absorbed each blow. Russell seemed an instant-gratification, live-for-the-moment kind of guy. She could get him to gush like Old Faithful and he'd never know he was spewing the secret to his brother's fall.

"Listen, we have a real security problem here." Russell's frown lifted his eyebrows into severe Vs that reminded her of drawings of the devil that had scared her as a child. "What are you going to do about it?"

"Call the police." Peter slammed shut the drawer. "File a report."

"Of course." Derision dripped from Russell's voice like acid. "It amazes me how someone so smart can be so dense. The police aren't going to do anything about this. You, of all people, should know this. The jerk could walk into their station, confess and he'd still have a hard time getting arrested. It's a criminal's world out there, not a victim's."

Peter grunted a noncommittal answer.

"So what?" Windmill hands chopped at the air. "You're going to wait until you actually get hurt to do something? What if he acts next time instead of writing?"

"It won't come to that."

"How do you know?"

Peter choked back a sigh. His aura was thin now—just a ring of ash-gray. "People who resort to this kind of threat rarely have the guts to follow through."

"You could take a vacation."

Peter plowed through the files on his desk as if he were a cultivator and they were earth that needed turning over. "Not now."

"Work in peace somewhere else, somewhere safe. I could run things here for a bit." Russell's voice was honey now.

Hoping to soothe the savage beast? Adria silently scoffed. Not likely.

"No."

"It's for your own good. For the company's good."

"I have too much to do before the financial-freedom seminar. It's only a letter."

"It's more than one."

"I'm careful."

Russell hit the side of his head with the heel of his hand. "Of course, what was I thinking? Peter the Great. Nobody can touch him."

"Russ—" Peter pivoted his chair to meet his brother's gaze head-on.

"This isn't one of your prissy gourmet recipes where everything is laid out and you know exactly what you're going to get before you sit down to eat it."

"That's enough." Peter hunkered behind his desk and bent back to his task. "I'm not going to give in to bullying."

"Forget it." Russell waved him away, slid off the desk and spun on the heel of his well-used boat shoes to leave.

"Call the police about the letters. At least there'll be a record of the complaint."

"Sure, Pete. I've got everything under control." Russell stormed out, brushing by Adria like a thundercloud, leaving behind a briny scent.

Adria waved Peter's note as she entered. "You wanted to see me."

"You weren't at your desk." The accusation in his voice irked her. Just how had he earned his reputation as Stamford's most-liked employer?

"I know." No explanations. No excuses.

His head snapped up and curiosity danced in his eyes. The tip of his titanium pen jittered on the pad of yellow paper. "I need the mortgage comparison chart."

"Coming right up."

"See if you can locate a file with notes on credit card debt in the cabinet behind your desk."

"Done."

"Oh, and I need for you to check out a few Web sites for me. Make sure the URLs are current before you add them to the resources section."

"No problem."

The morning flew by. Between tasks, Adria canceled Peter's lunch appointment, hoping to keep him safe in his office until she could ascertain the degree of danger these threat letters posed. The last thing she needed was to have someone kill him before she could make him suffer.

At twelve-thirty, Peter emerged from his office, wearing a beige trench coat and carrying a briefcase.

"I'm going out," he announced, punching the elevator button.

"Your appointment canceled." Adria dropped the file folder she was working with on the blotter and scooted the chair back from the desk. Her desk overflowed with folders awaiting processing into charts and graphs, chapters for the binder Peter planned to hand out to the seminar participants and a PowerPoint file for his presentation. Peter would breathe indignant fire if she didn't catch up with him—or worse, decide she wasn't good enough to hire on a permanent basis. That would screw up Phase Two. But she couldn't let him go out alone. Not before she'd had a chance to investigate if the threatening letters he'd received posed him or her goal any real danger.

"I know."

He flashed her his winning dimples, and a curl of heat fluttered in her stomach. *Figures.* A guy like him was used to manipulating with charm. Probably worked most of the time, too. But she had an unassessed threat to deal with. How could she make a judgment about the likelihood of danger if she didn't know what she was up against? Tension cranked up and squeezed her chest. Complications were part of the job. Opportunities for creativity, her grandfather called them.

"Why don't you join me?" The elevator doors

yawned open and Peter strode in. "Since you're working for free, the least I can do is offer you lunch."

"Thanks, I'd like that." She grabbed her briefcase
and raincoat and hurried to join him. When the elevator arrived at the lobby, she exited first, giving a quick
look around before she stepped out.

Without quite knowing how it happened, Adria fell
back a step as she would if she were guarding a client.
Protecting his vulnerable back. She shook her head, silently clucking at the instincts her grandfather had ingrained so deeply.

As Peter walked across the street to the Cosgrove
Hotel, she found it fascinating to watch the effect his
commanding presence had on people. His straight and
tall posture, his sure, floating gait, his supreme air of
confidence parted the lunchtime crowd before him like
a modern Moses. Almost everyone gave him a second
look as he walked by. Heads nodded greetings out of
respect—or was it fear?

Out of habit, she walked into the hotel ahead of him
and scanned the lobby. Before he'd finished smiling at
the woman manning the front desk, the manager himself came out to welcome him and treated him with the
deference a king might expect.

Missing nothing of the activity around them, Adria
followed Peter to the lobby restaurant, where she managed to maneuver him away from the windows and into
a small alcove to minimize his exposure. As she picked
up the menu, she discreetly checked for exits in case
of an emergency.

He ordered a steak big enough to feed a family of
four. She didn't know how he could keep his trim figure by eating that way. Of course, blowing all that self-
righteous fire used up a lot of energy.

Famished, she nonetheless ordered a simple sandwich. *Always finish your meal before the VIP you're
guarding.* In this case, very important perpetrator.

"Just a sandwich?" Peter raised an eyebrow. "Don't
tell me you're one of those women who don't eat."

It wasn't so much his deliberate zinger as her own
inability to put aside what she was that tweaked her
contrary nature to life. "I'm one of those women who
listens to her body's urges and eats when she needs to."

As soon as the words were out, she regretted them.
Grandpa was right. As usual. No good ever came out
of mean.

Peter's dimples deepened. "Do you always listen to
your urges?"

"I listen. I don't always indulge."

Peter gave a rocky chuckle. "Having you around
might prove interesting after all."

"And will I…be around?" She practically choked on
the vampish undertone. But he wanted intrigue, and she
had to pretend to give him what he wanted.

"I'm impressed with your work." His gaze, unread-
able beneath the slight tint in the shield of his glasses,
didn't leave her face as he stirred a spoonful of sugar
into the coffee that had appeared, as if by magic, with
the waiter taking their order. "You catch on quickly,
you pay attention to details and you're efficient."

The compliment pleased her more than it should
have. But everybody had a weakness and hers tended
toward pleasing. Every time she'd gotten into trouble
it was because she'd failed to listen to her instincts and
had given in to pleasing a client. "Impressing you with
my skill was the whole point of offering my services
free for the day."

The spoon paused against the side of the cup. The

smoky green eyes seemed to search for something just out of reach. "Seeing as my secretary has decided not to return to work after her honeymoon, I'm impressed enough to offer you the position full-time. If you want it."

"I do." How far had he dug into her background?

"Good. I'll inform Human Resources. You'll have to drop by their office sometime this afternoon."

She was in. Success warmed her the way it always did. *Move on, Adria.* Time to start collecting data. "The presentation you're working on doesn't seem to be in line with your usual work."

Peter took a roll from the breadbasket, broke off a section and slathered it with butter. She cringed and hoped he didn't die of a massive heart attack before she had the chance to make him pay for his family's sins.

"I'm taking the financial principles I use to rehabilitate companies and adapting them for use by the general public."

"Why?"

He buttered his roll pensively. "Really, this stuff is as basic as writing, reading and arithmetic. It should be taught in school. There's no reason for people to get their lives in such a financial mess. I want Joe and Jane Average to realize that financial independence is within their reach. All they have to do is make different choices."

What a load of baloney! "Why would you want to give away so much power?"

"Power?" He chewed thoughtfully on a bite of bread. "I'm not giving away my power. I'm endowing others with the knowledge that will give *them* power over their own futures. All it takes is knowing what you want and taking proactive measures to see it happens."

"What about the people who were left out of a job during your corporate healings?"

He was quiet for a long while. Too quiet. The intensity of his gaze had her insides squirming like a guilty child. She'd said too much. Where was her control? It was her grandfather's most basic lesson. She had to remember it now when it counted so much.

"I pride myself on being true and fair."

True? Fair? What did someone who was hiding the first half of his life know about truth? What did someone who built an empire on blood money know about fairness?

"I always found other employment for the people my financial surgery displaced." Dimples creased his cheeks. "For someone who claims to want a secretarial job, you seem well-informed about my work."

She reached for her water glass and twirled the stem. "I told you I did some research. Being a professional secretary isn't my life's goal."

"And what would be your life's goal?"

She shrugged and threw a half smile in his direction. Someone like him wouldn't understand a lowly goal like peace of mind.

"Your secret is safe with me."

She had a feeling not much was safe around him. "Someone with your success should understand that certain goals should be shared only with close and trusted friends."

He banged a closed fist against his chest. "You wound me. Here I thought I was making a good impression."

"Why would you want to do that?"

He cocked his head, leaned back and narrowed his gaze. "Something about you fascinates me."

Their lunch arrived, saving Adria from further comment. The last thing she wanted was to invite that kind of fascination. Intrigue was one thing. It was far and remote. Fighting off advances was another. How many of his past secretaries had ended up sharing his bed? She would bet none of them had stayed there for long. That much intensity could drain even the most eager gold digger.

While they ate, she kept the conversation focused on his upcoming seminar. As he spoke of his project, his face transformed. When he smiled, the sad lines around his mouth softened, his dimples deepened, his eyes vibrated with energy.

This man wasn't quite what she expected. One moment he was a terrifying western dragon, the next, he metamorphosed into the friendly eastern dragon of her grandfather's tales. As soon as she thought she'd figured him out, doubt trotted in and a race of questions jockeyed for position. What if his goals were truly as honest as he claimed? What if his work really served some good? What if her grandfather's wish for vengeance was aimed at the wrong target?

She shook her head. *He's the enemy. Don't start thinking about him in any other terms or you'll get yourself in trouble.*

"Dessert?" Peter asked as a waiter stopped by their table with a pastry cart.

"Uh, no. Thank you." Her appetite had vanished. Half a turkey club still lay untouched on her plate. Peter's didn't have a crumb left.

The hotel manager stopped by their table while

Peter savored another cup of coffee and a piece of apricot-almond torte. They discussed the final arrangements for his upcoming seminar. Adria found it hard to keep her mind centered on the conversation and was relieved when the scrape of Peter's chair signaled the end of the meal. She'd be glad when he ensconced himself in his office and she could get back to digging through his database. Only solid information would reveal the truth about the way he ran his business.

Peter made his way through the hotel lobby at a fast clip, eliciting the same silent awe he had when he'd walked in. She slipped through the door ahead of him, pausing to scan up and down the street.

Out of the corner of her eye, something caught her attention. Swiveling to the left, she spotted a fast-moving black Lincoln Continental. Mud covered the plates and front grille. Out of place. She couldn't see the driver's face, but instinct strung her body tight with foreboding.

Heightening her awareness, she sensed a tendril of virulence snaking out from the car. She pressed focused energy into her skeleton.

Just as she was about to pivot Peter out of harm's way, the car screeched to a halt in the No Parking zone in front of the lobby doors. The driver jumped out of the still-running vehicle, leaving the door open. Running by the doorman, he yelled, "Charlie! Park the car for me. I'm late!"

"I'll see to it, Mr. Brennan."

False alarm.

This time.

She released the contained energy back to the ground with what sounded like a static zap. Steam rose from the damp concrete, hissing before dissipating. One thing was clear. Peter had demonstrated at least half a dozen times this morning that he was open to attack. His hidden past, his rapid climb to power, the threatening letters sitting in his office all pointed to one thing: he was a walking target.

She hadn't counted on his disregard for safety to put her own plan in danger.

The Face sat on a park bench, feeding bits of crust from the deli ham sandwich to the beggar pigeons that plagued the city like flying rats. Rain pitted the dark gray skin of the river. The air's dampness swelled the scent of grass and earth. People, huddled beneath black mushroom umbrellas, scurried by as if no one sat here. That was the bane of The Face's existence, this invisibility. A face like this should shine, but everyone refused to see its diamond light.

Peter needed to notice. Diligent work had shown a worth beyond compare. How could he not see it? And what had the self-involved twit done? Peter had written off the more than equitable requests with one stroke of his titanium pen—not once, but three times. As if other people's ideas, dreams and hopes didn't matter. As if no one else mattered.

But Father had taught The Face well. *Use what you have.* If invisibility was a strength, then that strength would get The Face the rightful prize.

And victory was right around the corner. Five years of careful planning, five years of adapting to changing circumstances like a chameleon, five years of Oscar-worthy performances would soon come to fruition. Now that Peter was fixated on his quixotic goal, the perfect space had opened up.

The flock of cooing pigeons gobbled up the last of

the crumbs. Shoulders hunched against the rain, The Face trailed out of the park.

A little maneuvering room. That was all that was needed. That would prove The Face deserved to shine.

The right pieces were in the right place. They were just waiting for the first push of the domino. What fun it would be to watch the balance tumble.

Chapter 3

"Find Russell for me." Peter's voice roared from the other end of the phone. Barely twenty minutes had passed since they'd returned from lunch and already Peter seemed primed for another heated discussion with his brother.

"No problem." Although, it soon became apparent that finding Russell was a habitual problem. Russell's extension was busy, but according to his secretary, he wasn't in his office. Adria left a message.

As she dropped the receiver back onto its cradle, the elevator doors glided open. She glanced up automatically to assess its passengers. The man inside bumped a mail cart against the elevator door twice before managing to exit. The slow bob of his head matched his unhurried pace. As if he feared his height, his shoulders stooped over, swallowing his neck and adding to the turtlelike effect. As he muscled the cart in her direction, he lifted his head of scraggly auburn hair and smiled widely at her, and for some reason, the smile reminded her of water.

"Hi, I'm Ben. You're new, aren't you?" He picked up a stack of envelopes and held them close to his chest.

"Adria." She smiled back, offering a hand. Alienation wouldn't get her anywhere, but gaining his trust might prove helpful when she needed to prowl the mailroom.

Holding on to the mail with one hand, he stuck out his other. The cold and clammy feel of his noodle-limp grasp had her thinking of fish. She had to force herself not to wipe her hand dry on her skirt.

"I started this morning." She painted a pleasant expression on her face—one of her grandfather's lessons. *Everyone responds to a smile,* keiki. "How often do you collect the mail?"

He shuffled his feet and turned his long, affable face toward the carpet. "Mr. Dragon, he likes his mail when it comes in, so as soon as I finish sorting, I bring his up. Usually around one, but the truck was late, so that's why you didn't see me. I can pick up anything you have to go out."

The small, soft voice seemed out of place in such a big man. So did the pale coral of his aura. "Dragon, Inc. is lucky to have someone conscientious like you working for them."

"I love it here. Everybody's so nice." Pride swiftly turned to uneasiness, flushing the skin over his sunken cheeks red. "Well, I better get back to work. You need anything, you let Ben know."

"Thanks, Ben."

He made an awkward turn with his cart and headed

toward Peter's office. She picked up the first file her hand found and followed Ben's slow bob into the office. *Never leave a principal unguarded while on duty.* If she kept this up, she wouldn't have time to find the information she needed.

Peter, seated at his leather throne, greeted Ben in a friendly manner, but there was no mistaking that these two wouldn't share a whiskey and cigar at the club anytime soon.

Ben mumbled something. As if his attempt at conversation caused him great pain, his fingertips turned white on the pack of envelopes he held. With a clumsy shuffle, he aimed the envelopes toward Peter's in basket. Like an avalanche, the envelopes tumbled out of his grasp and fell between his cart and the desk.

"Sorry." Ben kneeled on the smoke-colored carpet and awkwardly thrust the envelopes he picked up from the floor onto the desk.

"Don't worry about it, Ben." Peter rose and stretched, emphasizing the lean musculature of his body, then started sorting through the mail.

At the sight of a lavender card-shaped envelope, a dimple-deepening smile folded the hem of tiredness from his face. He turned the envelope over and tore at the Easter lily sticker to release the flap. A flowery cross in spring pastels splashed across the front of the card. A tinny version of "He Has Risen" plinked out of the musical device nested in the cover.

Adria's heightened awareness magnified every note. Dropping the file she held, she bolted forward. "Peter!"

In slow motion, he turned toward her. With one fluid movement, she shoved Peter out of the way and deflected the card out of his hands.

Unbalanced, Peter sprawled to the floor. A small explosion like that of a child's firecracker ravaged the quiet of the office. Something sharp slashed the skin of her cheek. She batted at it as if it were a gnat. Ben pounced on the smoldering ashes eating at the carpet.

Adria turned to Peter. "Are you all right?"

He stood and brushed pastel-colored shreds of cardboard from his perfectly pressed pants. He straightened his glasses, centered the knot of his tie and nodded. "Ben, are you all right?"

Ben rolled from the heap that once was a card and batted at the ash covering his long-sleeved beige polo shirt.

"Oh." Ben pointed to the carcass of card. His eyebrows arched high and his mouth melted in a downward cast. "The carpet's ruined."

"Don't worry about it, Ben." He offered the man a hand up. Ben reluctantly took the offer and scrambled to his feet. "We'll get it fixed."

"But the c-carpet," Ben said, clearly ill at ease.

"It doesn't matter as long as you're fine."

Ben nodded stiffly, shuffling his feet and staring at the toes of his work boots. "I'm okay."

"Did this letter come with the regular mail?" Peter asked.

Ben's neck retreated farther into his shoulders. "It was with the rest of the stuff, and…"

"It's all right, Ben." Peter turned to Adria. "Have you found Russell yet?"

"He wasn't in his office."

"That figures. Try the yacht club."

As if speaking his name had conjured him up, Russell strode into Peter's office. "What happened here?"

"Seems as if our letter writer decided to send a message with more bang this time," Peter said in clipped tones. "Why don't you take Ben down to the first-aid station and make sure he's all right. Then I want you to call the police."

Russell started pushing the mail cart, but Adria stopped him. "Leave it here. The police will want to look at it."

"B-but," Ben stammered, pointing at the undelivered envelopes, "the mail!"

"It's okay, Ben." Peter signaled Russell with a nod. "I'll take care of it."

Craning his neck, Ben blinked at the cart as Russell led him out of the office.

Peter stared at the burnt spot on the carpet. His cheek twitched once. His stony gaze moved ever so slowly to her face. His rock-hard stare and impassive expression gave her no clue as to his thoughts. Before her eyes, the gentle eastern dragon transformed into its flesh-eating, fire-breathing western cousin.

There had been no time for a warning. She'd acted on pure instinct drilled into her since she was ten.

He looked at her as if she were an alien. "Who are you?"

"Adria Caskey."

He crossed his arms over his chest, a stern genie ready to blink her back to wherever she'd come from. "What are you? You sure as hell aren't a secretary."

"That's the position I applied for."

"I value honesty above all."

Yeah, right. Then why don't you go by your real name? But she fought back the quip tingling the tip of her tongue. "My training is in executive protection."

His gaze appraised her from head to toe and he raised an eyebrow in disbelief. "A bodyguard?"

Her chin hitched up. Her grandfather took pride in

his training. Anyone could say they were a bodyguard, few could do the job in a way that was both efficient and nonintrusive as possible. Executive protection required both art and skill. "A security specialist."

"I checked your references."

One shoulder shrugged up matter-of-factly. "Most of them owe me their lives or the life of someone they care for. They were more than happy to do me a favor. I don't abuse the privilege."

"Why leave it off your résumé?"

She cocked her head, narrowing her gaze. "Would you have given me a chance if you knew what I'd done before?"

"Probably not."

She hadn't expected honesty. "I worked with my grandfather," she said, and surprised herself with a touch of honesty in return. "When he died, I didn't want to keep doing what I was doing. So much of the business was my grandfather. It hurt too much." She shrugged, grief, pain, love spinning inside her like snow in a blizzard. The force of the storm choked her. Then she remembered where she was and why, and honesty had to take a back seat to her grandfather's last wish. "I wanted a fresh start, and not acknowledging my training was the only way to get a job like this. A chance to start over."

His anger peeled off him in fumes that mixed with the acrid tang of gunpowder and made the air heavy. Was he angry that she'd saved his sorry hide or that he'd lost face? Neither mattered when the relaxation of his skewering gaze told her he bought her bluff— which didn't mean he planned on living with it. If he was going to fire her as a secretary, she might as well give him a reason to keep her around.

"You should hire a security firm."

He shook his head and retreated behind his desk. "No, this is just a prank."

"Someone sent you a bomb."

"Head games." He plowed through the rest of the envelopes Ben had delivered, but she doubted he saw any of the addresses.

"Are the professionals you deal with in the habit of playing these types of games?"

His jaw flinched, but he didn't answer.

"I didn't think so. It's gone beyond head games. There's a pattern of escalation. That's how it works. First it seems innocent—like letters. Then pranks. Then, when the target doesn't respond in the desired way, it escalates to physical harm. Are you prepared to defend yourself?"

He shoved both hands on the desk, becoming a pyramid of power. "It won't come to that."

Her gaze flickered over the remnants of the bomb, a mess of ash, card confetti and pieces of metal from the musical device, on the carpet. Incongruous inside the destruction was a three-by-five card—white neon against a sooty background. "It already has. You need to take precautions to stay safe."

With a letter opener she snagged off his desk, Adria crouched and studied the device. "Someone altered the musical box so the final note of the tune would send an initiating impulse to a small charge of explosive and detonate." She rose, skewered the letter opener back in its holder and matched his pyramid pose on the other side of the desk. "You're in real danger, Mr. Dragon. Your security is shoddy. You're vulnerable, exposed. How hard do you think it would be for someone to walk into your office and blow your head off?"

He winced at the rawness of the image she'd painted. "I have checkpoints."

She crooked her head and knitted her brow. "Nobody stopped me this morning. Nobody questioned my presence. What if I'd had less-than-pure motives? That's the thing about bad guys—they rarely look like the monsters people expect them to be. Haven't you seen news reports after a murder? 'He seemed so nice.' That's what the neighbors always say." And something she had to remember. Behind Peter's good looks was a long trail of blood.

She dragged her gaze over her shoulder and back to the pile of shrapnel. "Whoever sent you this card knows a lot about you. What did the return address read?"

He took off his glasses and rubbed his eyes. "Burt and Angie Lonsdale, a business associate friend and his wife."

"The type of friend who would send you an Easter card? The type of friend you wouldn't think twice about before opening anything he sent?"

Peter nodded, streaming out a slow exhale. "Burt went through a rough time a few years ago. When he reexamined his values, he returned to his faith. Angie helps keep Hallmark in business. She sends out cards to everyone for any occasion."

Because he needed to understand the vulnerability of his situation, she pushed the point. "Whoever sent you this card knows who you do business with. He understands your relationship with them. He knew this man was a devout Christian. He knew you knew that and would have no second thoughts about opening an Easter card from him."

She toed the reinforced section of card that hadn't

come apart with the charge and flipped it over. "If you still have doubts, this should erase them."

In mismatched cutout magazine letters, the note read, "How does it feel to be a man without a face?" A group calling itself People for Resource Parity signed the card.

A frown crimped Peter's forehead. "People for Resource Parity. That sounds familiar." He revived his computer from its sleep function and punched open a file. "The Dragon Foundation refused them a grant six months ago."

"Revenge. A motive as old as time." *She should know.*

"I refuse more grants than I hand out."

"It only takes one." She leaned in, fixing her gaze mercilessly on his. "You're a financial wizard. Think of me as a security wizard. You need my expertise. Your presentation is important to you. I can make sure nothing goes wrong." That no one else could use her parents' blood money for ill. She needed to see good come out of their sacrifice.

"How do I know you didn't orchestrate this little charade to gain a contract?"

"You don't. But ask anyone who's ever needed executive protection about Caskey & Caskey and you'll understand that we don't need to orchestrate. Like you, we're—we were—the best in the business."

He sat in his chair, elbows on arms, fingers tented beneath his chin. Master and commander again. Little old security specialist put back in her proper place. "How will you go about improving the security of this building?"

She was in her element and his attempt to assert his dominance didn't faze her. She stood solidly grounded.

This was what she was trained to do. "I'll bring a team in. They'll do a threat assessment and provide a list of suggestions to secure the building. We'll establish employee security and safety procedures, limit the number of entry points. Those will be monitored by closed-circuit television. We'll implement an ID tag system and key cards for access to certain areas, including your suite of offices. Security personnel in the lobby. Of course, tighter mailroom security."

"Sounds expensive."

"Life is priceless. Yours and that of those who work for you. How much is your life worth to you?" *Isn't it worth parting with some of your precious blood money?* "What if your secretary had been the one to open that letter?" She let that sink in. His face paled and the possibility that someone else could get hurt seemed to sting. "We'll need to take similar precautions at your home."

He stood, turned his back on her to glare out the window and spread his elbows wide as if he wanted to impress her with his size. "I don't need a bodyguard at home."

She tilted her head to one side and injected lightness in her voice. "How about a protector who can type and help you get ready for your seminar?"

His smile, when he faced her, reminded her of a steel trap. "I have too much to do to have you hovering over me all day."

She suppressed her growing irritation. "I don't hover. You'll barely know I'm around."

"Somehow, I doubt that." He stalked toward her, as if she was a tasty prey. His gaze softened and focused just below her right eye. "You're bleeding."

Then he lifted his hand and brushed at the wound

with the edge of his thumb. The gentleness of his touch was so unexpected, her stomach quivered. "It could've been your eye."

She swallowed the knot of confusion swelling in her throat. "It could've been your face."

He ripped his hand from her cheek and she gasped at the startling husking feel of his flesh peeling away from hers.

The office door burst open and Russell marched in, gesturing a thumb over his shoulder. "Pete, the police are here. They want to talk to you."

Peter seemed relieved at the interruption. "I'll be right there."

He grabbed his glasses off the desk, settled them on his nose and strode toward his office door.

Adria stepped in behind him. "Do we have an agreement? Are you hiring me to take over your security?"

"Yes. I want to ensure my employees' safety."

With an insistent hand on his upper arm, she stopped him as he reached the door. "Are you prepared to take orders from someone you employ?"

His eyes narrowed and became an impatient storm. "I already said so."

"I want to be certain you understand that if you hire me, if I accept this position, I will be in total control of your every movement."

"I get it." He started to move away, but she held him in place.

"I have to insist. You're a man who likes to control. I have to be sure that if I say 'Down,' you'll obey without question. Your life will depend on it."

He ground his teeth, fighting the twin urges to control and protect. "I'm hiring you as my security specialist. I will follow your suggestions."

"Be sure you do because, once I accept an assignment, I see it to its end." Until this menace who jeopardized her plans was discovered. She released her grip on his arm. "Once you give your statement to the police, we need to talk about the letters you've received and who may want to harm you."

The sooner whoever sent the bomb was stopped, the sooner she could disperse Peter's financial wealth to worthier causes.

Resignation deepened his voice to a rich bass. "As my security specialist, please make sure you pass around the word I've left the building and won't return until whoever is sending these letters is caught. I won't let some foolish person who's bent on a vendetta against me jeopardize my employees. Then we have some packing to do."

She followed him to the knot of policemen by the elevator doors. "Remember, wherever you go, I go."

"Yeah, me and my shadow."

Two police officers took their statements and carried off the remnants of the letter bomb as well as the other letters as evidence. While Peter was busy packing cartons with files, Adria called her office and asked her ever-cheerful assistant, Julie, to round up two teams—one to correct deficiencies inside the building, the other to guard Peter 24/7.

"It's going to take time, Adria," Julie said, in way that made Adria think of a cat licking cream. She could just see Julie's blue eyes twinkling and imagine the blinding wattage of her smile. Julie lived for unpredictability and had found it at Caskey & Caskey. She craved action, but her organizational skills made her invaluable behind the scenes. "I've already let go most of the people we have on retainer."

"Call in the floaters." Adria could hear Julie leafing through her personnel book, ticking off possibilities. If anyone could coordinate this assignment, it was Julie.

"I've notified them of the office's closing, too," Julie said. "I've already pretty much settled everything. All that's left is closing the accounts and packing the boxes. The Realtor's already shown the place to a couple of prospective buyers."

"Put her off for a bit. I need you to keep the office open for a couple more weeks."

"If you insist," Julie said, and made it sound like a treat.

"Start with the Swans for the home protection."

"I was going to suggest them. And Sam Keane. She's just finishing up an assignment and probably hasn't had time to round up something new. How big of a team do you want?"

"I'd like five for around-the-clock protection."

"Five?" Peter looked up from his packing and frowned at her. "I can't have that many people wandering around my home."

"Guarding is boring, Peter. We'll need shift changes to keep everyone fresh." She turned back to Julie. "Call DeHaven Security for the building assessment. They'll appreciate the reference."

"I'm right on it. You know, when you said you were closing down, I just knew you'd change your mind. I can't tell you how happy that makes me."

"I'm not changing my mind. I'm still closing the business."

"And next week, it'll be another emergency," Julie said, in a way only the perpetually cheerful could. There was no point arguing. "There always is. I was counting on it. Anything else?"

"Send my ready bag with the team to meet me at Mr. Dragon's home. It's in my office closet on the top shelf. You'll need to add my weapon—"

"No." The simple word was a detonation more deafening than this afternoon's bomb. Peter grabbed the phone out of her hand and barked into the receiver. "No weapons."

"It's only a precaution." Adria stuck her hand out for the phone.

He pressed the receiver against his stomach. To keep Julie from hearing their argument? "No guns."

"I'm trained."

"No guns." The way his voice went cold and lifeless struck her as odd.

"In the nine years I've been doing this, I have not once fired my weapon on duty."

"No guns."

"What do you have against firearms?" She remembered him throwing up after seeing her mother's body. Had the killing gotten to him?

His eyes were pure steel and just as impenetrable. "If you carry a weapon, then our deal is off. I will not allow a gun in my home."

Had his father's brutality marked him? Made him deny the tools of his father's trade? She hadn't expected this scar in him and wasn't sure what to make of it. "Fine, no weapons."

She grabbed the phone back from him. "Julie, forget the Glock. I'll still need the bag with the change of clothes, my knitting bag and my laptop." Peter didn't need to know she kept a spare handgun and a knife in her computer case. Keeping a low profile and retreat were a protector's most important protective techniques, but it never hurt to have a backup—especially when she wasn't sure what she was up against. "Call me when you have details." She gave her Peter's home address.

"Knitting bag?" Peter asked, and returned to his packing.

"Knitting is how I relax." How she dealt with the excess energy anxiety fueled in her. "Off-duty, of course."

Before leaving, Adria cornered Russell, explained who she was and briefed him on his duties. "You'll need to limit access to information about Peter. Don't tell anyone where he is—for any reason. Cancel his publicity interviews for the seminar."

Russell saluted her. "Will do, Captain."

"I'll send briefings every day," Peter said as he closed his briefcase. "And I expect detailed reports every day."

"Of course."

Briefcase in hand, Peter rounded the desk and put a hand on his brother's shoulder. "I'm counting on you, Russell."

Russell's mouth flattened and he nodded, looking as serious as he could with his dimpled baby face. "I won't let you down. I promise."

As Russell left the office, there was a new bounce to his step. Maybe Peter should trust his little brother more often. Everyone liked to believe they counted for something.

Adria arranged to have the boxes transported down to Peter's car in the garage. Before she allowed Peter to enter the car, she inspected every box and the car itself.

"Is this necessary?" Peter asked, standing soldier-straight.

"Absolutely. We agreed. When it comes to security,

what I say goes." Once done, she opened the back passenger's side door for him.

He balked. "I'll drive."

She smiled at him—all teeth and no sweetness. "When was the last time you took an evasive driving course?"

He grumbled, but slid into the back seat. Watching clouds gather in his eyes hadn't been as pleasurable as it should've been.

She settled into the driver's seat and turned on the engine. "When was the last time you had your car serviced?"

"Why?"

She adjusted the rearview mirror and caught his stern expression. "I want to be sure I'm driving something I can depend on."

"My car maintenance is automated." He flicked open the latches on his briefcase and retrieved a file.

"Automated?"

"It's the only way to take care of what's important."

Automation? For important things? Was his personal life automated, too? Not that she was one to talk. She liked routine. She liked things done her way. She liked knowing what was coming before it got there. But he didn't have to know that. "Doesn't it take all the wonder out of life?"

"It takes the unpredictability of human memory out of the equation."

Ah, control. He needed it, depended on it. And there she was taking it away from him.

Chapter 4

The police's investigation had delayed their departure from the Dragon, Inc. building. Now the shadows of dusk darkened the already-gray sky as Adria drove the six miles to Peter's home along the shore in Darien. The boy had relegated his life on Oahu to the past, but it seemed the man still needed the calming rhythm of the sea.

After she'd insisted on driving, Peter, like a belligerent child, treated her like a chauffeur, ignoring her and burying his nose in paperwork. Which was just as well, Adria thought, as she relentlessly scanned the environment outside the car.

She drove slowly past the old stone two-story home where Peter lived to the end of the street where she turned back before stopping in front of the black metal gate. "Security certainly isn't your top priority, is it?"

Peter glanced up from the file balanced on his knees. "What do you mean?"

"There's not a single light shining on the property. And all those trees offer a perfect cover for an intruder. Not to mention your nearest neighbor might as well be a mile away for all they can see of your property."

"I like my privacy." Peter curled back over his work, a grumpy bear irritated at having been disturbed for something so trivial as personal safety.

To anybody else, the place would look pitch-black and deserted, but Adria had left her most important skills off the résumé she'd given Peter. Even on this dark night, to her honed senses, Peter's home appeared as clearly as if a full moon shone.

A spiked black iron gate protected the driveway. The driveway wound, twisting its way beneath a canopy of maple trees. In the background birches swayed their ghostly white limbs in sinister cadence to the sea breeze. Spring weeds spread uncontrolled through the overgrown lawn. The property vaguely reminded her of a wicked witch's home in fairy tales. Did he hope to bury his secret in this dark abode? Still, such a forbidding place was also a minefield of possible places to hide for someone with murder on the mind. "Do you have as much problem hanging on to a gardener as you do a secretary?"

His expression was puzzled as he looked up from his file. "I don't have any problems hanging on to any of my employees. Roberto retired and I haven't had time to interview a replacement." He shoved the file into his briefcase and snapped the clasps closed. "I was going to mow this weekend."

"Before or after the full day at work?"

He jittered the end of his titanium pen on the leather top of his briefcase. "The gate opener is in the glove box."

She reached into the glove box and pulled out the remote. Nothing happened when she pointed it to the gate and pressed the button. "When was the last time you checked the batteries in this thing?"

"They get changed every six months."

"Let me guess—at the same time you change the clocks."

He shrugged. "Makes it easy to remember."

"Automation." She kept her tone light, but already her senses were buzzing with the feeling that all was not right in the dragon's rocky lair.

She swiped the pen from his hand, jumped out of the car and headed for the gate. With a flick of the pen, she found the electric gate's weak spot and disarmed it. Shaking her head at the ease of entry, she pushed the gate open.

"What did you do that for?" Peter asked as she handed him back his pen. "Now I'll have to get someone out here to fix it."

She drove through the gate and decided to leave it open for her team—or in case she needed to make a fast getaway. "It proves how vulnerable you are. We're going to have to make some major improvements to keep you secure."

He grumbled and ignored her, looking out the window as if he was seeing his property for the first time.

A huge pine stood like a dark sentinel to one side of the tired house. Malevolent ivy choked the stone chimney. Rounded mounds of dark green shrubs with tiny pink flowers hid the foundation, spreading their untended fingers toward the front steps. She'd imagined he'd own a contemporary place that was all angles, chrome and glass or a showplace mansion complete with columns, marble stairs and a circular driveway, not this drab and lonely gray stone house.

No jeweled lair for this dragon.

For all his riches, what kind of a life did he have? From his biography, she knew he had no wife—ex or present—no children, no close companion and that Russell was his only living relative. "How can you stand coming home to such a dark house?"

"Do you always criticize your clients this way?"

"No, but then, they've usually made some effort at security. With you, it's like you painted a bull's-eye and said, 'Come get me.'" Did he regret his bloodthirsty ways? Did he have an unconscious death wish? That could certainly complicate things.

"I usually leave a light on. It's on a random timer."

She parked the car beside the house. "Stay here while I take a look around."

Not giving him a chance to disagree, she closed and locked the car door, then searched the shadows as she made her way around the property, pausing periodically to listen and look for anything out of place.

Something stirred in the night, bringing Adria's senses to full attention.

The peepers hushed. Even the breeze stilled. And the air took on a stagnant quality.

Something evil lurked close by.

She edged back toward the car. As she searched the night, her head swiveled in a slow, deliberate sweep. Her ears tuned in to every sound around her—the sway of the breeze through the trees, the slip of Sound on the rocky shore, the report of backfire on the narrow street.

And rubber soles on wet weeds.

The feeling of foulness came stronger now, enveloping her in its rancid arms. She tracked a shadow's path along the edge of the woods. But as fast as it had come, the feeling dissipated like sulfur from a match.

A peeper tentatively croaked. Others joined the chorus. The whirl of wind from the water ruffled the loose hair at her nape.

The danger had passed.

She returned to the car. "Give me your house key." Adria palmed a hand at Peter. "I'll secure the inside."

"It's under the pot of dead geraniums."

"Peter! What were you thinking of?"

"It's a quiet neighborhood. Nothing ever happens here. I leave the key there for the housekeeper when I'm away."

"You'd be better off giving her a set of keys than leaving it in the first spot an intruder would look for. I don't suppose you have an alarm system."

"I don't keep anything of value here."

"What if your friendly letter writer had decided to pay you a visit, used the key to get inside and was waiting for you when you got home?"

"Point taken." Peter looked at the dark house and the light disappeared from his eyes. "I bought this place to relax and get away from the city. I've always thought of it as safe."

A twinge of guilt nibbled at Adria's conscience when sad lines bracketed his mouth and eyes. "Once this is over, you can relax again."

"Can I, though?"

No, but he didn't have to know that now. She didn't like leaving him alone while she gave the house a quick, but thorough once-over, but she didn't have a choice.

She lifted the pot of dead geraniums, took the key from the pot's clay base and inserted it in the lock. With the flick of one switch, she knew they wouldn't spend the night there. No power. Breathing in deeply, she heightened her senses and moved through the house as if she carried a flashlight.

He was right; there was nothing of value in this house. The air smelled of lemon wood polish and pine cleanser, but not of cooking or living. Most of the rooms didn't even bear any furniture. Not a home—just a place to sleep. Maybe it was the age of the house or maybe it was the man who inhabited it, but the sense of loneliness weighed heavily on her as she walked upstairs. Part of her felt sorry for him. As much as he'd stolen from her, she'd shared a real home with her grandfather and her foster sisters. She packed a bag for him, stuffing a week's worth of clothes and his toiletry bag in a duffel bag she found in the bedroom closet. She locked the door behind her, pocketed the key and returned to the car.

"Power outage," she said as she slipped into the driver's seat. She reached into her briefcase for her cell phone and placed a call to Connecticut Light & Power. She bypassed the automated line and eventually reached a live operator who informed her in a droning voice that service at Peter's address was terminated that morning.

"Who placed the order?" Adria asked.

"Janine Taylor, Mr. Dragon's secretary. She has account access authority."

"Thank you." She turned to Peter. "Are you sure you don't have a problem retaining employees?"

"Never before. Why?"

"You must've done something to tee off your secretary. She had your power turned off."

"Janine?"

Adria nodded.

He frowned. "That can't be right."

"Right or not, she did—or someone posing as her did. Which doesn't alter the situation. We can't stay here. Not with the property so vulnerable."

"We'll stay at the Cosgrove then." He reached for his briefcase again and she had a feeling he used his work to shield himself from things he considered unpleasant.

"I would rather not until I learn more about this People for Resource Parity group. They seem to know you and your habits too well."

She placed another call to Julie who told her she'd rounded up the Swan twins and Sam Keane and that they were en route to the Dragon mansion. "Change of plan. There's a power outage here. We'll need a safe house."

"You're not making this easy for me," Julie crowed with pleasure. "All the leases were terminated per your instructions. You may have to spend the night at a hotel. I'll find you something for tomorrow."

"Okay. We'll meet the team at the Select Suite Inn just off I-95 in Norwalk. Can you make a reservation?"

"It'll be waiting for you when you get there."

"You're a gem, Julie."

"It's like old times, isn't it?" Julie's answer was more of a purr than a goodbye.

Adria felt it, too—that excitement that came with strategic planning. The quick hit of adrenaline before the hours of boredom set in. She rode on that high all the way to the hotel. Julie, true to her word, had everything settled—three suites on the fifth floor at the end of a hallway and away from both elevators and staircase to minimize foot traffic. Adria would stay in the extra room in Peter's suite. The twins would spend the night in the suite next to theirs and Sam would be in the one across the hall. She'd noted the exits and swept the three rooms in the suite while Peter poured himself a drink from the minibar.

He didn't look so fierce now. The creased worry lines on his forehead, the dusty smudges beneath his eyes, the downward cast of his mouth made him appear strangely vulnerable in the soft light.

Drink in one hand, he loosened his red power tie with the other and surveyed the room as if he wasn't quite sure how he'd gotten there. "So what now?"

She folded her arms below her chest, leaned against the doorjamb and observed the taut lines of his face. "Now we wait."

"For what?"

"For the rest of my team to arrive. We'll have to move again in the morning so don't unpack. Once we get to a safe house, we can start gathering information."

He dropped into one of the two gold-upholstered armchairs and his tired eyes stared at her for a long time. "Why do you do this? You could get killed."

"Without my help you could end up dead."

"You didn't answer my question."

Shards of anger spiked his aura. She admired his control, but the intensity of his emotions worried her. What would happen when they exploded? How much longer could he tame them? "My work saves lives. It's all I know."

The revelation didn't sit well with her. It would take more than dismantling her grandfather's business to set her free from the training ingrained in her since she was ten. What else *could* she do?

She certainly couldn't tell him about the fear that plagued her life when she had no one to watch over. It was as if her charges' fear neutralized her own. She'd never told anyone, not even her grandfather.

As Peter swallowed the last of the amber liquid in his glass, he shook his head. "Still, it's not right."

"What's not right?"

With deliberate precision, he placed his empty glass on the small marble-topped table beside his chair. "A woman protecting a man."

"I thought your biography said you were thirty-one." She took a seat in the chair opposite him.

"I am."

"With an attitude like that, I was starting to think you'd been around since the Dark Ages."

Peter rumbled an attempt at a laugh, raked a hand through his hair and massaged the back of his neck. "Sometimes I feel as if I have. Have you worked as a bodyguard for many men?"

How much to give away? *The best cover,* keiki, *is the one closest to the truth.*

"My grandfather specialized in training female executive protectors. Most of his clients thought of us as an asset."

"Really?" He seemed to find the concept simply unfathomable.

"Yes. Two for the price of one."

He slanted her a questioning look.

A soft smile gentled her lips. "Most businessmen hate wasting money. Having someone stand around doing nothing all day is a waste. Instead they hire someone like me. I double as secretary, receptionist or public-relations officer. People tend to show a woman more respect than a man. It's actually easier for me to get support from bystanders in a tight situation than it would be for someone with Schwarzenegger's build." She shrugged, getting back to what he would understand best. "Besides, it's cost-effective. Like I said, two for one."

"Can't fault the logic in that." He eyed the minibar with lust, but didn't move to refill his glass. "So where does one train to be a bodyguard?"

She closed her eyes and the watery images of her grandfather's cottage floated on the back of her eyelids. Home. Warmth. Security. "My grandfather was a protector. So was his father and so on. You could say it's a family legacy." Only her mother hadn't followed the path, choosing instead to nest in one place with her true love. "Grandpa says he can trace his roots back to some Egyptian pharaoh's defender, but I always thought he was exaggerating."

"He trained you?"

She nodded. "Yes, not just in self-defense. He made sure I could shoot, fly and jump out of airplanes, drive like a pro, but he also made sure I understood psychology, knew etiquette and learned several languages. I never went to regular school, but I got a much wider education than any college could give me."

The fingers of one hand formed an L against the side of his face as he considered her with a narrowed gaze. "What about your business degree at Yale?"

"I was guarding a foreign dignitary's daughter. I sat through the classes with her. The degree was my reward."

He rose, strode to the window and contemplated the nightscape outside.

"Move two paces to your left," she said, watching his broad back, wondering at the strange sensation swimming in her stomach. "Don't stand directly in front of the window."

He did as she asked, then slowly turned. The seriousness of the situation was finally sinking in. He was a target and he didn't like it. And he didn't like relinquishing control of his life to someone he saw as weaker. His voice was brutal, his expression granite-hard, his temper bubbling. "I want you to leave."

The bark to his voice wasn't unexpected. She made no attempt to move. His long stride swallowed the length of caramel-colored carpet separating them with contained restraint, then he stood elbows splayed out, dominant male to subservient female. "You're fired."

If she gave an inch now, she'd lose his respect. Without his respect, she couldn't do her job efficiently. And she had to keep him safe until she could separate him from his fortune. "Once I accept a job, I'm bound by honor to see it to its conclusion." Especially this one. It was for her mother. It was for her father. For the lives they'd lost due to greed.

Fury lit his eyes with boltlike spears. The effect ruffled her for an instant, the way lightning always did. Still, she didn't give in, didn't look away, not even when he invaded her space.

"I don't want you here." He brought his face a fraction of an inch from hers. Had he learned this intimidation technique from his father? "I don't need you."

"You don't want to need me." She matched his fiery heat with cool calm. "Nobody does because it means that something in their ordered lives has gone terribly wrong. But the fact is that you do need me. You need to understand this threat against you. You said you wanted to keep your employees safe. And you need someplace safe to go to finish your presentation. I can give you all of that."

"I am not going to let some two-bit thug chase me out of my home."

She leaned into him, eye to eye—his stirring with hot and flammable anger. "You've heard the expres-

sion 'the best defense is a good offense.' He knows
who you are, what you do, where you work and live.
He knows the weaknesses of your defenses. He knows
exactly what he wants to do. He has a plan. You
don't."

Adria softened her tone. "We're not running, Peter.
We're giving ourselves the opportunity to respond,
which as you know, is one hundred percent more
effective than reacting. Wouldn't you rather find the
source of the fires than tiring yourself putting them out
as he lights them?"

Hands still pressed against the arms of the chair in
which she sat, Peter slid his gaze away from hers.
Needing his cooperation to get her job done, she gave
him something to hang on to. "You want to win. The
key to winning is knowing your adversary. For that we
need a strategy."

He pushed himself off the chair, turned away from
her and kneaded the stiff muscles at his nape. "Brain
over brawn."

"Every time," she said, curious at the odd mocking
tone of his voice.

"I don't want you hurt."

She swallowed a chuckle. Her being female had
brought out the protective male in him. Sweet, but in
this case, also dangerous. For both of them. He needed
to trust her, to do as she said, to follow rather than lead.
"This is what I do, Peter. What I was trained for." She
rose and gently touched his shoulder, felt his exhaustion kiss her fingertips. "Why don't you get some rest?
Tomorrow's going to be a busy day."

"I suppose a swim in the hotel pool is out."

To her surprise, she regretted taking away his means
of stress relief. "For tonight, yes."

* * *

After Peter retired to his room in the suite, Adria walked into hers and threw her black suit jacket onto the bed. She was tired. She hadn't realized how much until she'd stopped moving. She hadn't misread the challenge in Peter's eyes that morning. He'd tested her without mercy all day. And she'd measured up.

But all this showing off had taken its toll on her energy. She desperately needed a nap. Yawning, she closed her eyes, and opened her ears to catch every nuance of the night. Until the rest of the team arrived, she couldn't relax.

A light rain fell outside. Streets glistened under the sheen of streetlights and headlights. Cars, zipping on the highway, provided a sort of white noise that even the hotel's soundproofing couldn't quite drown.

Her attention drifted. She recalled it, wishing her grandfather had taught her the art of living without sleep as well as the ability to fight without force, read auras, see through the dark and hear like a microphone.

She turned away from the window and wished for her knitting bag. The pink wool afghan in the bag was half-finished. The pattern was simple—a knit/purl combination that was easy to remember, yet still managed to look elegant. She needed the mindless click of those needles. Her personal variation of the biofeedback machine. No batteries needed. Somehow it managed to calm the madness stirring inside her, and that craziness was revving at full speed tonight. Plus she liked having something to show for her worries. The blanket therapy didn't go to waste. She donated each solid representation of her anxious energy to Project Linus and had the pleasure of knowing it would become a symbol of security for a child undergoing a traumatic event.

But her bag was on the road somewhere with her team and all her mind had to focus on was Peter.

She didn't want to feel anything for him. She didn't want to feel the edges of her heart softening, the corner of her fortress crumble. If she did, she couldn't do her job, and what purpose would she have left? How would she ease the pain threatening to destroy her?

She breathed in slowly to regain mastery of her undisciplined thoughts. She shucked her shoes and nylons, pulled the pins from her chignon and let the heavy wave of mane fall to midback. Then she untucked her white blouse from the black skirt. She stood in a horse stance, but the skirt bound too tight, so she removed it. Breathing deeply, she stretched through a warm-up. As she found her calm center once more, her awareness increased.

She heard the restless pacing in the room across the suite.

How could she possibly feel sorry for him after all his family had done to hers? Just her weary body's betrayal, nothing else. *Concentrate.*

She moved into the first posture of the Tai Chi form her grandfather had taught her so long ago when the nightmares had made it impossible to sleep.

She banished all thoughts from her mind, directed her consciousness to alert her to any change in the suite and flowed through each movement of the form. Twenty minutes later, her hands descended back to her sides at the end of the last movement. She basked in the soothing healing ocean of light washing over and through her.

But the calming effect didn't last long. Her rabbit mind started running again.

Though they had left the mark of evil behind, danger would follow them. She couldn't keep professional neutrality in this case. That much was clear. Too many emotions of the past were entwined with this man. Too many new ones attached themselves to her in her state of high awareness.

Fear, deep and primal, snaked like poison through her veins. If she thought of him as a man, as vulnerable, she wouldn't be able to finish her cathartic task.

Leave, an internal voice entreated. Oh, how she wanted to. The itch of the desire had her fingers raking her forearms, leaving red and white streaks on her sensitive skin in their wake. But if she didn't face the insecurities of her past, she would lose what little bit she had left of herself. She wanted peace, long and lasting. The only way to achieve that was to neutralize the Dragon empire. Then her parents' and her grandfather's ghosts could rest and she could finally start to live.

Chapter 5

The Swan twins and Sam Keane arrived half an hour later, armed with messages from Julie and enough take-out Chinese to feed the whole floor. Adria joined them in the Swans' suite, leaving the connecting door open to keep an ear out for Peter.

Whether by design or default, her grandfather had ended up collecting girls who'd somehow become outsiders and trained them in his art of protection. These lost little girls bloomed under his tutelage and grew into strong women who could take on anything and anyone who crossed their paths. Some left; some stayed and became part of the Caskeys' ragged family.

Jodie and Jamie Swan had come to him at fifteen as troubled foster children nobody else wanted. They'd lived a life of pain and misery and only they knew the extent of their scars. Jodie and Jamie never spoke unless it was absolutely necessary, yet could communicate with each other with just a glance. Their being flaxen-blond, slim and fey looking made it easy to assume you could bowl right over them. A mistake few made more than once. They always worked as a team. You couldn't get one without the other. It was both their strength and their weakness.

Sam Keane had arrived at the Caskeys' home literally by accident. The wreck not far from the cottage had taken the lives of both Sam's parents and her brother. She was driving and had never quite forgiven herself for her inability to avoid the collision in the evening fog. The other driver, lost and going too fast, had drifted over the median, causing a deadly end to Sam's family's seaside vacation. Ejected from the car, both legs broken by her fall, she could only lie helplessly as she watched her family burn. From her cinnamon hair to her green eyes to her Amazon-like body, there was nothing subtle about Sam. If the twins were smoke, then Sam was fire.

As they sat around the small table in the sitting room, Adria outlined the situation while Sam opened the cartons of Chinese takeout.

With chopsticks, Sam dug into prawns that dripped with orange sauce. "Any idea who we're looking out for?"

"There are several possibilities."

"Lucky man," Sam kidded, trapping another prawn between her chopsticks.

"Indeed." Though Adria was hungry, she had no appetite. She twisted the soft lo mein noodles around chopsticks and forced herself to eat. "The person who sent the bomb is aware of Peter's movements and habits. It has all the earmarks of an inside job. We'll need to run a check on all of his employees, paying special attention to Terry Atwell, who was Chief Financial Officer, and Janine Taylor, who was Mr. Dragon's secretary. She eloped with Atwell two days ago."

"Talk about inside job," Sam scoffed, and teased strips of sesame beef into her mouth. "Who've you got doing building security?"

"Daphne DeHaven."

The twins nodded their approval. Daphne, with her quick hands and quicker mind, had gone from thief to protector with only a great deal of patience on Nolan Caskey's part. But once she'd accepted her new role, she'd performed it with unparalleled dedication. No one could secure a building better than Daphne.

"The letter bomb was signed by a group calling itself People for Resource Parity," Adria continued, giving up on the lo mein. "He's received several anonymous letters that could be from the same group or from someone else. One mentioned a two-week window for his demise."

Sam reached for a bottle of water. "Popular guy."

"We've been hired to do the executive-sitting."

A crooked smile slanted Sam's wide mouth askew and her eyes twinkled with mischief. "So what happened to your plans to close the business?"

"Still ongoing. This is just an unexpected hitch." Adria pretended interest in the contents of the other cartons on the table. She wasn't about to tell them they were protecting this man just so she could collapse his empire.

Sam tucked her long legs under her, leaned back in her chair and fixed Adria in one of her patented squints of torture. "So just who is this guy?"

Adria stirred the contents of the cashew chicken with chopsticks. "Someone my grandfather knew. Let's leave it at that."

Chopsticks stopped in midair, the twins glanced at

each other and frowned in perfect unison. Jamie gave a small shrug and they both turned back to their food.

Adria was willing to bet that whatever language they shared wasn't English, but something that would sound distinctly alien. "Once we get to the safe house, I want to keep the shifts short and alternate between secretarial duty for Mr. Dragon, walking the grounds and monitoring the equipment."

Sam tore into an egg roll. "Julie had us stop by the office to pick up the two Suburbans that were left in the fleet like you asked. The guy at the garage gave her grief. He has a customer ready to buy."

"He'll have to wait a couple of weeks." Both armored cars were equipped with a GPS and communications electronics. Adria reached for a cup of green tea. "Julie'll let us know about the safe house as soon as she's located one."

Sam tossed back her long russet hair. "I hope it's not one of the wooded lots. Mosquitoes love me as much as I hate them."

"We'll take what we can get."

"Seems to me we had a good setup, a good business and a good reputation," Sam said, a hard edge to her voice. "Why break it all up when you know Nolan wanted us to carry on?"

Adria ignored Sam's question and went down her mental list. "I need some sleep. You decide who takes first shift tonight."

"You didn't answer my question," Sam pressed.

"Because I'm not him, okay." Adria stared Sam down. "I can't do what he did. I can't give all of you what you need."

Sam didn't flinch. "We need a center, some place to orient ourselves from."

"I gave you all the option to take over the business."

Sam cracked open a fortune cookie, discarding the fortune unread. "It's not the same."

"I know." Adria peered at the knot of her joined hands as if she'd find the right answer there. But she wasn't her grandfather. She didn't have the right words at the right time for the right person. "It's not the same for me, either."

She shook her head, refusing to let sadness envelop her. She needed to stay focused on the goal. Keep Peter safe. Take down his empire. Take away everything he cared about. And the ghosts would go away. "Let's get back to Peter Dragon."

Jamie tapped her chopsticks on a container of fried rice and cleared her throat. Jodie finished her bite of scholar's chicken, then fixed her attention on Adria and said, "Problem?"

Adria should have remembered their intuitive ability to sense currents of emotion. "Nothing that'll interfere. The only thing that matters is keeping him safe until we find the source of the threat."

Another silent exchange, followed by a mirror-image shrug.

Sam downed the last of her water and eyed the twins. "Flip you for first shift."

The twins shared a smile, silently deciding on which they'd prefer. Jamie threw Sam a quarter. Sam flipped it up and called heads. The twins followed the quarter's trajectory and when it landed tails on the table, they both grinned. Jodie said, "You go first."

Jodie and Jamie were creatures of the night, moving as silently as shadows. That they'd chosen the late shift didn't surprise Adria at all. How many nights had she found them wandering the beach?

"Good night, all." Adria rose. "We'll meet in my suite at seven tomorrow morning."

Adria retreated to her suite. She stopped by Peter's door to offer him a chance at what was left of the Chinese takeout. But all she heard on the other side of the door was the restless rustle of sheets. She walked away, knowing her night would be no more restful. Once on duty, she could never quite sleep. Something none of her grandfather's training had coached out of her.

She rose at dawn the next morning, moved through the long form of Tai Chi for calm and energy. The razor edge of anxiety still skated right below her skin. She showered, then answered Julie's page and made the necessary arrangements.

Ten days. That's all it would take. She could handle this.

Ten days and she'll have complied with her grandfather's wish.

Ten days and she'd be free.

Before she met Peter and the rest of her team for breakfast, she placed her Glock into her briefcase and strapped a throwing knife to her calf.

"This isn't going to work," Peter said after the rest of the team invaded the sitting room for breakfast. He paced the carpet as if he intended to carve a path into the nap. Adria let the fire vent itself, knowing he wouldn't hear until the heat had dissipated. Being a prideful male and depending on mere females for his well-being had to be a blow to his ego.

He pegged the end of his titanium pen at the twins standing sentinel by the door. "They look like they're twelve." Then swept it at an amused Sam, draped over an armchair, coffee cup in one hand, cheese danish in the other. "And she looks like a floozy in a one-star Western."

"I rate at least three stars," Sam said, licking danish crumbs off her fingers.

Adria shot Sam a warning glance. The man had no sense of humor and stirring his anger wasn't going to get them anywhere. Sam chuckled and shrugged one shoulder.

Peter ground his temples with the heels of his hands. "This is going from bad to worse."

With her voice even, Adria tried to soothe her client. "Jodie and Jamie usually guard VIPs' children, and executives with a craving for eye-candy prefer someone like Sam at their sides in a social situation where a bodyguard is needed. It's much more flattering to their image than a muscle-bound thug. These women are all highly trained and efficient."

Hands on hips, Peter stepped into Adria's personal space. "I'm not a child and I have no need for candy."

She matched his stance and showed him teeth. *Your disposition sure needs sweetening.* "Do you want to live?"

He spun away from her, swiping a hand through his hair. "This isn't going to work."

"It's going to work just fine. We have a safe house waiting for you. Once we're there, I'll need about an hour of your time, then you can work on your presentation. That's what you want, isn't it? Share your power? Teach Joe and Jane Average they have control of their financial futures? You won't know any of us are around unless you want to."

He shook his head. "How did I let you talk me into this?"

Because she needed his cooperation, she appealed

to his pretense of higher purpose. "You said you wanted to keep your employees safe and nail the guy trying to erase your face. I can make your wish come true." Before he could argue further, she turned to her team. "Are we ready?"

Her team nodded, all business, and shuttled Peter out of his suite and into one of the armored cars in an efficient ballet that did more than a thousand words to show the conceited dragon he was in good hands.

The attack came out of nowhere.

They'd waited until the snarl of rush-hour traffic had lightened before heading out. Adria drove the lead car with Sam riding shotgun—Sam never drove—and a surly Peter relegated to the back. The twins rode in the follow car.

Peter clicked open the clasps of his briefcase. "Where are we going?"

"You'll see when we get there."

"Great." He shuffled papers and made a great show of ignoring her and Sam.

On I-95, they slipped into the center lane of the fast-moving traffic. The sun glared out of an eye-hurting blue sky, bounced off the pavement and winked off chrome and glass in a dazzling show-off display. Spring was definitely in the air.

Ten minutes into their drive, a state trooper rode hard on Jamie's tail and pulled her over.

"Fabulous. Absolutely fabulous," Adria muttered. "What'd Jamie do this time?"

"She's a good driver," Sam said, adjusting the side mirror to keep Jamie's car in sight. "She'll catch up."

A black Hummer came up hard on their right and stuck.

Keeping her attention fixed on the horizon ahead, searching for maneuvering space, Adria said, "Can you catch the plate on this jerk?"

"Nope, and his side window's tinted, so I can't get a make on him, either."

At the adjustment of speed, Peter lifted his head from his work. "What's going on?"

"Make sure your seat belt's on," Sam said over her shoulder. "Looks like the ride'll get bumpy."

The volume of traffic narrowed Adria's choices. Peter was her priority, but no innocent commuter would get hurt if she could help it.

The Hummer's driver stuck to her right side, narrowing the space between them. Cars boxed her front, side and back. "Are they all together?"

Sam shifted in her seat. "Don't think so. One mother with a bawling kid in a car seat in the minivan beside you. Salesman busy on the phone in the Grand Prix behind you. He's not paying attention to anything."

Adria tapped her brakes with her left foot, hoping to catch the attention of the driver behind her. As she slowed, the Hummer scraped his side against hers, scratching paint, creating a shower of sparks that bounced against Sam's window.

Sam stiffened and went paper-white.

"Simply marvelous," Adria muttered, then gave Sam a shove. "Snap out of it."

"What's wrong with her?" Peter asked as he shoved his file back into his briefcase.

Adria ignored him. Her grandfather would have handled the situation with grace and precision. He'd have gotten Sam out of her stress response with dignity intact. He wouldn't have put her in this situation in the first place. Adria didn't know how to handle anyone's fears—all they did was make her feel helpless because she knew where they came from, why they hurt, and she loved these women as if they were her sisters. She couldn't run the business without her grandfather. She didn't know how to keep everything together. She needed him. They all needed him. Anxiety crawled beneath her skin like crazed ants. She'd done her homework. She knew the network of roads by heart, but Sam needed action. Adria shoved a map into Sam's hands. "Find me an exit."

Sam fumbled with the map. "You didn't have to hit so hard."

"First one to make a mistake loses. That's the way it goes in this business and you know it."

"I'm fine."

"The map."

Sam cleared her throat and unfolded the map.

"Forget the map." Peter leaned forward, wrapping a hand around each of the headrests. "We're nearing Bridgeport. If you take Exit 27A, we can lose him. He'd have to go over the bridge to turn around. We could make good time on Route 25 or switch to the Merritt Parkway to confuse him and lose him."

"Sounds like a plan."

The Hummer slowed, then bullied the salesman's silver Grand Prix into the third lane and wedged into his place behind her car. The salesman laid on his horn, then shook his fist at the Hummer. The Hummer swung back and forth along her bumper, making sure he filled all of her mirrors with his big, bad bulk.

A baseball cap and sunglasses pooled his cheeks with shadows. An overlarge handlebar mustache distorted the proportions of his face. No doubt fake.

He rammed her bumper, bobbling the car for a second. Adria held on firmly.

"Where are the cops when you need them?" Sam said, her voice straying high and thin as she was trying hard to strong-arm the remnants of terror still pecking at her mind.

Adria played along, pretending they were on a joyride, even when she noticed the driver's armed hand steadying itself on the side mirror. "How much you want to bet the Hummer put in a call to our friendly state trooper about some hazardous driving on Jamie's part?"

"You think?"

Peter's fingers sparked static against her shoulder. "He has a gun!"

"Someone wants to give you a little scare, Peter. Stay low. What I'd like to know is how he found out where you were. Who'd you talk to?"

"I checked in with Russell."

"After I told you *not* to tell anyone where you were?"

"I needed some information."

"And gave away your advantage and *our* safety at the same time."

But now wasn't the time for an argument. The shot from the Hummer's weapon hit her rear tire and smacked through the car like a cow kick. Good thing the tires were reinforced no-flats. They'd make it to the safe house without having to stop.

As they approached a curve on the road, the Hummer positioned himself to spin her out. A space opened up and before he could strike, she crammed herself into it and wove in and out of traffic, until a string of commuters spaced them from the Hummer.

"The 27A's coming up," Peter said.

Looking ahead, she formulated a plan, then maneuvered to the outside lane. She let her pursuer catch up to her, leaving one car between them. Her gaze flicked through all the mirrors, checking for traffic. "Hang on."

With a quick snap, she muscled the car across three lanes and onto the sharp right turn of the exit. To a raucous symphony of blaring horns, she left their pursuer with no other option than to drive on by. The exit cloverleafed onto the two-lane Route 25.

"Jesus! Are you trying to get us killed?" Peter roared from the back as his briefcase went flying out of his lap.

"I'm trying to keep you alive."

Once settled on Route 25, Adria dropped her speed and filed into the traffic. She made her way into Easton to a massive Colonial that looked like any other house in the high-end neighborhood. The two-acre lot sat at the bottom of a dead-end street in a quiet community of gated and manicured two-acre-plus lots. But unlike its neighbors, every tree was artistically arranged, every square foot of grass was strategically planned and every inch of the house was logistically engineered to hide enough electronic security devices to ensure that no intruder could enter the property undetected.

As she exited the car, Adria noted both the missing chaos of city noises and the bucolic chirp of birds. Sun warmed the earth, perfuming the air with its peaty scent. In the flower beds, daffodils bloomed gaily.

Deceptive, this quiet.

"This way," Adria said as Peter issued from the car, briefcase in hand. Sam punched the security code into the front door of the house, opened it and went inside.

Like a steel bracelet, Peter's hand snapped around Adria's wrist, turning her to face him. Her pulse bumped warm against his cold fingers. She recognized the storm of fury blowing in his eyes, understood how the loss of control over his fate grated against everything he was, but she couldn't let him use it against her or she would lose her advantage.

"You know they have classes for that." Adria held on to his gaze, cool and calm.

"For what?"

"Anger management."

His grip around her wrist tightened as he jerked it up tight against his chest and invaded her space. "I never had a problem with it before you showed up at my office."

And that was the crux of it all. Right now, she represented all that was wrong in his ordered world, and he wanted to reclaim some of that control. She didn't step back, but faced him squarely.

"Let go." She enunciated the word precisely, low and slow, so there would be no mistake of intent.

"Or what?"

"I'm here to protect you, not hurt you."

Faster than he could grasp, she inhaled, gathering energy. With an exhale, she freed herself from his hold as easily as if his hand were greased with oil.

The collar of her white blouse rippled under the rapid jog of her pulse. "You've hired me and my team to protect you until your seminar is over. I'm bound by honor to fulfill my duty." She slanted him a smile laced with contempt. "You understand the concept of honor, don't you?"

Danger shimmered around him, hot and red. "From now on, things are going to run differently."

"This isn't a business negotiation, Mr. Dragon. It's a threat situation."

"I'm not stupid, Adria. I was there."

"You have to trust that every decision I make is to keep you safe. You agreed."

"I didn't know it would feel like this." He swiped a hand to the back of his neck. "I'm not the type of person who sits back while all hell's breaking loose around him. I want to know what's going on. I want to understand the threat. I want a say in what happens. This situation affects me. I'm going to help defuse it."

"You want to help?"

The hum of challenge pulsed between them. Caged emotions danced brightly in his eyes and stirred something she'd long ago learned to cast aside. Another time, another place, another person. Maybe. But not him and not now. There was too much at stake.

He nodded.

"Good. Then let's go." She swept her arm in an arc to the side, guiding him toward the front door. "Time for truth or dare."

Chapter 6

"Is there a kitchen in this place?" Peter asked after Adria had shown him the command post on the first floor and his room and the safe room on the second floor.

"It's still early," she said, a little annoyed that he could want food at a time like this.

"I haven't eaten since lunch yesterday."

He'd gone to bed without dinner and was too riled by the sight of the twins and Sam to eat breakfast. "Right. This way, then." She led him down the stairs and to the back of the house.

The kitchen, like the rest of the house, was set up for efficiency rather than style. The color scheme was neutral. The surfaces easy to clean. There was nothing fussy or feminine, nothing that spelled home. The white cupboards, granite counters and stainless-steel appliances gave the room a masculine feel that made

Peter look right at home. He headed straight for the fridge and perused its contents.

"Julie should have stocked it with a week's worth of groceries," Adria said, watching the straight lines of his body as he stood illuminated by the harsh light of the fridge. The solidness of his stance made it hard to paint him as a victim.

"Your Julie has strange tastes."

"She knows what we all like." Root beer and corn dogs for the twins, bottled water and Brie for Sam, green tea and thin mint cookies for her. When faced with long hours of boredom, it was nice to find a few bites of comfort. Julie always remembered and they always forgot to thank her for her invisible efficiency.

"Thin mints?"

"What's wrong with thin mints?"

"In the fridge?"

"They're better cold."

Dimples creased his cheeks. And that strange turn of her stomach had her thinking she was coming down with the flu. She cleared her throat. "We need to talk."

"Truth or dare?" he teased as he poured water into the coffeemaker.

"Actually, more of a do-you-dare-to-tell-the-truth?"

"Ask away and I'll cook."

After he filled the filter with coffee, he plugged in the coffeemaker and set it gurgling. He looked around the cupboards and took out two cutting boards and a large pot. Next he raided the fridge and came out with a chicken, garlic, onions, carrots, celery and mushrooms. He moved with natural grace for someone who spent his days with his butt parked on a throne. He contemplated the ingredients he'd lined up on the counter with the enthusiasm of an artist facing the possibilities a blank canvas offered. "Julie knows how to shop after all."

Frowning, Adria slid onto a stool on the other side of the counter where he'd set up shop. "She's very good at what she does."

"So why are you closing the business?" He unwrapped the chicken and washed it, then placed it on one of the cutting boards.

"I told you already. It was my grandfather's business and it's not the same without him."

He picked a knife out of the block and tested its edge. "The assets are the same."

"But not the grounding force."

"Ah." He dissected the chicken into parts with a precision that was forceful—much like his financial surgeries. A shiver skated down her spine. Where had he learned the skill? From his father?

Someone like him wouldn't hesitate to kill to get what he wanted. Was that why he was now in danger?

If you lie to yourself, keiki, how do you expect to read the truth in someone else?

Grandpa was right, of course. She didn't know that the father's evil flowed through the son's veins. But if not, why had her grandfather asked her to tear down Peter's empire?

What is the first thing you must do when you're trying to read someone, keiki?

Become aware of your prejudices and projections.

Very good. It is normal not to want to see anything good in those we dislike, but it is not the way to get to the truth. What are your prejudices now, keiki?

I hate him because of what his father did to my parents. I hate what he's done with his father's blood money. I hate that I have to protect someone like him.

Can you put this aside? Or should someone else ask the questions today?

No, I can do this.

You need to get to the intimate layer, keiki. You need to get him to tell you things he wouldn't reveal to a stranger, maybe not even to a friend. He will drop his defenses only if you drop yours.

Communications was more than ninety percent non-verbal. How often had her grandfather made her watch programs like *20/20* with no sound and made her tell him what the interviewees were feeling by their body language? The words could easily tell tall tales, but the body didn't know how to lie. The trick was having the patience to read the cues and listen to what lay beneath the words.

Let him relax. Ask the easy questions to get his normal pattern of behavior.

"Don't you need a recipe?" she asked as he poured a measure of oil from bottle into the stockpot with a show-off arc, then turned on the burner.

"Not really." He pushed aside the cutting board, leaned over the counter and skewered his gaze to hers. "Close your eyes."

The unexpected punch of power in his gaze startled her and she leaned away from him. "Why?"

"I won't bite. I promise." He was laughing at her from his dimples all the way to his green eyes.

"I'm on duty," she reminded him.

"It'll only take a minute." He was chuckling out loud now, a low rumbling sound that somehow managed to ruffle and please. He gently dragged two fingers over her eyes, cajoling them into closing. He smelled of the lemon soap he'd used to wash his hands after cutting up the chicken. Every inch of her body was on alert, ready to flee or attack. "Imagine the taste of chicken."

"What?" Her eyes sprung open. He touched them closed once more.

"Chicken. Imagine the taste of it in your mind."

"Okay." Where was he going with this?

"Imagine the taste of tomatoes."

Much to her surprise, she could somehow meld the imagined taste of chicken with imaginary tomatoes.

"Now add onions and carrots and celery."

It tasted rich, but left her wanting. "Something's missing."

She could picture his smile widening. "Add oregano, parsley, thyme. Some wine. Can you taste it?"

Her stomach growled her answer. The hum of his chuckle sang inside her.

"Now add cinnamon."

She winced. "You ruined it."

His laugh was full now, round and rolling. "That's why you don't need a recipe. You can feel the taste before you start." He tweaked the tip of her nose and her eyelids flew open. With the comfort of someone who'd done this many times before, he dropped the flour-dredged chicken pieces in the hot oil, then poked them with a fork as they sizzled. He reached for a couple of mugs, filled them with coffee, handed one to her, then savored the brew from the other.

He was at ease; she had to keep him there. *Start with the easy questions.* "Where did you learn to cook?"

But already there was evasion in the careless shrug of his shoulder. He pushed aside the coffee and fixed his attention to the sizzling pot. "I like to eat, so I taught myself."

She watched his hands as he chopped an onion into rough pieces and reminded herself that he was a dangerous man, a man with a bloody past.

"I have to ask you some questions." She twirled the mug of coffee between her cupped hands and concentrated all of her focus on the cues his body might give up. "I realize that you're a very private person, but if we're going to keep you safe, I'm going to have to intrude."

"I understand." His gaze flicked at her, hard and sharp.

"How long have you lived in the Stamford area?"

"Almost fourteen years."

"How did you end up there?"

"New York was too busy for me. Stamford seemed the perfect compromise between the convenience of the city and the ability to live in relative quiet without the long commute."

"Before, where did you live?"

He turned away and stiffly peeled carrots over the sink. "Here and there."

"Peter, this isn't idle curiosity. I need to know if something in your past is affecting your present." *If you can trust me with the truth.*

"No."

Everything about him said No Trespass and if she didn't get back on track, she would get nothing more out of him.

Why do people lie, keiki?

Because of a conflict with self-image, a resistance to revealing the true self.

Little lies, big lies, they all have the same root. He is lying, keiki. He is ashamed of his past.

Ashamed?

Read the body, keiki, *not the spoken words.*

The signs of stress were there in the way he chopped the carrots. His posture was defensive, distancing, like a boxer trying to block a punch.

"Do you know if there's any wine around?" Peter asked.

"None. We don't drink while on assignment."

"Too bad." He found chicken broth in the pantry and set it aside.

What motivates him, keiki*?*

He made a good living, had a home and had easy access to food. The basics were covered. He had a brother, but no other family—no wife or children. "Are you seeing anyone at the present?"

His stance loosened as he cut the celery stalks into bite sizes. His head tilted over one shoulder and a smile, rich and warm with charm, slid down one side of his face. "Why—are you interested?"

Here was a man who was used to having the attention he gave women welcomed. She couldn't have him think of her in that way—even if it would provide a shortcut to the intimacy needed to bring him down. The lines would blur and she didn't want to get caught in the trap of emotions. Too messy. She raised an eyebrow and encapsulated a world of warning in the gesture.

"No," he said, his voice ringing with amusement, "I am not seeing anyone at the present. And no, there is no spurned woman from the past who might seek revenge." His face tightened, fixing his smile, giving it a plastic quality. He slipped a clove of garlic beneath the side of his blade and pounded his fist against the metal, crushing the garlic. "I've never let a relationship get that serious."

"Why?"

"It's not part of the plan." He rested an elbow on the counter and dragged a finger along her jawbone. Something jolted in her gut. "But for you, I could make an exception."

She shook her head, dislodging his finger. "Not part of my plans, either."

He leaned in closer. "How about a torrid affair then?"

"Sorry. Against the rules." She slid off the high stool and opened the pantry. She reached for a box of crackers, tore open the inner bag and chomped on the crispy wafer. Obviously, he wasn't pining away for love, so that left professional respect and achievement of life goals. "We're here because someone wants to hurt you, Peter."

Address his need, keiki. *Form the bond of trust.*

"What you're doing is important." The cracker tasted like chalk dust. "It could help a lot of people. If you want the chance to present your seminar, then we have to figure out who may want to harm you. What can you tell me about Terry Atwell?"

"Terry? He's bright and ambitious. Young." Peter opened the fridge and took out the round of Brie. He grabbed a handful of crackers from the box she held like armor, spread some of the soft cheese on a cracker, then handed it to her.

She shook her head. "Dairy allergy."

"Really? No ice cream, no pizza, no cold milk with your thin mints?" His dimples deepened.

"No."

"What do you do for cereal?"

"Soy milk. Rice milk. Oat milk."

He made a face.

"Is Terry ambitious enough to want to roll over you

and take control?" Adria asked, idly picking salt off a plain cracker.

"He couldn't. My business is privately owned." He bit the cheese-laden cracker, and she watched, fascinated, as he made a sound close to purring while he savored the treat.

"But if he damaged your reputation, wouldn't that make it easier for him to take over where you left off?"

Peter added the chopped vegetables to the browned chicken, perfuming the air with a rich aroma. "Maybe. But he doesn't have the vision and that would soon become apparent. Terry is good at what he does—and that's crunching numbers. He doesn't have the patience or the skill to deal with people or other aspects of the business."

"So he gets a partner. Your brother maybe. If you were dead, Russell would inherit, wouldn't he?"

Peter poured chicken broth into the pot, wafting a plume of fragrant steam between them. "He would. But Russell has no business ambition."

"I heard differently yesterday morning. He was asking you for more responsibility."

"He doesn't really want it." A flash of anger, impatience and, surprisingly, sorrow sparked through his eyes. He cared about his brother. "That's why everything is in trust. He'd rather spend his days sailing than working. Even if Terry took Russell on as a partner, even if they cooked up a scheme to take over my business, it would fall apart."

"Maybe neither of them is smart enough to accept that."

"I just don't see it."

"What about your secretary? Janine Taylor."

He peered into the pot, adjusted the burner's temperature and settled a lid on top. "She's smart and efficient, but she's not the kind of person who'd want to take over. I always knew she wasn't there for the long run. Working was a temporary necessity until she found a man who would fulfill her dream of the big house in the suburbs with the white picket fence, the two point five kids and the dog. I just didn't think she'd leave me without notice."

Adria leaned her backside against the high stool and chewed on a cracker. "Were you sleeping with her?"

"Janine?" He waved her question away as if it were stupid and turned to the fridge. "She wasn't my type and she knew I couldn't give her what she wanted."

"She left with Atwell and, according to Connecticut Light & Power, she had your utilities turned off. Maybe there was some resentment on her part that you wouldn't pay her any attention."

He found an apple, cut it up, then took the high stool beside hers and proceeded to spread Brie on an apple slice. "Anyone could've pretended to be her. She had definite plans. She wouldn't have wasted her time on me."

"Then who had enough access to your private information to use her name to make life difficult for you?"

He pointed his apple slice at her. "What about someone from the People for Resource Parity group?"

"What do you know about them?"

He shrugged. "Just that their goals didn't match the foundation's, so we rejected their application for funds."

"What were their goals?"

He took his time spreading Brie over another slice

of apple. "They wanted grant money to petition the government for access to certain lakes by motorboat. Many lakes restrict motor use to protect fragile ecosystems."

"Are they related to Mystic Pleasure Crafts? I heard you and Russell arguing about them."

His gaze narrowed. "I don't know, but we could certainly look into it."

"Can you think of anyone who works for you who might have a grudge against you?"

"No." He offered her a slice of apple—cheese-free.

Before she quite realized what she was doing, she let him slip the firm flesh of apple into her mouth. She pulled back abruptly, remembering her grandfather's rules. "What about the people you had to downsize when you rehabilitated companies?"

Temper smoldered in his green eyes. "As I've told you before, I always provided employment fairs. If they wanted a job, they could get one."

"Still, it's a disruption and people tend to dislike change. Maybe the new job wasn't to their liking. Maybe they were angry enough to seek revenge."

He pushed away the remnants of the apple and dusted his hands together. "Put that way, it could be any one of a thousand people."

"Jealousy. Greed. Anger. Something's pushing someone to act out against you. Once we find a motivation, we know his weakness. Once we know his weakness, we can exploit it to bring him down while minimizing your exposure to risk. You said you wanted to help."

"Any way I can."

She glanced at the simmering pot on the stove. "How long before lunch is ready?"

"About an hour."

"Let's get started then. I want you to go through your personnel files and see if there's anyone who would want to harm you."

Adria led him to the command post. The electronics cramming the room made it look smaller than it was. She sat at the console, scanned the closed-circuit television screens from each of the cameras monitoring the perimeter. Sam was walking her round. Everything else was quiet—just as it should be.

Adria punched in a sequence into the computer. The screen in front of her came to life.

Peter stood next to her chair, watching her every move. "I'll have Russell send me a list of employees that were recently fired or have recently left."

She pointed to the wall-mounted phone. "The phone in this room is secure. Have Russell send you his findings by e-mail. My friend Romy's security program will cloak your location in case anyone is trying to find you through your electronic footprint."

Romy's image appeared on the screen. Her short, spiky brown hair reminded Adria of a hedgehog's. Her brown eyes seemed too big for her face, lending her a doll-like fragility that had people falling over themselves to take care of her. Of course, it was all an illusion. Romy was never a victim, even when life had tried to make her one. She could take care of herself and had for a very long time.

"You summoned me, o mighty princess." Romy's laughing voice filled the room.

Peter chuckled. "She's got you pegged."

"Very funny." Adria elbowed Peter in the hip. His laughter rolled in her ear, sending a spike of pleasure arrowing to her stomach. He draped an arm over the back of her chair and leaned over her shoulder to look at the screen, enfolding her in his scent of leather and spice. "Peter, meet Romy Mirren, information specialist. Romy, this is Peter Dragon, our VIP."

"Nice to meet you, Mr. Dragon. How can I help?"

"Peter's going to tell you everything he knows about a group called People for Resource Parity, then I need you to dig up anything else you can find on them. We also need some electronic tracking of a Terry Atwell and a Janine Taylor. Peter will give you their personal information. Russell Dragon, too."

Peter stiffened. "Russell doesn't have anything to do with this."

"We check everyone."

Adria twisted the chair away from the screen, dislodging Peter's casual touch from her shoulder, and rose.

"I'll leave you to it, Romy. I have a date with a tire." She turned to Peter. "If you need anything, you can reach Sam on the radio." She showed him the unit in the cradle on the desk. "Jodie is across the hall. Jamie is upstairs. I'll be in the garage."

Adria was acutely aware that every bit of information he would dig up she would eventually use to bring him down.

He would be handing her the keys to his demise.

From the outside, the garage looked like any other garage in the neighborhood. Each of the three bays had its own automatic door. Except that no grease stained the concrete floor. No tools littered the walls. No toys or bicycles cluttered the edges. Stark lighting gleamed from fluorescent fixtures, draining color from the gray floor, the cream walls and the beige cars. Inanely, the place reminded Adria of the sterile hospital emergency room where she'd last seen her grandfather.

Don't think about that.

She removed the full-size spare from its well, took out the jack and loosened the nuts on the wheel. She positioned and raised the jack, then took off the wheel. Working with quick efficiency, she put on the spare, tightened the nuts and lowered the jack. After she'd given the nuts a final tightening, she put away the equipment. It wasn't until then that she studied the tire she'd removed.

With her knife, she reopened the sealed wound made by the bullet. She dug around until she found the shell, then popped it out. Holding her palm flat, she rolled the object in her hand.

"Marvelous," she muttered, closing her fingers around the cylinder. "A tracking device."

Carefully, she planted the gadget on top of the door-frame until she could decide how to use it to her advantage. By now whoever was tracking them had most likely already located the safe house. She went back into the house to put Sam and the twins on high alert and call Julie.

Their safety was compromised. They would have to move.

The dot had stopped moving hours ago. Only a stationary blip blinked on the screen of the laptop, quiet and unconcerned. Adria would find the device. No doubt about that. She was proving a more worthy adversary than the original target.

Looks could be so deceiving. Her porcelain-white skin, almond-shaped eyes the color of kukui nuts and midnight hair formed an undecipherable ethnic stew.

That face seemed to belong to the world rather than a specific country. That face could easily get lost in a crowd—an advantage for a bodyguard. Few people would give her a second look. Who would have guessed at the steel core beneath the long, lean lines of her body?

She, more than Peter, was a threat to success. The defender of kings had taught her well. She must have compartmentalized her grief and fallen back on her in-bred need to protect and finish her grandfather's duty of honor. But she could not interfere with the plan.

If she did, she would have to die, too.

The Art of Warfare. The Illiad. The Odyssey. The Crusades. Even the Nicomachean ethics. They had shown The Face the traits of an ethical person—temperence, courage, prudence and justice. The old mentors had taught patience, strategy, how to maneuver and manipulate. And the lessons had stuck.

The Face had researched and prepared to meet the enemy. Had learned all there was to learn about Peter, then Adria. Her weaknesses. How to break her. How to make her cry.

The thrill of the coming exercise revived the inner fire they'd all tried to quash. The throbbing sensation of looming victory pounded with the pulse of a strong and fair heart.

See, I am worthy. I deserve what you withheld. I'm just like you.

Peter would never know what hit him until it was too late. But Adria would, and she would be helpless to stop the course of rightfulness.

The Face could not be stopped.

Time to move in for the kill.

Chapter 7

Knowing someone was out there watching tingled between Adria's shoulders—an itch she couldn't quite reach. Adrenaline flowed but had nowhere to go, so it stewed and bubbled through her veins as restless energy. Julie needed time to find them another safe house. They had to move, had to put a buffer between them and their pursuer. But for the moment, they were safe enough there, enveloped by all the state-of-the-art electronic protection. They'd already cooked up an escape plan that would confuse their pursuer. There was nothing to do but wait for an opportunity and be ready to move.

By nightfall, the anxiety ants were crawling fast and furiously under Adria's skin and it took all of her discipline to keep from clawing her arms raw to dislodge them. When it was her turn to sleep, she took forever to slip into slumber and the trip was anything but restful.

Her dreams were getting edgy again, popping up like ghosts in a haunted house. Somewhere middream, the hand of panic reached out and nearly choked her, jarring her awake. She tore herself from the blood and the darkness and dragged herself out of bed. In the bathroom, she downed a glass of water, refusing to look at her reflection in the mirror, knowing she would find a scared little girl. Better to stay up rather than risk another fall into the waiting memories.

The stress of the situation was getting to her and her dark dreams were a warning. Someone was going to die. And she was going to end up alone, dealing with all that blood. The nightmares wouldn't go away until Peter was out of her life. Maybe when his empire was dissolved, they would disappear permanently.

She dressed and checked on everyone—Sam in the command post, watching the screens; the twins, walking the perimeter. Her team had everything under control. They were well trained. They knew what they were doing. So why couldn't she just relax? She shouldn't waste her turn at sleep. She might not get another chance to rest for a while. But a glance at the bed and the ripple of nightmares caught in the snarled sheets had her backing away and reaching for her knitting bag.

You must face your fears, keiki, *or they will eat you alive.* So she sat in the living room, in the dim light and long shadows cast by the security lights shining outside, and let the click of her knitting needles and the rote of the pattern soothe her ragged nerves. The pink wool pooled in her lap, warming her, unwinding her, quieting the rabbit thoughts.

In that calm state, the scratch to her left came as loud as thunder. Instantly, her needles froze. Still holding the needle she'd just emptied at the end of a row, she slipped from beneath the wool and stood. Her head swiveled to the left at the short hallway that led to the command post. If there was anything wrong, Sam would have noticed. Sam would have reacted and notified the rest of the team. The house had stood empty for a while. Had some rat or squirrel taken up residence in the walls?

It came again, that scratching noise like a mad mouse. She peered in the direction of the bathroom off the kitchen. Not the window. Too small, except maybe for the twins. Besides, the alarm would have sounded at pressure against the glass, at anything trying to force the frame. Then what? Cautiously, she started for the bathroom, then heard the same scratching noise coming from the other end of the living room—the window by the front corner of the house.

Not mice, but rats on two legs.

Where were the twins? Why was Sam not sounding the alarm at the intrusion? How had the intruders gotten past the motion detectors, the cameras, the seismic sensors along the fence and those implanted in the lawn?

If she called for Sam, she would give away her chance to nab at least one of the intruders. Were there more than two? Were they armed and dedicated to kill? To get to the living room intruder, she would have to pass two windows and risk her silhouette giving away her presence. Instead she went for the bathroom, hugging the shadows until she reached the door left ajar.

The scratching ceased, replaced by a quiet that was too deep—as if the intruder was holding his breath, listening for her.

Movement again. A foot carefully placed in front of

the other, crushing the pile on the decorative mat in front of the sink.

She rotated the knitting needle in her right hand so that it lay between her middle and ring fingers, its knobby end in her palm. The shine of the outside security lights reflected off the glossy paint. The mirror caught a slim black-clad shape skulking toward the door. She waited patiently for the right time.

He reached for the doorknob. With the speed of a striking snake, she discharged the energy gathered in her center out through her left hand. The door cracked into his face, pitching him backward into the wall with a gasp of surprise and a howl of pain. He hung there for a second, then crumpled to the tiles, swearing between gritted teeth as he wiped the blood from his nose.

More quickly than she'd expected, he sprang to his feet, dropped his handheld computer and swung at her with a knife.

Fast, like a spring uncoiling, she turned her body away from her attacker and struck. In one fluid, continuous motion, she impaled her knitting needle through his hand and into the wall. The knife rattled to the tiles while its owner screamed in pain.

The noise of the scuffle had drawn Sam out. She intercepted the living room intruder and neutralized him. The twins charged through the front and back doors simultaneously and flicked on every light in their way. Peter scrambled down the stairs, wearing only a pair of jeans.

Without taking her gaze off the intruder, Adria picked up the discarded knife and slipped it into the pocket of her black pants. "Didn't I tell you that if you heard anything wrong you should lock yourself in the safe room?"

"Sorry," Peter said as he stared at the blood flowing from the intruder's impaled hand. "Force of habit."

With a snap of her hand, Adria whipped off the black balaclava the intruder wore. His nose was swollen and bleeding. His hair was blue and spiked with gel. His beard nothing but peach fuzz. He was just a kid. "Do you recognize him?"

"No."

Adria patted down the intruder for weapons and took away a penlight. She yanked the knitting needle from the wall. He toppled into a heap, hugging his hand to his ribs and moaning. His body was thin enough for him to have slipped through the small bathroom window. He had to have known ahead of time that he, rather than his huskier companion, would have to go through this entrance. "How about the other guy?"

Peter glanced at the living room where Sam hefted the second, unconscious, intruder into an armchair. The natural coal-black of his skin had made wearing a mask redundant. "No." He turned back to the kid lying on the bathroom floor. "He needs help. Where's the first-aid kit?"

"In the kitchen."

Peter nodded and left. "Jodie, stay with Peter. Jamie, give me five minutes, then call the cops and get ready for Plan B."

Adria glared down at the kid whose face was contorted in pain. "Who are you?"

"None of your frickin' business."

"I have your knife. Your partner's unconscious. You really don't have much bargaining room here. Especially if you want some relief for your pain." She brought her face close enough so he could read the coldness in her eyes, but not close enough for him to strike. "Do you like pain?"

"Wendell." He panted like a woman in labor, clearly afraid now that he was cornered. "Don't hurt me."

"Wendell who?"

"Wen-dell Gra-ham." The name seemed to stick in his throat, but once it was out, it dislodged a flood that was intent on spilling out on one breath. "It wasn't supposed to happen this way he said no one was going to get hurt he said it was a test."

"He who?"

Wendell choked on swallowed blood. "The guy from the security company."

"What security company?"

"DeHaven."

For a second, the name was a jolt. How could anyone know Daphne had installed the security systems in that particular house? No, whoever Wendell had spoken with, it definitely wasn't someone who worked for DeHaven Security. Daphne didn't have any men on staff. And she used no security stickers. Someone had to know who protected the house. The thought didn't sit well. The target was no longer simply Peter, but all who protected him. "What's his name?"

Wendell flinched at the sharpness of her voice. "Henry Poole."

"What does he look like?"

Wendell tried to put distance between them by crab-dragging his body sideways, but his hopes of escape were short-lived when his head bumped against the toilet. "Don't know. Never saw him."

"How did you get the job?"

"He called." Wendell curled into a fetal position and rolled back and forth like a baby being rocked. "He—

he said he'd heard we were good at bypassing security and he wanted to hire us."

"How did Poole find you?"

"Don't know. Didn't ask."

"Surely you don't advertise."

In spite of pain, a spot of pride shone in his eyes. "No need to. Word of mouth."

"And from whose mouth did he get his recommendation?"

A shrug and a wince. Pain squeaked his voice. "Didn't ask."

"That's where you made your first mistake."

His gaze narrowed and his sneakered foot slipped in his blood when he tried to sit up. "I needed the cash and Jack's always looking for places to test his equipment. And DeHaven—well, it's the best, so how could we say no?"

As warped as that logic was, she could almost understand the thrill of besting the best. "Does Jack have a last name?"

"Heron."

"What exactly did Poole ask you to do?"

Wendell snorted, then hawked up bloody phlegm. "Just break into the house and bring back the computer's hard drive to prove we'd done the job. He said the house was empty. It was just supposed to be a test."

"But you saw the guards outside. You must have considered the possibility someone was inside and this Poole person was lying to you."

"Yeah, well, you know, we got caught up in the moment."

This had started out as a game and the thrill was fading fast in the face of reality. "How exactly did you get past all the security?"

Blood had pooled and dried over and around his lips, giving his smile of pride a clownish bent. "Easy."

"So, show off."

Peter, followed by Jodie, walked in with the red-and-white first-aid box. Jodie shot Adria a questioning look. Adria nodded and Jodie left. As Peter opened the first-aid box, Adria told Wendell to sit up. He obeyed too fast and tipped over in the opposite direction like a drunk, cracking his head against the wall. Peter proceeded to crouch by Wendell, steady him and examine the hand wound. Wendell watched Peter's every move with suspicion, his body poised for a flight he couldn't possibly make.

"I used an electronic pulse to jam the motion sensors," Wendell said, blowing puffs of air between every few words, as Peter tended to his hand. "Jack beamed a stronger frequency at the cameras and programmed them to show what he wanted to show—a loop of what they'd already seen." He glanced at the handheld computer at her feet. "We clipped the computer to the window alarms, cracked the code and faked the system into thinking the windows were still closed."

Adria grabbed the small palm-sized computer. It weighed no more than her PalmPilot. How could something so small cause so much damage? Daphne would want to decipher their code. If something good came out of this, it was that DeHaven Security would become stronger. "What about the seismic sensors in the ground?"

"Jack's newest toy told us exactly where they were. All we had to do was avoid them."

Not good. Daphne would swear a blue streak when she found out. "Where were you supposed to meet Poole with the hard drive?"

"No meeting. Drop off. On the doorstep of the De-Haven Security building."

"Let me guess. He paid cash for the job."

Wendell nodded, preoccupied by the antibiotic cream Peter slathered over the hole in his hand.

Poole hadn't wanted the computer. He'd wanted something else, something more insidious. He'd wanted to let them know that they weren't safe. A cold knot anchored in her chest.

Peter finished bandaging Wendell's hand, then ran a washcloth under cold water and scrubbed as much of the blood from Wendell's face as he could. "He's going to need stitches."

"The cops'll be here in a minute. They'll get him the care he needs. Go up and get dressed. We need to get out before they get here."

Peter started to ask a question, but she cut him off. "Whoever set up this caper figures we'll do one of two things. Call the cops and stick around to explain or hightail it and leave the garbage behind. I don't like either option. Dress in dark clothes. Hurry."

He tapped the doorjamb once and obeyed.

"Get up," she ordered Wendell. When he didn't seem quite steady on his feet, she helped him up, then hauled him to the couch where Sam had his partner-in-crime tied up.

"You know what to do?" she asked Sam.

Sam nodded and proceeded to truss up Wendell. "The twins are already rolling. I'll stay and deal with the cops, then call for a rendezvous point."

Whoever had paid these guys to penetrate the safe house's defenses would have stuck around for the show. There was a lot of ego involved in setting up something like this.

He was there. Watching. Waiting.

The question was: What exactly did he want?

The flashing blue lights from the cruisers flickered on the walls and cut short her musings. "Time to go."

Adria didn't like splitting the team in three. There was safety in numbers. One of grandfather's rules. But above even that was "Keep the principal safe." In this case, that meant dividing and, if all went well, leading their pursuer in the wrong direction.

Sam had stayed to deal with the police. When they left, she would have Julie pick up the remaining armored car and travel a circuitous route to the rendezvous point, making sure she wasn't followed. Jamie was driving the other armored car while Jodie sat in the back bulked up in layers of clothes to resemble Peter at a quick glance in the dark. Adria had planted the tracking device on the bumper when they'd packed the cars earlier. The twins would lose the device somewhere along the way. That gave the mysterious Mr. Poole the choice of two targets to follow on a wild-goose chase.

As Sam let in the cops, Adria led Peter out the back of the house and into the woods. She'd disarmed the system for the cops, so no alarm shrilled as they made their escape.

"Where are we going?" Peter asked, dressed, as she'd asked, in dark blue jeans, a black turtleneck and a black windbreaker.

"Shh. I need to listen. Just keep going straight and be quiet. Can you go faster?"

He nodded and started jogging. He had an easy gait that handled the uneven terrain well. His breath was steady and strong. He wouldn't wimp out on her after a quarter mile. She angled away from the more populated area toward the conservation land that abutted the neighborhood. Now and then he glanced back at her. She could read the questions in his eyes and was glad he had the sense not to ask them.

A mile later, when she smelled water, she touched his arm and stopped him. She leaned into him and whispered in his ear. "We'll wait here for a minute."

Then she blended into the shadow of a tree and heightened her awareness. Her breath was maddeningly loud in her ears. His, off to her right, was an echo of her own. Up ahead a raccoon and her kits squinted at them, then changed course. A trio of deer stirred in a thicket off to their left. Above, an owl whoo-whooed as if he expected an answer. Something quick and small splashed into the lake.

"How can you do what you did back there and remain so…unaffected?" Peter stood on the other side of the tree, staring at her as if she were an alien from a faraway galaxy.

She hated how she lost herself when a situation called for a response, how she could tuck all her feelings, all her fears somewhere inside herself and react like a robot. In that state, she could kill. And had. That made her no better than the man who'd popped her mother. Darkness swamped her heart, leaving it cold and hard. Somewhere inside, she could still hear the little girl cry for something more, something different, something…warm.

She glanced at Peter and, even through the dark blanket of night, the hardness of his gaze struck her as sharply as a slap. He saw the ugliness in her, saw through the dress of good intentions to the empty core. And she didn't like it. Not one bit. Superiority of pur-

pose was her guiding light. If it didn't exist, then…
With a resolute shake of her head, she chased away the
doubts and focused on her task. "I can't afford emotion if I'm going to keep you alive."

She turned away from the hard lines of his face, the
thoughts she didn't want to read, and listened to the
night. Footsteps on the forest floor. Fast and sure. Did
their pursuer have night-vision goggles? "Someone's
coming."

She nudged Peter toward the edge of the lake, then
pointed left. "Keep going until you hit a boathouse."

She didn't like to run from the faceless pursuer, but
the objective was to keep the principal safe. Getting
close enough to put a face on their attacker would place
Peter in jeopardy. She pushed him hard until they
reached the boathouse. A survey of their surroundings
showed no one was home—no car to borrow—and the
boathouse was locked.

"Do you know how to paddle?" she asked him, for-
mulating a plan.

Peter nodded.

"Good." Adria had the lock picked open in less than
ten seconds. "Grab a kayak and head for the water."

Peter stuffed a paddle and a vest into the kayak,
then hefted it over his head, bracing his head against
the seat, and carried it to the water's edge. After re-
locking the boathouse, Adria did the same.

He slipped on the vest, then snapped the two halves
of the paddle together. "It's dark. No moon. How're we
going to see where we're going?"

"Use the light across the lake as your target."

"Then what?"

"We'll see what we have when we get there."

"Doesn't sound like much of a plan."

"The object is to put distance between him and us. Get in." He boarded the kayak as if he'd done it once or twice. With a dip of his paddle, he pushed himself out of the shallow water, then floated, waiting for her.

"Go on." She pushed the kayak into the water, hopped in and caught up with him.

The slap of his paddle on the water made it easy to keep track of his progress. He wore his boat well. Of course, his family had owned a fleet of boats—everything from outboards to yachts. *Not now, Adria. Concentrate.* She matched his rhythm, then slowly increased hers to subconsciously engage his competitive drive. Predictably, he increased his tempo.

They were three quarters of the way across the lake when something slammed into the stern of her boat with a hollow thump. "Faster!" She propelled her kayak so that her boat and her body shielded his. The next two gunshots plinked around them.

As soon as Peter hit the shore, he started to get out of his boat.

"No! Wait." She grabbed his paddle and held it so that they floated side by side in the darker shadows of the trees, the pulsing wash of water slapping against the side of their boats. "I need to think."

"What's wrong?"

"We don't have many options. There's one road that travels around the lake. If he's smart, he'll wait for us there."

"It's a long road. We could be anywhere along it."

"Exactly."

"So what's the problem? We'll just come out where he isn't."

"That's the plan."

"He'd expect us to take the shortest path." Peter

pointed to the bend of road that kissed the shore. "And get out there. Run to the main road where a car would pick us up."

But so far, their pursuer hadn't acted as she'd expected. "Let me listen."

Heightening her senses, she strained to hear a car engine, footsteps, searched for headlights, for the beam of a flashlight. Her reward came in the low growl of an engine accelerating in the distance to their right.

She freed Peter's paddle and pushed him forward, away from their pursuer. "Stay as close to the shore as possible." The overhanging trees would provide some cover.

Watching her so he wouldn't slam her kayak against the shore as he shoved off, Peter plunged the paddle into the water, but didn't stroke. "You're taking on water."

Cold water lapped at her feet and skimmed her buttocks, but she ignored the discomfort. "We're not going far. Go."

For an instant his body froze, the picture of gallant hesitation, but he obeyed. Five minutes later, she tapped her bow to his stern. "Out."

The lot was empty and had the most woods between the shore and the road. Using this exit point was counterintuitive and might give them the edge they needed. They tugged the kayaks onshore and left their vests and paddles behind. Crouching low, Adria led them to the edge of the woods. "Down."

He followed her lead, got down on his belly and crawled until they could see the unpaved lane that circled the lake.

From the fringe of winter dead weeds, she studied the road, listened for noises, but didn't hear their pursuer's engine. "Why did the chicken cross the road?"

"To get across?"

His body was much too close to hers. The heat he generated was a tempting target for her icy limbs, compliments of the footbath in April waters. "You go first. I'll watch your back. Stay low."

Crouching, he sped across the road. Gravel spit out from his sneakers. Once on the other side, he dropped to his belly and waited. For a man who spent his life behind a desk, he was in good shape.

Darkness seemed to swell around her, becoming thicker, heavier. The noises of the night hushed, as if the thousands of night creatures had turned as one to watch the impending show. An acrid taste filled her mouth.

Evil was nearby and she'd left her principal unprotected.

Try as she might, she couldn't hear an engine or see headlights or smell exhaust. Only the strong sense of danger clung to her like a too-tight skin. She rose to a sprinter's stance and raced across the road.

At her first step, an engine roared. At her second, a transmission shifted. At her third, a black monster of a truck shot out of its hiding place and charged at her. Just as it was about to collide with her, she shot off the road and rolled into the underbrush on the other side of the road. On her back, she pulled her weapon from its ankle holster and aimed it at the truck's taillights.

"On your feet," she called to Peter. He snapped up, poised for flight—until he saw the weapon in her hands. Anger radiated from him as he stared at her Glock.

"Run parallel to the road until you get to the curve," she ordered. "Then head back across the road."

"No guns. That was our deal."

"Peter. Run."

"That'll put us back where we started? Not smart."

He was questioning now and that wasn't good. She needed his strict obedience. "Just do it!"

The truck braked, spewing gravel and blazing its taillights. "Now!"

Peter's glance darted to the truck, back to the weapon in her hand, then he ran.

She sprang to her feet and followed him. At the lake's edge once more, she asked, "Can you swim?"

Before she quite realized his intentions, Peter grasped the barrel of the Glock, rolled it from her hands and pitched it into the water. It splashed and sank. "We had a deal. No guns."

She didn't bother looking at the spot where the Glock had disappeared. There was no time for regret. Instead, she skewered her gaze to Peter's. "I'm trying to save your life! I'd appreciate a little cooperation in the matter. Can you swim?"

He gave a brisk nod.

"Get in the water, hug the shore."

"The water's cold. We won't survive long."

"It's the only way to hide from his night-vision goggles." Or infrared, for that matter. "Keep your face in the water as much as possible."

Doing so would rob them of heat faster, but it would also help hide them.

Twelve minutes later, she prodded him and pointed toward the shore. He was cramping up, but too proud to say so. She had to get him out immediately. Another ten minutes and they wouldn't have to worry about their pursuer; they'd be fish food.

Peter slid on the bank, his movements jerky and awkward. She had to get him warm before hypothermia set in too deeply for him to keep moving. "Take off your clothes."

Shivering, he mustered a crooked grin. "I thought that wasn't part of the plan."

"Wet clothes right now are worse than none at all." She stripped off her pants and shirt, leaving on her sports bra, Lycra shorts and shoes, then stuffed the wet clothes between two trees. Cold air licked at her wet skin, raising an army of goose bumps. He stripped down to his gray boxer briefs and stowed his wet turtleneck and jeans next to hers.

"Can you keep walking?" she asked, studying him for signs of worsening hypothermia.

He nodded and soldiered on. She had to give him points for persistence. For a spoiled dragon, he was holding up well. She wrapped one arm around his waist, huddling close, surprised again by his hard leanness. He shot her an odd look.

"Body heat," she said, forcing herself to ignore the false intimacy of skin against skin.

Nodding, he reached around her shoulders and tucked her in closer. She fit neatly there and they seemingly merged into one as they pressed on through the dark woods.

"Do you think he's given up?" Peter asked.

"Depends how badly he wants you dead."

"That's not very reassuring."

"Do you want reassurance or truth?"

His teeth clacked and his hand tightened around her biceps. "Truth."

As they neared a butter-yellow gambrel with oxblood shutters, Adria studied it for signs of life. Two horses grazed in a paddock attached to a small barn. She scanned the yard for a dog, but saw no doghouse, no chain, no stray bone or bowl. No warning barks echoed through the house to alert its owners of intruders. A gray cat flapped through the small pet door on the side of the barn, sniffed at the air and prowled to the other side of the building. At her side, Peter's teeth chattered. Shivers racked his body. "Hang on. We'll get you warm."

Peter eyed the two horses that had wandered to the edge of the fence and were inspecting them curiously. "I have to warn you. I don't know how to ride. But I'm game if you are."

She chuckled. "Their body heat would warm us up nicely. But where there's a horse, there's usually a barn."

He smiled back, but the effort showed. They both needed shelter fast. Cautiously, she led the way inside the barn into a tack room that smelled like leather and sweet feed. She handed him a rough horse blanket.

"Keep it," he said and reached around her for another. Their gazes met and something in his eyes gave her pause.

"I'm sorry," he said as he wrapped a blanket around his shoulders.

"For what?"

"The gun. I never thought it would get this serious."

"I can't argue with your values. In a perfect world, there'd be no need for guns. But we don't live in a perfect world and sometimes they're needed to defend a just cause." The topic would need further addressing, but not now. They had to get out and they had to get warm.

She spotted a phone on the wall by the door and called Julie. She didn't want to linger there. Any moment, a light would go on, someone would come out to investigate strange noises in the night.

She gave Julie the location where she wanted Jamie to pick them up. After she hung up the phone, she inched open the barn door to scan the yard. No shifting shadows. No furtive silhouette. The night remained quiet. No sneaky footsteps. No prowling engines. No sleepy owner armed with a shotgun. She edged the door open wider and cleared the yard, then shirked the blanket off her shoulders, instantly regretting the loss of its prickly warmth. "Let's go."

Chapter 8

With all the company's leases broken, the only house Julie was able to round up for them on such short notice was her stepfather's. He and his new wife were still wintering in Florida and wouldn't arrive back in Monroe until late May or early June.

Adria didn't like the feeling of vulnerability as she patrolled the wooded lot. Though they weren't followed to the house, the scent of something evil seemed to hang in the air. Still, they had no choice but to stay there for a day or two and reassess the threat. She'd already asked Julie to keep looking for a better location.

As she headed back toward the house, Adria noted its many faults. For one, the mustard-yellow ranch sprawled into an L. It sat on a corner lot. The population was denser there. More traffic traveled the narrow roads. No fence other than a foot-high stone wall protected the property. Too many trees offered a place to hide. An alarm system was present, but it was the kind that would detract only honest people. And to top it all off, the grounds were littered with gazing balls, lawn dwarves and plaster animals.

Midmorning, the twins relieved her, and though Adria knew she should get some rest while she could, too much restless energy raced through her veins and too many knotty questions tangled in her mind.

How could their pursuer know their next step seemingly before they did? Her grandfather had believed in a person's ability to transport his spirit into the future to gather information, but she'd seen no evidence his research had borne any tangible results. Was Peter talking to Russell and unwittingly giving away their location?

Her skin went cold and her step faltered on the winding slate walkway that led to the front door. Was someone on her team helping the enemy?

No, impossible. She strode through the door and closed it just shy of a slam. She knew these women. She knew where they came from. She knew what they'd gone through. They were as fiercely loyal to her as she was to them. Once they took on a job, they would give their lives to protect their principal.

Yet the intimacy of this dance between them and their pursuer kept looping back to the same niggling suspicion. Someone wanted Peter to die. And only someone who felt personally and deeply wounded would go to such elaborate lengths for payback.

Which brought her back to Russell. How did the brothers truly get along? Having a controlling big brother who insisted on watching over him as if he was still a child couldn't sit well. But how could someone as lazy-seeming as Russell have come up with such an intricate plan? Did he have the malleability of mind to adapt so easily now that the plan was in motion and each move less easily predictable?

On the surface, no, but then few people presented their real selves to the world.

The scent of apples and toffee and cinnamon infused her senses as she stepped into the hallway. The sweet aroma transported her back to her mother's kitchen, to the gentle breezes that wafted through open windows, to the warm sunshine that spilled over the checkerboard of tiles...and laughter. Mama singing, her voice as pleasing as a canary's, as they twisted King's rolls into coils, pressed faces into sugar cookies with chocolate chips and macadamia nuts, baked coconut cupcakes and topped them with cherries. Mama's fingers were swift and sure; Adria's slow and awkward. But the end results never mattered to either of them. Only the joy of sharing time and closeness. Tears stung Adria's eyes, but she blinked them away.

With purposeful steps, she followed the trail of sweetness to the back of the house where she found Peter in full command of the kitchen, a tea towel slung over his shoulders, his expression as serious as if he was in the middle of negotiating a deal. As if she was a pirate digging through a treasure chest, Sam sliced through a toffee-and-apple-studded loaf that sat on a cutting board on the pink Corian counter.

After the night he'd gone through, he should be sleeping. Instead, his perpetual motion, the stiff set of his face and the gold, red and blue spikes in his aura told her he was relieving his frustration by converting every food item he could get his hands on into a different form.

Alchemy. Transforming unwanted feelings into something useful. Ailing businesses to thriving entities.

Don't go there, Adria.

Although they use different forms, for the most part, martial arts don't go beyond the strong oppressing the weak and the slow resigning to the swift. Remember, keiki, it is only when instinct transcends technique that a force of four ounces can deflect a thousand pounds.

Alchemy.

Adria brushed away the mosquito of empathy buzzing around her conscience and eyed the butter melting on the slice of bread Sam savored with orgasmic approval.

"Early lunch or late breakfast?" Adria asked Peter.

"Both." Peter cracked a dozen eggs into a bowl and beat them, along with some Parmesan cheese and Italian herbs, as if he were picturing some unnamed enemy. Shredded potatoes, broccoli florets and slices of green onions sautéed in a skillet.

Adria picked out a nub of toffee from the slice of bread Sam handed her. Her gaze never left Peter's solid back as the toffee melted against her tongue. "What are you making?"

"He's making a frittata," Sam said with undisguised lust. "When this assignment is over, I think we should kidnap him and chain him to a kitchen."

"You'd get bored with him before the end of a month."

Sam bit into the bread and hummed her satisfaction with eyes closed. "I'm thinking this one would last a wee bit longer."

"If he's going to be around for a kidnapping, we first have to keep him safe. Your turn at the command post."

Sam's mobile face drooped with disappointment. Her gaze flicked to the skillet into which Peter was pouring the egg mixture. "After lunch?"

"I'll let you know when it's ready."

"Spoilsport." Sam stuck her tongue out at Adria, grabbed another slice of bread and reluctantly ambled toward the command post.

Peter's restlessness was contagious and Adria found her skin starting to itch. Concentrating on the shift of muscles beneath the forest-green turtleneck Peter wore, she asked, "Did you get any sleep?"

"Enough." He stuffed the skillet into the oven.

"We need to talk."

"I know." He shucked the mitts and dropped them on the butcher-block island separating them. A symbolic throwing of the gauntlet?

"Have you talked to Russell lately?" Adria slid her unfinished slice of bread onto the island. The sweetness seemed somehow wrong for the coming conversation.

Peter crossed his arms over his chest, hands clamped on opposite biceps, as if loosening his hold would allow his anger to fly unchecked. "We communicate through e-mail and everything's filtered through Romy's program."

She pressed her lips tightly together. Confrontation wasn't going to get them anywhere.

You need to get to the intimate layer, keiki. You need to get him to tell you things he would not reveal to a stranger, maybe not even to a friend. He will drop his defenses only if you drop yours.

She mimicked Peter's unyielding pose and stepped back into a time she'd tried hard to forget. "When I was a kid, my parents died. After that, I was scared of everything—darkness, being alone, being in a crowd, riding in cars, thunder, water." Lost in the inner landscape of her childhood fears, she chuffed a mirthless laugh.

"Of my own shadow. My grandfather tried everything from therapy to tough love. Nothing worked. I was just one big blob caught in a web of my self-perpetuated terror."

"Obviously, something succeeded." His voice was filled with caution, his body primed to block.

"We moved—away from all the memories." She remembered the islands shrinking away to pinpoints in the ocean. She remembered her shuddering sigh of relief when clouds enveloped the airplane. She remembered thinking that the monsters would stay trapped down there and, wherever she and Grandpa landed, the bad dragons wouldn't be able to follow. "But I still couldn't let go."

"What happened?"

The thought of her grandfather's determination triggered a soft smile. "My grandfather was a very stubborn and, shall we say, traditional man. A man protects his family and he'd failed. A man is responsible for his family's happiness and there I was reminding him each day that he was a failure."

"Everyone is responsible for his own happiness."

"I agree."

"So what did he do?" Peter's grip on his biceps loosened.

"My grandfather knew one thing well. Protection. He was taught that the business of protection was the domain of males. I think I already mentioned that his lineage, if he's to be believed, goes back to some Egyptian pharaoh's protector."

"He sounded like a noble man."

"He was." Her gaze connected with his, but his eyes were a steel door against his thoughts. "He read an article about Dagger Ladies. How they were all the rage

in China. Practically a status symbol among affluent
Chinese. And there was the added bonus of them being
a good investment."

"Two for the price of one."

"Exactly. He did some research and saw how confi-
dent these women grew after their training."

"So he trained you."

"Yes. From the time I was ten. He started with Tai
Chi and kept adding. Did you know that with years of
training, you can teach yourself to see in the dark?"

He slanted her a doubtful look.

"He thought that the training would eventually
shrink the fears."

"Did it?"

Her fingers nervously scratched at the black slacks
covering her thighs. "Mostly."

Frowning, he leaned across the island, contemplat-
ing her eyes much too closely. "What are you still afraid
of?"

Her gaze slid away before he could see too deeply.
"The same thing as my grandfather—not being there
when it counts."

"You were there yesterday. Besides, I'm responsible
for what happens to me." He cupped her jaw in both his
hands, turned her face to meet his and drilled his gaze
into hers. "I'm paying for your expertise, but I don't expect you, or anyone else, to die for me. Is that understood?"

She grabbed his wrists, fully intending to push his
prickly grasp away, and instead, held on tightly to them
as if to transfer the depth of her convictions. "My grandfather took his role as protector seriously. When you
take on a job, you take responsibility for that person. It's
a matter of honor. A promise made cannot be broken."

And when her obligation to Peter ended, she would have to keep her promise to her grandfather. She found that hatred no longer fired her purpose.

Peter studied her face as if seeing it for the first time. "You don't look Oriental."

"I'm not specifically. More of a melting pot than any one nationality. But my grandfather's philosophy isn't eastern, it's universal. He believed in what he did and the responsibility that it entailed. He passed those beliefs on to me, to all of the girls he trained. When I accept a job, I see it to its end."

"Even if I fire you?"

She nodded. "About the weapon—"

He pushed himself away from her as if she'd suddenly become repugnant. "I'll pay for a replacement."

"That's not the point. The point is that you overreacted and your overreaction could have cost you your life. And mine."

"It won't happen again." He crossed to the fridge where he grabbed lettuce, a cucumber and two tomatoes.

"I need to know where that fear of firearms is coming from."

"It won't happen again." He cranked on the water. It gushed into the sink, cutting off conversation.

Adria raised her voice. "I have to be sure. Convince me."

His shoulders sagged as if someone had loaded them with a boulder too heavy to carry. He finished rinsing the lettuce before turning and facing her. Both his hands gripped the edge of the counter. Controlled anger shook through his voice. "When I saw the gun…" He closed his eyes as if shutting off a bad memory. "All I could think of was…"

She waited, sensing that pushing him would only close him down.

When he looked up, sadness crimped painful lines around his eyes and rendered his pupils nearly black. "When I was a kid, I saw someone killed with a gun. All that blood. All that senseless violence."

In her mind's eye, Peter appeared as a young boy once more, hanging over her parents' bedroom window, retching.

Ragged pieces of what she'd thought of as Peter—the man, the dragon, the oppressor—rearranged to form a different picture. She shifted, erasing the unwanted empathy, trying to dislodge the uncomfortable itch between her shoulder blades. *Grandpa? What if you're wrong?* "I'm sorry, Peter."

He reached for the cucumber, turned to the cutting board and chopped the hapless vegetable until it was nothing but mush. "I swore that I'd never use force to get what I wanted."

"You've used your brain to build your business."

The blade of Peter's knife slowed and the tomato fared better than the cucumber. "Every situation can be win-win."

She frowned. Win-win, a nice ideal. But still at the beginning of the Dragon empire was all the money that came from blood—her parents' blood. And that money needed to go back to its roots, to people like her parents who lived an honest life helping others. "My job is to anticipate threats and take evasive actions when a situation occurs. I will only draw my weapon or fight if I have to. Confrontations with you over my decisions put your safety in jeopardy."

"I understand." He dumped the cut vegetables into a teak salad bowl. "But I have to insist. No guns."

The man was too stubborn for his own good. "You don't get a vote. I will kill if I have to."

He stilled, the lettuce in his hands forgotten. "Have you?"

The million-dollar question. "Yes."

She could read nothing in his steeled gaze. Even his aura had disappeared against the sun-filled window. "How?"

"With my bare hands." She waited for the shock to register. He showed no response. "When I was guarding that dignitary's daughter last year, she let herself fall in love. The boy of her dreams was hired by her father's enemy to seduce her, get past me and kill her."

"What happened?"

"He tried and failed. I broke his neck as he was trying to break hers."

Peter nodded, paying great attention to tossing the salad he'd put together. "I've seen enough death. I'd rather not witness any more."

More than her father's? More than her mother's? How much death had he witnessed at his father's side? "Then let's work together and find who's after you and why. You have to trust me."

"Got it." The buzzer on the oven rang. He brought out the golden-topped frittata and set it on top of the stove. When he turned toward her again, the light of determination burned in his eyes. "Let's find the bastard and get this over with."

After lunch, Daphne called with an estimate for the cost of upgrading Dragon, Inc.'s security. Peter listened thoughtfully, then approved the expense without flinching at the cost. He told her to implement the changes right away, starting with the ones that would do the most to ensure the safety of his employees while they were in his building.

Another layer of mask or his true concern?

Adria dialed up Romy and arranged for a videoconference. Minutes later, Romy's hedgehog haircut and big brown eyes filled the computer screen. "What's up, princess?"

"Have you made any headway on the People for Resource Parity group?"

"They're a two-bit outfit that's not well organized. There are a few chapters scattered throughout New England, but no central head office or anything." Romy glanced over to her right. Probably looking at one of the dozen computer screens that surrounded her. "I found three citations listing PRP. One on a group of ATV enthusiasts who destroyed a cranberry bog in Madison, New Hampshire. Another on a group of dirt bikers who ruined a farmer's cornfield in Townsend, Massachusetts, after the farmer refused to grant them access to his land for a trail. And the third was on a boating club who spilled drums of gasoline on a nature conservancy lake outside of Weston, Connecticut, after they were refused Jet Ski access to the lake." She snorted. "As if wrecking private property was going to endear them to the landowners."

"Were you able to track down the membership list?"

Romy shook her head. "Not a complete one. Like I said, these people aren't well organized. They're more into destruction than record keeping. I'll send you what I have."

Peter looked up from the notes he was taking and said, "Russell sent their file. I'll see if there's anything more on their application to the foundation."

"The only name that appears more than once is

Hank Waters," Romy said. "He's a lawyer and represented both the New Hampshire and Massachusetts cases."

Adria and Peter looked at each other and said, "Henry Poole."

The mystery man who'd hired the two university students to breach Daphne's security system.

"Romy, do a check on this Hank Waters. See what comes up." Adria glanced down at her list. "Anything on Wendell Graham, Jack Heron and the Mr. Poole who hired them?"

"The kids are exactly what they said they were. College kids with more brains than good sense. Nothing so far on Henry Poole. He doesn't seem to exist, but I'll keep digging."

More than likely Henry Poole was an alias. Adria ran a finger down her list. "What about Mystic Pleasure Crafts?"

"I'll send you what I have on the company, its officers and employees. None of the names matched the PRP list or the list of Dragon, Inc. employees. So far, nothing makes me think someone's out for blood."

"How about Atwell?"

Romy switched screens. "Still working on his electronic footsteps. Right now he's in Cancún, sunning himself with his new bride." She brought both hands up, splayed them against her heart and batted her eyelashes dramatically. "Looks like true love."

"My company has a contract with a private database service," Peter offered.

Romy chuckled like a little girl with a secret. "I am that service, Mr. Dragon. I'm on it, don't worry. If there's anything that doesn't add up, I'll find out."

Peter took off his glasses and gestured at the screen. "Atwell has access to offshore accounts."

"So far he's made three transfers. All domestic. All under the reportable ten thousand dollars. All from stock sales."

"He's good at juggling numbers and accounts."

"I'm even better at digging up information. Give me a few days and I'll have more details."

Romy signed off and Adria printed the files Romy forwarded. She and Peter spent the next few hours poring over them, Adria questioning him about every name. His memory for even the lowliest of employees impressed her. He knew his people and they served him well. But as the last page dropped back into the folder, all they were left with was more questions.

The weather couldn't be more perfect. Winds howled through the trees like an ancient Druid priest intoning. The stir whipped up eddies of dried leaves, dirt and twigs as concealing as fog. Tree limbs bowed and shook as if prostrating in prayer to some angry pagan god.

Hidden in the maelstrom, The Face waited, watching. The titian Amazon patrolled her territory as well as any guard dog. After observing her for three hours, the surprise was timed for maximum impact.

Right on schedule, she rounded the corner of the house. She thought her patrol had no rhyme or reason, but there *was* a pattern to her randomness.

And soon it would collide with her most frightening demon.

"*Samantha Alison Keane.*" The name unfurled like a sough from a nightmare, rode on a gust and right into her heart.

She stopped and listened to the echo. At her hesitation, the heavy branch released.

Here it comes.

The broken branch surfed on the wind, right on target, and snapped the power line feeding the house. The wire popped, becoming a snaking cobra, spitting sparks as it arced toward its prey. One fiery lick swooped down at her, caught the sleeve of her coat and ignited the wool. A scream worthy of a horror flick ripped across the night. She dropped. She rolled...right into the waiting live wire. Then she twitched like a crazed rag doll.

One down. Three to go before the prize.

The twins, like some miniature ninjas, descended on the scene from opposite sides of the house, ready to slay the foe that had felled their sister. Too bad such thoughtful action didn't extend beyond that narrow sisterhood.

And right on cue, came the Dragon's guard.

Chapter 9

The scream ripped through Adria's unsettled doze, jolting her off the couch before her eyes could even open. The finished blanket of pink wool pooled at her ankles. Her heart drummed hard against her ribs. Her breath choked high in her throat. The darkness of the room, the howl of the gusts banging against the siding and the windows of the house disoriented her. For a second, she was back in her childhood home, on the outside looking in, a storm raging all around her. The ghost of her mother's scream reverberated in her ears. Then the present slammed back into her body. The safe house, Peter, her promise. The scream hadn't come from her nightmare, but from outside.

Sam.

Adria drew the throwing knife from its sheath and slunk out the door, alert for danger. The chill of the April night bit deep into the bone. Fragments of pale moon broke through the scud of dark clouds and sliced patchwork shadows on the ground, making the yard appear surreal. A neighbor's chimes clattered an unearthly cacophony. Out of the spin of wind, reeled a scene straight out of a horror movie. A live hydro wire belly danced at Sam's fingertips. Her left sleeve was ablaze. Her face was contorted in a mask of terror. The twins circled the undulating wire unsure how to rescue their friend.

"Jodie, call the electric company," Adria said, scouting the perimeter. "Jamie, find a dry stick. Watch where you put your feet."

Peter rushed out of the house. Wind ruffled his dark hair and flapped the tails of his white shirt. For once, why couldn't he just stay put? "Get back inside. You're exposed and vulnerable out here."

He ignored her order. "Electricity's tricky. I can help. Follow me and drag your feet. That way you have less chance of getting zapped. The voltage can vary in different spots, depending on conductivity."

Adria sheathed her knife and trailed him, shuffling her feet. The wind had probably knocked the line down, but she kept scouring the woods and the road for intruders. They needed to save Sam, but Peter was still her principal.

Jamie met them with an old broom handle.

"That'll do the trick." Peter took the stick from her and pushed the twisting wire out of the way.

Then he grabbed Sam's shoulders, Adria her feet.

"To the driveway," he said. "The asphalt won't conduct as well as the damp ground."

They placed Sam on the hard surface.

"Sam!" Adria shook Sam's shoulders. "Wake up! Sam! Wake up!"

Placing a hand under Sam's neck, Adria tilted back her forehead to establish a clear airway. She pressed her fingers against Sam's carotid artery, feeling for a pulse and found none. "You can't die, dammit. Sam, wake up!" She stared at Sam's chest, willing it to move up and down. "I can't feel a pulse. She's not breathing. Do you know CPR?"

Peter nodded. "I'll compress. You ventilate."

He kneeled at Sam's side. Adria attempted four quick ventilations. "Come on, Sam. Wake up!" But she didn't respond.

Peter shoved aside the lapels of Sam's coat. He located the compression site, interlocked his hands, stiffened his arms and rocked forward, pressing on Sam's sternum. Adria counted out loud. "One, one thousand. Two, one thousand. Three, one thousand..."

Trying to pump life back into Sam, they worked in perfect unison until the ambulance arrived and the paramedics took over. A bit of color had pinkened Sam's skin, but she still looked dead as the paramedics loaded her into the ambulance. The doors shut with a slam that sounded like a clap of thunder. Adria's heart knocked hard. Her limbs went cold. Her chest burned. Would she ever see Sam again?

They were on duty. They couldn't leave their principal unguarded. But Sam shouldn't be alone. Not now. "Jamie, call Julie and have her meet the ambulance at Bridgeport Hospital."

Grandpa, please, watch over Sam. She needs you.

The wail of the leaving ambulance mingled with the lament of the wind and swelled through Adria, tearing a piece of her soul. In the fifty years her grandfather had served as a protector, he'd never lost a team member. Kicked up grit and the whipping ends of her hair irritated Adria's eyes. Tears welled up. She rubbed her eyes, trying to clear her vision. Sam would be all right. She had to.

Peter put a hand on Adria's shoulder and squeezed. "Let's get inside."

"You go. I'll be right there. I need to find out what happened."

Jodie sidled up to Adria and jerked her head toward the sturdy oak whose broken limb had plunged Sam into the midst of terror. "I found this over there."

The light green paper fluttering in Adria's hands was stained with water and mud, but the lettering was still visible: "People for Resource Parity." Coincidence or warning? Either way, they couldn't stay there. Not without power.

"Take Peter inside. Be ready to leave in fifteen minutes."

Jodie nodded, then she and Peter hurried back inside.

Adria stepped toward the broken branch, dodging the hissing wire still spewing sparks. Splinters jutted out the shattered joint at all angles as if the break was natural. Dead wood. A fall long overdue. With all this wind, no one would suspect duplicity. What were the odds of finding the flyer at the same place at the same time?

Someone knew they were there. Someone had planned and executed the incident. Someone had succeeded in eliminating part of the security team guarding Peter.

Why had their pursuer not terminated Peter while he was in the open? What was his objective, if not following through on his threat of death? Why had he hurt Sam if his target was Peter?

Her grandfather had trained Adria. He'd coached
procedures. He'd drilled tactics. He'd tutored her in the
ways a criminal mind works. She should've anticipated this and dealt with it. But she hadn't. And because of her lapse, Sam was hurt and their principal's
safety was compromised.

Choking the vile piece of paper in her hand, Adria
stood and confronted the shifting shadows and the
tacking winds darting through the wooded lot. She
breathed in and softened her gaze. The woods bright-
ened, but refused to give up the trace of evil swirling
through their midst.

She challenged the faceless monster. "What do you
want?"

A breaker of wind pelted her and on its sweep
flowed the baleful scraps of a murmur. *"You. I want
you."*

Julie had wrangled the use of the house of Adria's
sociology professor friend for a few nights while Caleb
was out of town, researching. The catch—they had to
feed and walk Norm. Adria didn't want to take on the
added responsibility of a dog in case they had to leave
in a hurry. Especially not when the wind's eerie threat
seemed to have pursued her all the way to their present location.

How safe were they there?

Caleb's house was in a quiet West Haven neighborhood a half dozen blocks from Long Island Sound.
He'd lived there since Adria could remember and she
suspected he'd never actually moved out of his childhood home. It was still furnished as it had when his parents were alive, and the air smelled...forgotten. The
maddeningly slow tick-tock of a grandfather clock

marked time in the hallway. Every room was piled with books and papers. The threadbare furniture desperately needed a dusting and the forties décor updating. The alarm sticker was a fake and security measures practically nonexistent.

With her options limited, she didn't have much choice. Julie needed time to find something better.

But both Peter and Norm seemed pleased with the arrangement. Norm basked in Peter's lavished attention as the golden retriever spent hours having his tangled coat combed through.

The day droned by. At lunch, Julie dropped off a sack of groceries and an update on Sam. Her burned arm would need intensive care, but otherwise, Sam would be back to her old self in no time. Wanting to hurry the process, she refused to blur her mind with drugs and was managing to drive all her care staff crazy.

Daphne and Romy checked in. Progress on the security installation at Dragon, Inc. was coming along. Romy had unearthed Atwell's scheme of accepting bribes in exchange for a favorable assessment of their company's assets and a better chance at Peter's magic transformation. He'd received payment from two companies, including Mystic Pleasure Crafts, before Peter fired him.

His CFO was good with numbers, Peter had said. At little too good, it seemed, and not loyal enough. Experience told her that, once Atwell returned to the U.S. and was apprehended by the police, his motivation would boil down to a feeling of dissatisfaction or a perception of exploitation. And the conversation she'd overheard between Peter and Russell in Peter's office supported that belief.

But Atwell was still in Mexico, sunning on the beach with his new bride. He wasn't the one tracking their trail. Someone from Mystic Pleasure Crafts who wanted something for their investment? Someone Atwell had hired while he basked in his alibi? No matter how much they looked at the evidence they'd collected, no new insight appeared.

At five, Peter put out a plate of crusty Italian bread, slices of fresh mozzarella and dipping oil while he prepared a dinner of rosemary-roasted chicken, garlic red potatoes and green beans almandine. The enticing aroma filled the house with warmth and had Adria's stomach growling with anticipation. She had to admit there was something alluring about a man who could create such culinary delights out of ordinary ingredients.

They ate in shifts, the twins going first. While they slept, Adria kept watch. As she patrolled the yard of Caleb's house, her grandfather's voice reverberated in her mind. *Look closer for answers.*

But close where? Close to Peter? Or close to her? If the threat wavering on the wind was real, then whoever was chasing Peter also wanted something from her. But what? What did she have to offer? She was a protector. That was all she knew. That was all she was. All she had been since the age of ten.

She rubbed away the gnaw of emptiness stirring in her gut. She would have plenty of time to think about her life after her duty was fulfilled.

Her ties to Peter were distant and long ago. No one else could know about them. In any case, no one who was close to her was also close to Peter.

All the combinations and permutations of possibilities shawled her with a sense of impending doom, heightening her caution. She examined the dark corners behind the detached garage, walked the chain-link fence and peered around the giant holly bush, sprouting in the corner of the yard.

All the while, the foreboding of approaching danger continued to stalk her.

The dog became sick first, vomiting all over Peter's shoes as Peter worked on his presentation at his laptop. Whining, Norm retreated to his plaid beanbag bed in the corner of the living room. Body stretched out, head extended, brows furrowed in misery, he panted.

The twins fell ill next, puking their guts out, one in each of the two available bathrooms. Their foreheads spiked with fever. Their joints ached. All they could think of was sleep. Adria sent them back to bed and took on their shift. Her skin itched and she couldn't stop herself from scratching at her arms. Peter offered to watch after the twins while she kept up the security patrols. His offer relieved part of her stress. Walking her beat displaced some of the anxiety ants trooping up and down her bloodstream.

The feeling of evil crawled up her spine and had her searching into every corner to ferret out danger. *Who are you? Where are you? What do you want?* The last time she'd felt this helpless, she was six and scared of her own shadow.

She couldn't take care of two ill protectors while keeping her principal safe. Yet she couldn't abandon her foster sisters when they so obviously needed attention. How sick were they? Just a touch of stomach flu? Should she compromise their location and find a doctor to look at them? She checked and rechecked each possible entry point into the house, making them as secure as she could. If the twins weren't better in an hour, she would have to get them some help.

Half an hour later, Peter, too, succumbed, heaving up his dinner. After a round of the outside perimeter, Adria found him paste pale and sweating at the kitchen sink. A jag of nausea rippled through her stomach. Her hand automatically cradled the phantom pain. Was she next? Then what would happen to Peter? To her plan?

"Peter?"

He seemed to concentrate all his efforts on staying upright. "I'm all right."

"You really don't look good."

"I'll be fine," he insisted, staring at the sink as if it were an antidote.

"Why don't you sit down?" She reached for his elbow. The heat of his fever burned through the cotton of his shirt. The stutter of her pulse shot up. Just a bug. Nothing more. He'll be fine. "I'll get you a cool cloth for your forehead."

For once he didn't question her orders. He simply drew out a Windsor chair and collapsed into it. Adria swiped a facecloth from the top of the dryer in the small laundry room off the kitchen, ran it under cold water and pressed it against Peter's forehead. The heat of his fever soon warmed the icy cloth.

"You're burning up." Her pulse leapt with concern. She fought to keep her thoughts centered on the present rather than zooming back to the past.

"I'll be fine."

Typical male. Hadn't her grandfather said the same thing? "No, you're really burning up. Let me find a thermometer."

She frantically searched Caleb's medicine cabinet. All she found was a vial of expired aspirins, an empty bottle of Pepto-Bismol and an empty box of antihistamines. She couldn't leave three sick people—four if she counted the dog—unguarded to run out and get supplies. That would leave Peter exposed and the prime directive was to never leave the principal unguarded. She checked in on the twins, who lay like two moaning ghosts in their beds.

She marched back into the kitchen, weighing her options. "How's your stomach?"

His attempt at a smile turned into a skewed grimace. His skin had a greenish cast. "It feels as if someone is in there playing with razor blades."

Wasn't that how her grandfather had described his stomach pain? Hadn't he looked green and sunken, too? Worry crimped her forehead. "Where? Show me."

He pressed a hand over his belly. Was he favoring the right side? Appendicitis? Her heart knocked hard once, then drummed a warning tattoo.

"Any other symptoms?" she asked, watching every shift of expression for cracks in his stoic mask.

"My head hurts." He squinted up at the fixture shining over the sink. "Could you turn off the light?"

She reached for the switch and dimmed the light. Her grandfather's symptoms had started the same way. Stomach pain, vomiting, fever. He'd insisted it was nothing, that he'd be fine. Too late he'd admitted the pain was getting worse. He finally agreed to let her take him to a hospital. Hours later, he was dead of a ruptured appendix.

"I think you all need to see a doctor."

Peter shook his head. "Food poisoning. Maybe the chicken. It'll be over in a few hours. I just need to lie down for a bit."

He started to get up, but she needed him still while

she made up her mind, so she rubbed his back. He rocked back into the chair, braced his hands on his knees and sighed in appreciation. "Feels good."

Sweat soaked his shirt. Too warm. He was too warm.

"Can't be the chicken," she said, frowning as she reviewed the day. "We all ate the same thing."

He glanced up at her over his shoulder, eyes narrowed with pain. "Except the cheese. You didn't have any."

But he had, and so had the twins. Even the dog. She'd seen Peter slip Norm a sliver here and there.

The trapezius muscle in Peter's back suddenly stiffened under her hand. He shot out of the chair, rushed to the sink and dry-heaved. He clutched his stomach as if to support the pain and rested his head against the spigot. Sweat beaded along his hairline. His limbs were starting to shake in spite of best effort to hide his growing weakness from her.

"Okay, that's it." She helped him back into the chair, rewet the cloth and pressed it against his forehead. "Don't move."

The taste of disaster was metallic and bitter on her tongue. A compulsion to waste no time dogged her heels. She sprinted to the bedroom where the twins were resting, bundled them up in blankets and helped them into the car. An ambulance wouldn't let her ride with Peter, so she had to drive him and the twins to the hospital. She came back into the kitchen for Peter, wrapped her arm around his waist to help him up and started to lead him to the car.

He gamely followed her, resisting her offer of support, then stopped as she opened the back door.

"Are you all right?" she asked, tightening her hold

on him. "Do you need to… Are you feeling sick again?"

He glanced toward the living room. "The dog. We can't leave Norm here alone."

"We can't take him to a hospital, either. Come on. Lean on me." A sense of urgency prodded her. Time was of the essence. He and the twins needed help now before their condition worsened.

"Norm," Peter insisted. "He's sick."

"You're my first priority."

"He needs care."

What was she going to do with the dog? She shouldn't have let Julie talk her into adding a dog to her responsibilities. Not when so much was already going wrong. And Julie couldn't come fetch him because she was with Sam. "You're right. We'll take the dog."

Gritting her teeth, she yanked the phone book from the counter and flipped through the Yellow Pages. She found a listing for an emergency animal hospital and tore out the page.

The deadweight of a golden retriever, she soon discovered, was quite a workout. By the time she had stuffed the panting Norm into the back of the car, she was perspiring.

When she returned to the kitchen, Peter was nowhere in sight. Adrenaline shot through her veins. Was this a setup? Was the food poisoning no accident? Were they all supposed to fall victim to the bug, then become easy prey? She reached for her knife and stalked the paper noises coming from the living room. "Peter?"

"In here."

He was on his knees stuffing his presentation materials into a box. She didn't like the glassiness of his eyes, the ashen cast of his skin or the roll of sweat streaming down the side of his face.

"We don't have time for this."

"It's almost done." Strain crept through Peter's voice. "I can't leave it behind."

"Is it worth your life?"

"Yes."

Exasperation had her gritting her back teeth. He was just like her grandfather—putting everything ahead of his health. "Get in the car. I'll get this."

Peter sucked in a breath as he rose to his feet, grabbed the laptop case and turned toward the door. The echo of his pain wavered through her, but he didn't utter a sound. She admired his resilience, but feared it would also become his undoing.

"Did you know that dragons fear nothing but elephants?" Adria asked as she rammed the car in gear.

Eyes closed, Peter rested his head against the cool glass of the passenger's side window. "I'll bite. Why would a dragon fear an elephant?"

"Because an elephant's fall can crush a dragon to death."

His fingers skimmed her forearm. "Don't worry. There aren't any elephants around."

In spite of his reassurance, Adria couldn't shake the feeling that a whole herd of elephants was thundering right on their heels.

She dropped Norm off at the emergency animal clinic, parking the car directly in front of the door so she could keep an eye on it. She'd have to remember to have Julie check on him in the morning and call Caleb.

Weighing stealth against expediency, she opted for

the most direct route to the hospital. She kept scanning the mirrors, but no one seemed to be following them. As she steered the car off I-95, the seat belt cinched garrote-tight against her chest. *Too fast, Adria. Stay in control.* She eased her foot off the gas pedal. The sight of the sprawl of stucco-and-redbrick buildings making up the hospital complex teased her long before she turned onto York Street and found the circular emergency entrance.

She parked in front of the doors and tried to rouse the twins. Neither responded. She crashed through the doors and yelled for help.

A flurry of activity followed. The twins and Peter were plunked on gurneys and rolled past the receiving desk.

Someone grabbed her sleeve and wouldn't let go. "Ma'am, you'll have to move your car."

"I can't leave him." Keeping her attention focused on Peter, she jerked her sleeve free and started toward the hall where he was wheeled.

Beefy hands once again wrapped around her biceps. "You can't go with him, so you might as well go park your car. We'll take good care of him."

Her instinct was to coil her energy and let it fly, freeing herself from the attendant's hold. But that would get her kicked out permanently and she needed access to Peter. "Where are they taking my husband?"

"To an examining room. A doctor will be with him shortly. Go park your car, then we'll take you to him."

"Thanks."

Reluctantly she left her principal behind. A wife would obey a figure of authority. And the cover would allow her back to Peter's side.

Still, she didn't like leaving him. Worry shadowed

her every step. *This is the situation. Deal with it.* She
fell back on her training, mentally ticking off her plan
of action so she could return to Peter as fast as possible.

Finding a parking space took longer than she'd expected. She finally jammed the car into a spot in the
garage. There was no way to watch the car and protect
Peter. She reached into her briefcase, took out a sam-
ple-size container of baby powder and sprinkled a thin
layer of talc around the car. If anyone tampered with
the car, she'd know.

Her mind on Peter's ashen face, the twist of pain in
his eyes, his vulnerability, she plowed through the
emergency entrance doors.

The bright lights, the neutral color scheme, the smell
of death assaulted her senses. Her hands shook. Her
stomach pitched. Her head spun. The crackling of the
P.A. system threw her back two months to the day
she'd rushed there with her grandfather.

To the same hospital.

To die.

Grandpa.

*His sweaty palm squeezed her hand. His pain-filled
eyes pleaded. His dread-filled words came out in a
choked rush.*

*The gurney squealed down the hall toward the oper-
ating theater. She trotted beside it, hanging on to its
metal rail, reluctant to let go. Her grandfather reached
for her hand. His voice was pinched with stress and
was flash-flood-fast. "Adria, you must promise."*

"Shh, Grandpa, don't talk."

*He shook his bald head, his dark eyes pearls of ur-
gency. His sweat-slicked hand squeezed hers harder.
His need to speak lifted him off the gurney. The atten-*

dant tried to push him back. "Danger. Peter Dragon. Hauxwell."

The name Hauxwell brought a cold surge of fear flooding through her veins. They hadn't spoken of Rudy Hauxwell and what he'd done to her family in over twenty years. "Grandpa, it's okay. You can tell me later."

He gasped in a breath. "You must—" Pain bent him in two. "Promise."

"Anything, Grandpa. Rest, please. Let the doctor take care of you."

The attendant banged through a set of doors and she had to let go of her grandfather's hand.

"Take care of—" He hissed in a breath and reached for her. Beads of sweat rolled down his leathery face. "Danger."

She wiped the sweat from his brow. His face was so pale, so gaunt. Tears hitched her breath. "Yes, Grandpa. I promise. I'll take care of the danger."

"Peter Dragon." He writhed in pain.

"Grandpa, please." She cradled his cheek, willing him to heal.

His eyes urged her to understand. "In danger. You."

"I'm safe, Grandpa." She tried to reassure him, to let him know he could stop worrying about her and take care of himself. "You taught me how to take care of myself. I'm not afraid anymore."

He shook his head, dragged her closer to his fading voice. "Need you to. Destroy. Threat."

"I will, Grandpa. I'll destroy the threat."

"Dragon. In danger."

"Grandpa, please."

"Saved you."

"Yes, I know. I won't let your hard work go to waste. I promise. I'll destroy the threat."

Her promise vibrated in her skull. I'll destroy the threat.

A tug on her sleeve reeled her back to the present. She turned to see a pear-shaped nurse looking at her quizzically. "Mrs. Dragon? Your husband's asking for you."

Chapter 10

After blood, urine and imaging tests, Peter and the twins were admitted. The twins needed hydration and the doctor wanted to keep both Peter and the twins overnight for observation because of their high fevers. Adria stuck protectively at Peter's side from the examination room to the ultrasound room and finally to his hospital room, all the while playing the worried wife.

The worry part wasn't hard. There was enough there to multiply into a festering colony. The wife part was harder. How would a proper wife act? A wife would comfort. A wife would support. A wife would stay close. She'd never imagined herself in that role. Being married, having children, had never been part of her plans. On the other hand, the description of duties seemed similar to a protector's. A good wife was vigilant.

She sat next to Peter's bed, positioned to view both him and the entry. Her body shielded his from anyone entering the room.

He was sleeping. Not a peaceful sleep, but at least he was resting. His dark hair cut a stark contrast against his skin—more gray now than green. Rays of pain spoked out from his closed eyes. An IV line snaked down from a pole and dripped fluids into his arm. A bruise fanned out from beneath the tape holding the needle in place. She brushed away a hank of sweat-soaked hair from his brow. A wounded dragon. One who looked sick enough to die.

Just as her grandfather had.

Don't go there, Adria. Reassessment of what had gone wrong would come in the debriefing phase of the assignment. Peter was young. Strong. He would recover.

The hospital was a surprisingly quiet place at night. Once in a while, a patter of hushed voices drifted down the hall. Rubber-soled shoes squeaked like rushed mice on the linoleum, approaching, then retreating. She blocked out the nasty olfactory cocktail of sickness and disinfectant, attuned herself to the sounds of normal and programmed her brain to alert her to changes in the pattern.

Awkwardly, she adjusted the thin hospital blanket over Peter's shoulders. "You'll be fine."

Self-conscious of the echo of her voice in the dimmed light of the room, she cleared her throat. "The doctor doesn't think it's appendicitis."

Peter's even breaths filled the void of her voice. She should have listened to her grandfather and practiced the talking part of small talk more often.

"Julie's working on another place for us so we'll

have somewhere to go when you're discharged in the morning," she said, resuming her one-sided conversation with her pseudohusband.

Peter turned in his sleep, his head swiveling as if it were an antenna trying to catch the signal of her voice. A sigh—or was it a moan?—escaped him as his head found a new home on the pillow. Her pulse jumped. Was he in pain? Should she call the nurse?

"I'm afraid we'll be on our own. The twins will be too weak to work."

She didn't like the situation at all. The strain of the events of the past few days weighed her muscles and drooped her eyelids. A yawn escaped her. How would she keep Peter safe? She couldn't stay awake and alert 24/7. When was the last time she'd slept? Not since Sam's screams had jolted her out of a nightmare. Too long to remain one hundred percent effective.

Her resources were drying up faster than water in a desert and a week remained before Peter's seminar presentation. A week of treasure hunting for clues and playing keep-away from a faceless foe.

Elbows on knees, hands dangling in the stretch of space between the bed and the chair, she frowned. "I've been so busy reacting that I haven't had a chance to focus on what's real and what's smoke screen."

Peter flung a hand across his body, tightening the coil of IV line. His fingers brushed hers on the edge of the mattress. His fever had gone down. His skin no longer burned, but gave off a pleasant warmth. She reached up and unkinked the IV line, then let her fingers drift back to that small crackling contact of knuckle against knuckle.

"What's the common thread behind all that's happened over the past few days?"

She breathed in, softening the borders of her consciousness, trying to tap into the web of the collective unconscious. Dreamlike images of the past five days streamed like a movie. Viewed that way, the common denominator stood out, startling her. Her spine went steel stiff. Ice flowed through her veins.

No, it couldn't be. Why? There was no good reason.

Still, there it was.

Julie.

Adria had asked for Julie's help every step of the way. Julie knew where they were going. Julie had chosen their destinations. Julie had stocked the pantry and resupplied groceries. Julie knew the weaknesses of each member of the team. Julie had coordinated every detail of the assignment.

And Julie knew where they were now. Where they would go next.

She hadn't wanted Adria to close the business. Everyone had understood Adria's reasons, except Julie.

Her motivation became sun-bright.

The girls who worked for Caskey & Caskey had come to them as bruised and broken children and shared the common bond of Nolan Caskey's training. All except Julie, who'd come into the business as a full-grown woman five years ago. She commanded the office with the skill and efficiency of a four-star general. They all depended on her for the smooth operation of their assignments. But Julie hadn't seen it that way. She'd told Adria more than once she felt like an outsider looking in, invisible. She'd often voiced her desire to be out in the field, not stuck behind a desk.

She wanted action. She wanted adventure.

Wanted it enough to fabricate it? Did she think creating chaos would make Adria change her mind? If anything, this assignment was cementing her decision. She wasn't her grandfather; she couldn't take his place as guide and leader.

How far would Julie go? Far enough to risk electro-cuting Sam? Far enough to risk killing the twins?

Adria looked at Peter's too-white skin, ran a finger along the furrows still rippling his brow, touched the strangely vulnerable sandpaper roughness of his beard. A cold lump settled in her chest and iced down her gut. The food poisoning was no accident. Julie had brought their supplies. Julie had done this. Someone she'd counted on with absolute faith.

Adria had to get Peter out. Soon.

Sneakers kissed the linoleum with messy smacks out in the hall. Slower, this time. Heavier. The door opened with a whoosh and a tall, broad-shouldered male nurse in green scrubs trundled in. A thick mop of blond hair sat on his head like a dead cat and brushed the top of the doorframe. His face and arms sported the tan of a sun salon worshiper. His smile was probably meant as reassuring, but made her think of an eager beaver looking for a log to gnaw.

"Hello, there." His British accent floated into the room. "I'm Victor and I'm here to take the patient's vitals."

"Oh, someone was in not long ago." Suspicious, Adria stared at the badge hanging from Victor's chest. The photo ID appeared genuine. Victor Robbins. Friend or foe? As she coiled her energy, ready to strike, she added his name to the list she'd have Romy run a check on.

He fiddled with Peter's IV bag. "Change of shift, love. We have to check and make sure the last crew did their jobs right." His coarse laughter seemed wrong somehow.

She softened her gaze and sought out his aura. Green often shimmered around those who were healers. She could see nothing around Victor, except a muddy line of gray.

"I'll be here for a few minutes," Victor said as he aimed a digital thermometer at Peter's ear. "Why don't you run down to the cafeteria for a break? It'll do you some good to get your blood circulating."

Her gaze never left Victor's hands. She rose, feigned a stretch and repositioned herself within striking distance. "Thank you. I'm fine."

"How long has he been asleep?"

Every snail-like second ticking by since Peter was admitted had echoed in the beat of her pulse. "Three hours."

"Has he been comfortable?"

"He moans once in a while." And every time, the gut-wrenching sound had sent an adrenaline shot spiking through her bloodstream.

Victor flashed her a toothy grin. "He'll be all right, you know."

She nodded, anticipating the ABC course—airway, breathing, circulation—of Victor's ministrations, shifting, ready.

"Listeria is rarely fatal," Victor said as he pressed a stethoscope against Peter's chest.

The nerves along her spine perked. Her gaze jerked up to meet Victor's. "Listeria?"

His brow beetled as if offended. "Didn't anyone tell you?"

"No, they said the results wouldn't be in until morning."

"They're in his chart." He tapped the clipboard on the nightstand with the tip of his pen. "Just a touch of food poisoning."

The way this bug had felled a strong man like Peter as if he were an axed tree seemed more violent than a "touch" to her.

Victor picked up Peter's wrist and counted his pulse. "How are you holding up, love?"

"I'm fine."

"There are some biscuits and cranberry juice at the nurses' station. Or I could brew up some tea."

"Thank you. I'm fine." To prove it, she sat down once again and resumed her vigil at her beloved husband's side.

Victor scribbled his findings on the chart. "Anything at all I can do for you?"

She forced a smile and twirled Peter's fingers in hers to imprint her worry for her dear husband. "No, just make him better."

Victor flashed her a toothy grin. "The symptoms are harsher than the disease. All he needs is a bit of rest and time. He'll be as right as rain in the morning."

"I'm glad."

"All right, then. If you need anything, press the bell-push. Someone will answer."

"Thank you."

Victor's creaking gray sneakers with lime trim retreated. The hum of the fluorescent bulb in the light fixture over Peter's bed rattled along her nerves. False alarm. Not an enemy, but a nurse for Peter's care. Still the incident highlighted her need for rest and the urgency of getting Peter into a secured environment as soon as possible.

"Here, love." Victor squeaked back into the room. "I thought you might want a pillow."

"Thanks." The unexpected act of kindness caught her off guard. Still sitting, Adria reached for the pillow Victor handed her.

But Victor didn't let go.

Arms extended he shoved the pillow against her face and rammed the chair backward until the wall jerked its momentum to a halt.

Back jammed against the chair, head pressed against the wall, hands trapped, nose and mouth plugged by the pillow, Adria struggled for breath, kicked at her assailant and connected with his shin. Unfazed, Victor drove his knee into her stomach and clamped the pillow tighter against her face.

She freed one hand, groped for the nightstand and fumbled for the glass of water she knew was there. Her fingers connected with glass. She palmed the bottom of the glass, spilling the water onto the floor. Letting go of muscle tension for speed and energy, she thrust the glass at Victor's head.

The rim of the glass thwacked against his temple, biting into his skin, dazing him, loosening his hold. Blood streamed down the side of his face. The pillow slipped, freeing her other hand and part of her face. She gasped in air and followed the glass thrust with a shoulder strike that knocked him back. She was up and out of the chair before he could rebound.

Shaking his head, he grunted and lunged at her.

She leaned her body in his direction. Bending her forward knee, she unleashed her coiled energy and let it flow through her hand and into his face. "Who are you? What do you want? Who sent you here?"

His breath burst out like a deflating balloon. He pitched backward, landing heavily onto his hip. One hand slapping at the blood flowing out of his nose and cut lip, he scrambled like a crab on his free hand and feet.

"Help!" Adria pressed the call button and rushed at Victor.

At the door Victor rolled onto his hands and knees, popped up like a sprinter and took off down the hall.

Adria's pursuit halted at the door.

Victor turned in his flight and tossed her a mocking smile. "I'll be back."

He had her and he knew it. She couldn't chase after him because she had to stay with her principal.

"Help! Security!" Adria yelled.

Two nurses burst out of different rooms. Adria pointed at the fleeing form pounding through the stair exit. Knowing that Peter's health was their first concern, she said, "That man tried to smother my husband."

The stick-thin nurse with the white cardigan that flapped at her sides like wings sprinted toward the desk to alert security. The nurse with the ruddy cheeks and grandmother face bustled into Peter's room to make sure he was okay.

Every muscle in Adria's body cracked with the need to rush after Victor Robbins and crush every bone in his body. Reining in her aggression and reminding herself she was defending, not assaulting, took all of her discipline.

She turned back to Peter and the nurse who was hovering over him.

I'll be back. The echo of Victor's mocking laugh reverberated in her mind.

No, you won't. This time, no one would know where they were heading.

* * *

Outside the window, pink brushed at the purple clouds, painting dawn's arrival. One security guard, his supervisor, then an officer from the local police department had made Adria repeat her statement in whole and in parts as if she were a child with the attention span of a gnat. The exercise had further drained her of energy.

To stay awake, she forced herself to keep talking. She'd run out of trivia and was now at the nonsense stage, babbling about her grandfather.

"When I was a kid," she said, her voice scratchy from overuse, "I thought that lightning was the tongue of a dragon and thunder its growl. I was scared of both, so my grandfather found every dragon story he could and read them to me. Kind of like immune therapy for allergies." He'd piled her room, both in Hawaii and at the cottage, with dozens of books—all of them illustrated with everything from golden Chinese dragons to the rainbow colors of faerie dragons to red fire drakes.

"He told me about the gentle eastern dragons and the scaly-skinned western dragon. And he told me that every dragon has a weak point. All you have to do is hit him there and he'll die. He made me visualize spearing my dragons' soft underbellies."

The mock battles had really been the beginnings of the self-defense strategies of Kuta.

"Did it help?" Peter asked, his voice gravelly with sleep.

His awakened state shouldn't have surprised her, but it caught her like a mugger on a deserted street. She needed at least one hour of sleep to regain her edge. "Not really."

Silence hummed between them.

"Talk to me," Peter said, his eyes still closed. Pink had returned to his cheeks. The ridges of pain had softened. "The sound of your voice makes me forget the meat grinder in my gut."

"It still hurts?"

"Only when I move."

"We'll have to soon."

"I know." He shifted sideways. The IV line lifted the sleeve of his johnny, showing off the cut of his biceps. "Are the twins okay?"

"They'll be fine." Because of their smaller size, they would need more time to recover. Should she tell him about the deliberate food poisoning? About Julie's involvement? Adria couldn't assume that Victor had told her the truth about the Listeria. Maybe Victor had supplied Julie with the bug to infect the cheese and he'd wanted to crow about his coup before smothering her. Adria was still having a hard time accepting Julie's involvement in Sam's electrocution and the twins' poisoning. What did she hope to gain from hurting friends?

"Something wrong?" Peter asked.

"You're not safe here. Someone tried to suffocate me last night."

His eyes sprang open. He lifted himself off the pillow "You?"

She shrugged one shoulder and pushed him back onto the bed. "Standard practice. Take out the protector and you have free access to the principal." She cracked a stiff smile. "Obviously, he didn't succeed."

His forehead crimped in a fierce scowl and his lips compressed into a grim line. "No one dies for me."

"I'm not planning on dying. Know anyone named Victor Robbins? Bushy blond hair, tall, British?"

"Doesn't sound familiar." The flare of nostrils and the stern set of his mouth said he didn't like the weakness of needing someone else's help. "When do we leave?"

"In a few hours. As soon as we can get you discharged." She needed to verify Listeria as the cause of Peter's poisoning with his doctor and ensure that Peter's discharge wouldn't lead to a relapse. Leaning back in the chair, she pretended a relaxation she didn't feel. "Get some rest while you can."

He nodded reluctantly and closed his eyes. "Tell me more about dragons."

She chuffed a scrap of laugh. "Look in the mirror and you'll see all you need to know."

"Do you really think so?"

She studied the lines of his face and read them like an oracle. "Your forehead, cheekbones and nose say you're a man of power, boldness and success. You're energetic, decisive and ambitious. Those are all qualities that need tempering. The heavenly dragon is yin. It needs the tiger's earthy yang for balance."

His forehead scalloped. As if the words were coming from a great distance, his mouth opened, and for an instant, nothing came out. "Did you notice the pewter dragon in my office?"

"Yes." Russell had wanted to use it as a baseball when his brother had frustrated him. "It held a crystal ball in its front paws."

He licked his dry lips. "The first apartment I moved into when I left home wasn't furnished. It was a tiny studio. Just one room. And right in the middle of it, there was that dragon. I thought it was a good omen."

"Because your name is Dragon?"

He nodded. Beneath the johnny, his deltoids and

pecs knife-edged with tension. "I was a disappointment to my father. He called me a spineless wuss, a gutless brat, a jellyfish. And those are the PG versions. He thought muscle was the only way to get what he wanted. He beat my mother. He beat me. He beat anyone who got in his way. That pewter dragon reminds me that there are alternatives to breathing fire and roasting your opponents."

His choice of pseudonym was starting to make sense. He'd wanted a rock-solid foundation, hence Peter. But he'd tempered that shift to independence with the dragon to remind him of the path he wanted to avoid.

Power versus force. He understood the difference.

"In the Chinese culture, a dragon is a symbol of long life and prosperity," she said, not understanding why she wanted to reassure him. "Dragons are guardians of treasures."

A smile crinkled his face, amplifying his dimples. "That's me, guardian of financial prosperity."

He opened his eyes and fervor burned in the warm green depths. His fingers reached for hers. "Now you see why this presentation is so important. It's my destiny."

The spear that would slay his father's bullying ways.

Her chest swelled with a deep ache.

If a dragon's eyes reflected the treasures they guarded, then Peter's eyes were just and good.

And if his quest was also just and good, then hers was unjustified and wrong.

Chapter 11

Arranging for Peter's discharge took longer than Adria had anticipated. First the doctor, who confirmed that Listeria had poisoned both Peter and the twins, then the forms, then the endless lists several nurses insisted on reading to them as if they were illiterate. Sleep deprivation and the constant psychic cattle prod to get Peter to a safe place had her nerves snapping and popping like Rice Krispies. Every cell wanted to scream at the hospital staff to hurry. *Bite your tongue. These people are doing their job.*

She couldn't trust Julie to help coordinate transportation of the twins or new accommodations for her and Peter. Not if Julie was involved in the incidents that had decimated her team and poisoned Peter. To keep her suspicions from Julie, Adria called her assistant and had her make arrangements she had no intentions of using.

The twins would recuperate at a former client's house. The executive's husband was an ex-cop and they lived with two retired K-9 dogs. Julie knew Adria hated calling in favors and wouldn't think she'd seek out a client's help. Norm, Caleb's golden retriever, would stay at the animal clinic until Caleb returned home. She and Peter would hole up in a hotel until she figured out their next move.

An aide with arms the size of ham hocks insisted—hospital policy—on pushing Peter's wheelchair to the exit and having Adria retrieve the car for curbside service. Leaving him unguarded, especially after the past night's event, grated against her already-raw nerves.

Her anxiety hit overdrive when she reached the car in the garage and footprints disturbed the talc she'd sprinkled around the vehicle. Big footprints made by oversize sneakers like the ones Victor had worn. Her clammy palms itched and the back of her neck tensed. She breathed in deeply so she could relax enough to sense if the threat had passed. But all that reached her was the slam of her own anger. Who was Victor? Had Julie hired him or had the letter bomber? How did all this mess fit together?

Later. Figure it out later. First, get Peter to a safe place.

She fell back on the rote of procedures to settle her nerves. A cursory inspection of the car showed no apparent bombs affixed to the undercarriage. The smooth belly-pan not only gave the added bonus of aerodynamic efficiency, but also covered all the cavities under the car's body, eliminating the easy puncture of the gas tank, gas line and brake lines. A structural shield protected the radiator. She spied no puddles of fluid pooled under the car.

Last night, in a hurry to get Peter and the twins help, she'd left the Maxim Detection Device in the car with the rest of her gear. The device monitored sensors affixed to critical parts. A glance at the remote receiver would tell her if any of the doors, hood or trunk were opened, if the battery had failed or if a bomb was wired into the car's electrical system. But the MDD didn't do her a whole lot of good locked in the trunk.

As she eased the key into the lock, the crooked looseness of the tumbler told her she couldn't use the car. Someone had forced the lock open and shoved it back into place. One of the car's few weaknesses and someone had exploited it. She drew back the key and half the tumbler screaked out of the metal door. She opened the rear door and checked their belongings. Nothing seemed disturbed, but without the time to get a mechanic to go over every system in the car, they would have to find alternate transportation.

She scanned the parking garage and the fleeting thought of hot-wiring a car crossed her mind. One look at the cameras monitoring the area and the guard at the exit canceled that plan. She couldn't risk being caught on tape performing a felony. Jail wasn't exactly the fresh start she had in mind after her assignment was over.

Nor could she fall back on Julie to arrange for alternate transportation. Once again her assistant's betrayal caught her in the center of the chest and knocked the wind out of her. How could she not have seen it coming?

She couldn't trust anyone.

Heart heavy, she swallowed hard. *Grandpa?*

But her grandfather's soothing voice didn't fill her mind with comfort. Her only answer was the lonely whistle of wind, skittering an empty chip bag across the concrete floor of the garage, and the drone and bump of traffic outside along York Street and Howard Avenue.

Choking the keys in her hand, she strode back toward the hospital. Rules, codes, tactics. That's what she needed to concentrate on. Processing facts was her job. There was no room for feelings. Not if she was going to see Peter safe and appease her family's ghosts. *Call a taxi and head to a well-secured hotel.* From there, she and Peter could depart for another destination, leaving no trace.

After collecting Peter's presentation and their bags from the trunk of the car, Adria gave the taxi driver Long Wharf as their destination. There they would find a collection of hotels, restaurants and offices. They could hopscotch from one to another, confusing anyone who might have followed them. Once she secured the use of a car, I-95 was right there for easy escape.

Eyes closed, Peter rested his head against the taxi's window. He looked gaunt despite his night's rest. She needed to get him to a safe place so he could rest and regain his strength. Others might like to see him this subdued, but she preferred him in full dragon mode. The why of that inclination puzzled her, so she forced her attention back to the driver.

Letting someone else do the driving went against all her training and had her muscles tied up in knots that were already too tight. As they wound their way through one-way streets to Frontage, traffic was stop-and-go and much too slow for her taste. Speed was protection. A stationary car made too easy a target.

What did a taxi driver know about offensive driving? Especially one with an attitude. Did he know how to make J-turns and Y-turns? How to avoid a ramming, a collision or an ambush?

Her muscles ached. Her head pounded. Her eyelids had suddenly transformed to heavy metal that wanted nothing more than to slam into place and shut out the world. Forcing alertness, she scanned the road ahead for warning signs.

Each traffic light revved her concern. Every parked car held a possible pursuer who could spring out into the center of the road and cut them off. The man bending behind the blue mailbox and the teenager crossing the street wearing a heavy parka in fifty-degree weather became possible assassins.

"Would you mind driving in the center lane?" she asked as the taxi turned onto Frontage.

The driver rolled his unlit cigarette from one side of his mouth to the other, narrowed his eyes and glared at her in the rearview mirror. Stubbornly, he stayed in the right-hand lane.

As the next stoplight approached, Adria scrutinized the street and the intersection. She noted a parked car with a man at the wheel. Two nurses in purple scrubs were sharing an animated conversation and one man in a business suit was waiting for the cross signal to change from an orange hand to a white walking stick man. Were any of them acting oddly? A woman came running out of a doughnut shop, carrying two to-go cups with arms extended. Hidden explosives? The woman didn't head into the taxi's path. Instead she jumped into the car with the waiting man.

The light turned green. The driver pressed the gas. Just as they nosed into the intersection, a black Dodge Ram charged through his red light straight at them.

Adria's heart leapt to her throat. The taxi driver slammed on the brakes and twisted the steering wheel to the right, sliding them through the intersection at an angle. She shoved down hard on Peter's shoulders to lower him against possible gunfire and covered his body with hers. With squealing of brakes and blaring horns, the Ram smashed the taxi's left headlight and popped off the front fender. The taxi's back end crashed into the Subaru in the next lane, denting its side.

To the crush and grind of metal, the Ram continued to race through the intersection. He plowed into a compact car in the third lane as it was turning. The compact spun around like a whirligig and smacked into the light pole at the corner of the street. The Ram continued on as if nothing had happened and disappeared at the next intersection.

Once the mangled orange-and-white taxi came to a stop, the driver picked up his radio and barked into it with seal-like yaps. Adria released her protective stance and calculated her options. Peter shouldered his way out of the door. Adria caught his upper arm and held him back. "We can't stop to help anyone."

"There's a hurt woman." He jerked his chin toward the twisted wreckage wrapped around the light pole.

A woman lay slumped against the steering wheel. Blood spatters decorated the crazed windshield and stained the woman's yellow sweater. A child strapped in a booster seat howled from the back. Her face was a harrowed twist of torment. Her arms stretched toward her mother, hands splayed and shaking from her terror. A crowd of people stacked the intersection, pointing at the wrenched carcass of car, frantically pressing cell phones buttons and adding their screams for help to the madness.

"Let the paramedics handle it," Adria said, gathering her briefcase and hauling the straps over her shoulders like a backpack. She couldn't get involved. She had to keep Peter safe. "We have to get away from this crowd."

"There's a kid in there."

Swallowing hard, she tried to block out the sharp, escalating cries of the panicked girl and closed her eyes against the rawness of her ordeal. *Don't listen. Don't hear. The child isn't part of this job.* No reprieve came, only the image of herself at six, alone and frightened in the dark while her mother lay dead in the house. She muttered a string of expletives that would have her grandfather threatening to wash her mouth out with soap.

"It could be a trap," she said, but her voice held no conviction. The little girl's cries pierced her heart. She would help. She had to. The Ram had done its damage and wouldn't chance a second pass—not with both the hospital and a police station so close by. "You're still weak from the food poisoning."

"They're worse off than I am." Peter made his way to the car on legs that seemed unsteady. *Why did guys like him always have to play the hero?* She snatched the pink wool blanket from her knitting bag and rushed after him.

Every inch of her skin itched with foreboding. *Get out of there. Fast.* But of course, she couldn't. She couldn't leave that frightened child all by herself. Not with her mother hurt, maybe dying, in the front seat. Not when every cell of her body understood what that little girl was going through.

Adria surveyed the crowd, looking for a secondary attack. The wind picked up, wedging a ridge of dark clouds across the horizon. Broken glass and sharp metal edges bristled out of the compact car like porcupine quills. People, too many people, in all shapes and sizes, milled about like a nest of exposed termites. Not optimal circumstance for client safety. They had to get away.

Peter, the taxi driver and the man in the suit worked furiously to check on the hurt woman. Someone shored the wheels to keep the car from moving. Peter pushed—way too hard for someone just released from the hospital—while the other two men pulled at the driver's door until it gave way and allowed access to the interior.

Adria rounded the back of the car. The passenger's side was relatively unharmed and the door opened with a sharp tug. With her knife, she cut the seat belt holding the booster seat in place. Taut arms reaching forward, tiny body convulsing with anguish, mouth open wide, the child bawled. Every tear, every blubber, every keening cry shredded Adria's insides to ribbons. "It's okay, little one. You'll be all right."

She wrapped the pink blanket around the little girl's shoulders. She brushed away the dark curls from the tear-dampened cheeks, pressed the small trembling body against her shoulder and rocked the toddler. Every shuddering convulsion echoed through Adria's body. "Everything's going to be okay."

The child's tiny arms wrapped around Adria's neck and clutched tight as if she would never let go. She smelled of peanut butter and baby shampoo. The salt of her tears soaked into Adria's blouse. Adria's heart contracted. Her soul bled. She wanted to cry, too. "Shh, it's okay. Everything's going to be okay. Your mother will be okay. Everything will be just fine."

The mother was still unconscious. Adria prayed her promise wasn't a lie. Even so, it was a lie she'd wanted to hear twenty-one years ago. Guilt needled her as she held the crying child. She'd led Victor—if he was Victor—into their path. Their misery was her fault. But what else could she have done? Peter was her number-one priority. She had to get him to a safe place and a taxi had seemed the best way. She kissed the girl's damp hair. "Your mother will be okay."

She had to be, or Adria would add another scar to her soul.

The wail of an ambulance and the counterpoint ululation of the police cruisers approaching from two different directions cut across the hysteria of the multiplying crowd. Paramedics and police officers soon swarmed the scene. The child was ripped from her arms, pink blanket and all, leaving her strangely bereft.

Then she remembered who and what she was. Shaking her foggy mind clear, she grabbed Peter. "Let's give our statements to the cops and get out of here."

"I'm sorry about your grandfather," Officer Carl Zimmerman said as his cruiser rolled to a stop in front of the hotel where Adria had directed him to drop them off. Her grandfather's sterling reputation preceded him and caused the officer to go out of his way to see them safely to their destination. Not exactly an inconspicuous way to arrive, but she didn't plan on staying there long. "I heard he passed on a few months ago. He was an honorable man. Aren't many of those around anymore."

"Thank you." Adria retrieved her briefcase and scanned the area. Peter scrambled out of the cruiser and hefted his presentation box and the duffel bag now stuffed with their combined clothing. For ease of travel, she'd left most of her things in the mangled taxi. "Thank you also for the ride."

Officer Zimmerman nodded his salt-and-pepper head. "With the description and partial license you gave us, we'll catch the scumbag and throw the book at him."

"I appreciate that." But somehow she doubted their pursuer would hang on to the Ram. He'd probably stolen it to start with and had most likely already discarded it.

"Anything else I can do for you, Ms. Caskey?"

"No, thank you. We're all set. Have a good day."

The officer pulled away from the curb. Adria turned to Peter. "How do you feel about cross-dressing?"

Both his eyebrows lifted. "What's wrong with the clothes I'm wearing?"

"Too Brooks Brothers."

His face screwed up tight. "What did you have in mind?"

"Frumpy octogenarian."

He thought for a moment, then nodded stiffly. "If it means getting to where we're going next safely, then I'm all for it. I hope to God that woman will be okay."

"The paramedics were hopeful."

His mouth flattened into a taut line. "We have to find whoever did this."

"We will." She worked at infusing certainty into her voice. She led him through the marble-floored lobby, past the central fountain gushing water, colored blue and gold by well-placed lights in the catch basin and into the navy-carpeted hallway leading to the hotel shops.

Soft generic music played over hidden speakers.

The air smelled of money and musk. Cascading brass holders dripped with a rainbow of evening gowns and rounders groaned with more casual wear. Peter set down the box and bag he carried. His sagging shoulders betrayed the weakening effect of his illness.

Adria headed toward the rounders. Tiredness blurred her vision and had her feeling like a wrung-out rag. That near-miss had shown her fatigue was affecting her judgment and two innocent victims had paid the price for her mistake. "See anything you like?"

"How about this?" With a finger, he hooked the hanger holding a red-sequined dress with a plunging neckline and spaghetti straps. His smile was stilted and his eyes reflected the evidence of his concern for the hurt woman and frantic child. Was he blaming himself as she was? Still he was trying hard to lighten the mood and play the role of carefree tourist for the saleslady, so she gamely went along even if her heart wasn't in it.

"Not exactly your style. You don't have the chest to hold it up."

"Um, I see your point." He looked her up and down, but she doubted he actually took in anything. "But you do."

"Ha, in your dreams!" Was the saleslady buying any of this?

He hung the dress back up on its hanger. "And what sweet dreams they'll be. You and me dancing. Do you own stiletto heels?"

Ignoring both his question and the staged quality of his voice, she held up a hanger with a purple skirt that would hit him about mid-calf and another with a loose lilac blouse topped with a Chinese collar. "How about this?"

He eyed the clothes dubiously. "I'll defer to you."

"I'm going to have to guess at the size."

He gravitated closer to his presentation box. "How about the golfer look?" He draped a beige windbreaker over green plaid pants and slapped a floppy black cap over his head.

She angled close to him so the curious saleslady doing her best to pretend she wasn't listening wouldn't overhear. "Whoever's after us is looking for a woman and a man."

"Right." He pursed his lips. "So you dress as a man and we'll pass for two men."

"This is more unexpected."

He fired a killer glare at her. "Payback is a bitch, you know."

A shudder rippled through her as if she'd shot down a glass of brandy too fast. Payback was still in the cards. As she wrestled with her crisis of faith, butterflies fluttered in her chest. *Facts, Adria. Stick to the facts. Do not let emotions overcome reason.* With a steady hand, she added a paisley scarf and a pair of tights to the pile of purchases. They headed for the public restrooms, where she herded him into the ladies' room and braced the door against entry by anyone else.

"So what's your disguise?" Peter held the purple skirt as if it carried the plague.

"Soccer mom."

"You don't look a thing like a soccer mom."

She caught her hair in a high ponytail and wrapped a black neckerchief around it, took off her raincoat and added sunglasses. "How about now?"

Wrinkling the purple skirt in one hand, he plucked a heather-gray V-neck sweater from the duffel at his feet and handed it to her. "Try this."

She slipped the sweater over her head. The cashmere hugged her body with comfort and added just the right touch to her black pants. The wool fibers had trapped his scent of spice and leather and her instinctive appreciation embarrassed her.

"Back there. With that little girl." He brushed a loose strand of her hair behind her ear and cocked his head. His eyes softened and peered at her with an odd kind of fascination. "You're not what I expected at all."

The rich rumble of his voice confused her. His interest spooked her. She stepped back and his hand curved around her neck, cradling her in place. "When this is over—"

"I don't do relationships." Too messy. Too complicated. Too…risky. She jerked her head toward one of the stalls. He didn't really want her; he simply needed to replace the horrid pictures of the accident with something life-asserting and she was handy. "Get changed."

"Pity." He brushed a kiss against her lips, then slipped into one of the stalls.

Her fingers reached up and touched the electric buzz still tingling her lips. The contradiction of firm softness shook through her in a slow wave of warmth. The yearning that licked through her jolted her back to reality. That he, of all people, should have that effect on her wasn't right. With a shake of her head, she dismissed her physical response as nothing more than errant adrenaline.

She never got close to a client—one of her rules. But he was different. He was more than a paycheck. He was more than a body to protect from harm. He was supposed to save her in return. His destruction would buy her peace. Wouldn't it? She couldn't let his past contaminate her future.

"What's taking you so long?" Adria asked, tapping her foot against the caramel-veined marble floor.

"It's not exactly my usual style." He opened the stall door and exited.

Even dressed as a woman, he painted a formidable picture. Rather than a frumpy grandmother, he came across as a stiff-backed matriarch who ran her household with an iron fist. "I think you'd better shave."

He ran a hand along his jaw. "What's the matter? Grandma doesn't have whiskers?"

Despite the weight of her weariness, she found room to laugh. "Not the clientele in this hotel."

After he'd shaved, she helped him stuff a T-shirt into his blouse to form a low bosom and tied the scarf around his head. She used the talc in her briefcase to lighten his eyebrows.

"I don't see how you women wear these things," he said, plucking at the waist of his tights. "This isn't going to fool anybody."

"Most people are too busy worrying about themselves to notice others. The skirt and blouse will register as old woman and that's all we need until we can get to the next hotel and make a plan."

His face skewed into a doubtful look as he plumped his fake breasts into place. "I sure hope so."

"We'd better get going."

He nodded. "Right."

Adria opened the restroom door. A wave of guilt clouded her thoughts. For an irritable dragon, he was taking all these setbacks with grace. The need for vigilance boomeranged her into action and she inspected their surroundings for possible witnesses, but no one was paying attention to them.

* * *

Adria stepped into the hallway and reflexively glanced both ways. Behind her, Peter pulled and tugged at his skirt. At the mouth of the lobby a tall man lingered. His hands were stuffed into the pockets of a gray windbreaker. The hair sticking out of the black baseball cap was brown, not blond, but something about the man's demeanor sent adrenaline spiking through her veins. Though the cap was lowered over his eyes, the motion of his head gave away his true intentions. He was searching for something or someone. And if he were a normal person meeting someone, his attention would steer toward the lobby, not the hallway. Her gaze shot down the baggy pants to his feet. Sneakers. Gray sneakers with lime-green trim—just like Victor's.

"Let's go out the back way," Adria said, trying to sound casual.

Peter's head snapped up. "What's wrong?"

"Just walk beside me. You're old, so take short, unhurried steps. Pretend you're fascinated with what I'm saying."

"I am because your behavior obviously means there's trouble."

"Ah, yes, I do believe Victor somehow found us. Don't look behind you."

He checked his head movement and his grip on her elbow became a vise. "Victor?"

"The assassin nurse from last night."

"Are you sure?"

"As sure as I can be. Please let go of my elbow. I'll need my hands free if he comes this way."

"Right." Peter reshuffled the box and bag in his arms and walked beside her with a checked gait.

Adria studied Victor's form in the small mirror attached to her sunglasses. He hunched his head down, pushed himself off the marble column and strode into the hallway in their direction.

They neared the double doors leading to a back parking lot. Clouds had chased sunlight away. Road sand from the past winter swirled in eddies. Raindrops splotched black on the gray asphalt.

"Once you're outside, go left," Adria said as she pushed the door open. "There's a strip of shops. Mix with the crowd as best you can. Head toward the hotel across the road."

"Where are you going to be?"

"Right behind you." Victor's steps stretched long and ate up ground fast. "Pick up the pace."

She and Peter dashed to the front of the strip mall. They zigzagged through the people milling about the protective overhang window-shopping. The scent of doughnuts and coffee gave way to perm chemicals and nail polish, then grilled beef and fried potatoes. Past the steakhouse, the street with its crisscross of traffic beckoned.

Peter glanced behind. The effort of the chase was turning his skin a sickly white once more. "He's catching up."

The slap of Victor's shoes got nearer and nearer. Adria grabbed Peter's elbow and desperately looked for a hole in the traffic. When the hint of safe passage appeared, she darted off the sidewalk and onto the road. "Cross. *Now.*"

Brakes squealed. A horn honked. Still Adria prodded Peter forward. At the midpoint of the four lanes, wind from the rushing cars tugged at Peter's head scarf, flapping it loose. Adria urged Peter on. They rounded the hotel and headed toward the back courtyard decked out with white patio tables, but no chairs. A blue gate guarded an empty pool. A set of glass doors led into the hotel.

"Where to?" Peter huffed beside her. This was too much strain for him so soon after his discharge. Irritation wormed its way through her chest. If he wasn't so married to lugging that box, they could run farther. But he wouldn't leave the stupid thing behind and she couldn't carry it for him in case Victor caught up to them.

"Let's go into the hotel." She weaved them through the lobby, down escalators and into a crowd of people registering for some sort of convention. She slowed, scanning the escalators, the elevator doors and every doorway. They couldn't stay there forever, but Peter would have a chance to rest and she to think.

Grandpa?

In spite of the buzz of voices around her, her mind remained eerily silent.

Fury shot through her at her need for her grandfather's guidance as if she were still that frightened six-year-old. The edge of tears made her angrier still. *Focus! You've done this hundreds of times before. You can do it again.*

"I know someone who can help us," Peter said, breathing hard into her ear.

"You can't trust anybody."

"I can trust this man."

"What makes you think so?"

"The same reason you could trust the twins' care to your former client. I saved his neck and he'd jump at the chance to pay back the favor." He shoved her into an alcove and dumped his box on the floor. "Got any change?"

At this point, they were running out of options. But depending on an outside party she hadn't had a chance to check out twisted her guts into knots. She fished into her pocket and brought out an assortment of nickels, dimes and quarters. He fed coins into the pay phone. After running through a gauntlet of secretaries and assistants, Peter finally reached his intended party. "David, it's Peter Dragon. I need a favor."

While Peter talked to his associate, her sense of dread multiplied, making her light-headed. There was no way Victor could've found them—unless he had help. And he was keeping up with them much too closely. Was he that good of a tracker?

Facing the crowd, she rummaged through the bag and box Peter had insisted on carrying. The answer to Victor's skill soon became clear. Beneath the files in Peter's presentation box, her hand collided with a metal object the size of her palm. A green light blinked, suggesting the device was operational. An electronic tracker.

Marvelous. Absolutely marvelous. Someone had tampered with the armored car while it sat in the hospital garage. What had she expected? That they'd done it just for the exercise? She should have taken the time to search their belongings more thoroughly. A rookie mistake. She was losing her edge and putting Peter in danger.

Five minutes later, Peter, his associate and Adria had worked out a plan. Peter changed back into jeans. In one of the meeting rooms set up with merchandise for sale by the confectioners' association hosting the conference, Adria bought him a brown hooded sweatshirt that read, Who Needs Therapy When You Have Chocolate?

As they left the registration area, Adria spied Victor's shoes coming down the escalator. Urging Peter into the open elevator, she dropped the tracking device into the canvas bag one of the attendees toted.

Chapter 12

"Sleep," Peter ordered a few hours later, once Adria had checked out the house and made sure they could occupy it safely for the time it would take her to formulate a new plan. That he could wield his voice as a weapon didn't surprise her. He was used to being the one in charge and taking a back seat to someone like her had to grate against his ego. That she wanted to obey grated against all she was.

"I can't." Fighting a yawn and the exhaustion seeping deep into her bones, she propped her computer on the dining room table. From there she would have a view of most of the lower floor of the house. David Porter, Peter's associate, had let them use his home and offered them one of the two cars in the three-bay garage. "This is my job."

Peter stood at the doorway between the kitchen and the dining room, chest puffed out ready for a challenge. "A little leaning isn't a weakness."

She snorted even as a shiver of warmth crawled down her spine. "Really? I practically had to force you into accepting my help."

"Then I know what I'm talking about." He skewered his gaze to hers as if his will could hypnotize her into compliance. "Besides, you won't do me much good if you're exhausted. I'd offer a back rub to unkink the stiff muscles in your neck, but I have a feeling you'd turn me down."

She rolled her shoulders as if she could dislodge the lead apron of soreness pressing down on them. Her eyes were dry and gritty. Her fingers responded to her orders as if they were slugs drunk on beer. She did need downtime and she resented his noticing. Resented, too, the image he'd planted in her mind his strong fingers breaking apart the knots in her muscles. She was getting soft and that wasn't good.

"I have to plan first—"

"You said we were safe here."

A regretful sigh sank to her heels. Peter might trust David Porter, but she was learning she could trust no one. "Not for long."

"So sleep while you can. I can keep watch for a bit."

"You need the rest more. You're just out of the hospital."

"I'll sleep later."

The determined set of his jaw told her she wasn't going to win this battle. While she hated to admit he was right, she did need to refresh her tired brain. They were relatively safe. At least for a bit. They weren't followed. Of that she was sure. Peter's associate had a good security system protecting the house. And even if someone tried to follow the chain of taxis they'd taken to get there, it would take them a while to unearth this address.

"All right," she said, closing the cover of her computer, reluctant to give up control. "I'll take a nap. Just for an hour. But we need some ground rules." She drilled his gaze and steeled her voice with authority. "First, you will *not* go outside for any reason."

The tense line of his face relaxed and he became agreeable now that she was giving in. "Check."

"You will not turn on any lights at the front of the house."

"Check."

"You will not look out any window."

"Check."

He was taking all this much too docilely. The wounded hero charm was digging in like a burr she found hard to ignore. The returning color to his cheeks and the relaxed set of his mouth made him look so reasonable—approachable even. All illusion. Tricks of a tired mind. Of all the people she shouldn't trust, Peter topped the list. "If you hear anything, and I mean *anything* at all, you will wake me up."

He cocked his head and narrowed his gaze. The fierceness of his expression was muted only by the sporting gleam in his eyes. "Do I look stupid?"

Not stupid, just…determined, and that couldn't be good. "No, but you tend to get involved in your work and tune out the world."

"Check." He nodded once. "No work. I'll stay alert. I'll wake you up if so much as a leaf hits a window."

She frowned, wishing she didn't so desperately need the rest. "One hour. That's all I need. Wake me up in one hour."

He took her by the shoulders and pointed her up the stairs. The warmth of his fingers melted into her stiff muscles, making her regret her inability to accept his offer of a back rub. "Go."

She shook her head, ricocheted out of his crackling grasp and aimed for the couch in the sterile white-on-white living room. She sank into the butter-soft leather of the couch and yawned as she slipped a decorative pillow under her head. They were heading toward crossing a forbidden line.

She had to preempt any attempt on his part to compromise her goal.

He'd lost them. For now. But eventually, they'd resurface. Had to. Few people could work in a vacuum. Even someone like The Face had to resort to using the shield of others to guard precious invisibility.

Always it was the little things that tripped people, made them vulnerable. All those human emotions that made them needy also made them betray long-standing trust.

Are you hurting yet, little Adria? Are the monsters creeping into your dreams? Are they breathing down your neck with their hot breath?

Details. It paid to be good at details. All those things that few people noticed. The rejected pennies on the ground because they were too lowly to weigh down a wallet. The blind looks that saw right through a person because of an accident of birth. The imperceptible ties that sucked a spirit dry because everyone was so afraid of what could happen if a secret came to light.

Shame was the easiest of all emotions to exploit. And a study of history showed that men in this warrior society thrived on the avoidance of shame and the garnering of glory through battle. Honor by death was so stupid.

Soon all the secrets would be exposed. They would make Peter die in shame. The Face would rise from Peter's ashes like the proverbial phoenix and take his rightful place waiting at the head of the line. No longer would The Face fester unnoticed in the shadows. The Face would shine in its full glory.

All that was required was the last bit of proof. And now that the connections were so clear, Adria was the link to follow to find that one important piece.

A reprieve. For now.

Where are you, Adria?

Laughter rocked as nimble fingers dialed the number from memory. *Come out, come out, wherever you are.*

The nice thing about pride was its predictability. Peter wouldn't be able to contain his temper. And his faithful guard wouldn't be able to stop her principal from blowing their cover.

When Adria woke up from her dream-tossed sleep, morning had given way to night. The room was dark and the patter of rain tapped against the living room windows, gently reminding her she had business to tend to. A glance at her watch reproached her for oversleeping.

Damn, Peter. He hadn't listened to a word she'd said. One hour wasn't half the day. She threw back the chenille afghan and planted her feet into the rich pile of cream carpet. The stiffness rusting her body demanded six more hours of remedial rest. She countered the claim by stretching as she rose.

She pushed herself through the routine of a perimeter walk around the house. A carpool minivan disgorged two teenaged baseball players three houses down. A few cars swished by to disappear into the gaping mouths of neighboring garages. The preteen walking the black lab exerted all her energy trying to control the animal. All was in order.

Back inside, she found Peter in the kitchen stirring noodles in a pot of boiling water while monitoring the stock ticker on CNN. Some sort of tomato sauce simmered in a saucepan. His color looked better. Too good for a sick man who'd been up for six hours. "You were supposed to wake me five hours ago."

He shrugged, but there wasn't a shred of apology in the gesture. "You needed sleep."

"That's not how this works."

He shrugged one shoulder carelessly as he tested the doneness of the noodles. "I fell asleep, too." His dimples deepened. "Feel better?"

"That's not the point."

"Yes, it is. If you feel better, if your mind is clear, then we have a chance to finally get some tracking done. There was a report on the local news about the accident."

"What did they say?"

"The mother is listed in serious condition, but they expect her to live."

The relief in his eyes mirrored the one buoying inside her. Her mistake hadn't caused a child to suffer through the horrifying loss of her mother. "That's great."

"Are you hungry?"

She glanced at the feast cooking on the stove. Her stomach growled in anticipation. She frowned, knowing that bachelor David Porter hadn't left a stitch of fresh food in the house. "I told you not to leave the property."

"I didn't. It's amazing what you can make out of a couple of cans, some spices and some frozen vegetables."

Making something out of nothing. He was good at that. "You went into the wrong business."

"There's a difference between an interest and a passion." He plucked a strainer from a cupboard and placed it in the sink. "Cooking is an interest that came out of necessity. Finance is a passion. As much as we'd like to deny it, money rules. Ask anyone who doesn't have the means to support themselves."

"Speaking from experience?" she scoffed.

Frowning, he turned his back to her and poured the noodles into the strainer as if it required all of his attention. Had she hit a nerve? "I've seen the whole spectrum."

But not personally. The one thing Peter had never lacked was money. Even when he'd chosen to deny his past, he'd taken his inheritance with him.

She'd grown up believing that her grandfather had only modest means. Though they'd never wanted for anything, they'd lived simply. As far as she could see, money had only complicated the lives of the people she protected. People like Peter, who grew empires from inherited money, were forced to protect their borders from jealous invaders. She studied the sharp sculpture of his features as he drained the cooked spaghetti, and read the network of sadness lining his eyes. "Money doesn't buy happiness."

His mouth twitched. "No, but it gives you control over your own life. If you're financially independent, then no one can dictate what's right for you."

She thought of her father, of the way her grandfather had said her father had worked so hard to run his business, always just one step ahead of the creditors. Because he'd refused to let Peter's father bully him, he'd died. If he'd had financial independence, would the story have had the same ending? "Do you really believe that everyone can achieve that kind of independence?"

"Yes, I do. Which is why I'm not going to let whoever's trying to kill me stop me from giving this seminar." He piled spaghetti and sauce onto a plate and handed it to her with a stiff smile.

They ate at the breakfast bar and went over the facts of the case. She plowed through her portion. He picked at plain noodles and unbuttered vegetables.

"It's someone close," she said, pushing her empty plate away. "Someone who wants you to hurt before you die."

His face went marble cold. His eyes were steel stones. His chin cranked up and he all but put up his fists like a boxer trying to block a punch. "We've looked at everyone with a fine-tooth comb. Even Romy couldn't come up with anything on anyone, except Atwell. And that has nothing to do with the threatening letters, the letter bomb or anything that's happened since he left."

"Then we need to look at it again from a different perspective."

He shoved plates into the sink and scowled at her. "What other perspective is there?"

"Time."

"Time?"

"We need to look back farther." She eyed him steadily and didn't miss the stiffening of his features. "Before you started Dragon, Inc."

"There isn't anything there."

"Are you sure?"

"Of course I'm sure. If there were, I'd be the first one to bring it up."

She shrugged matter-of-factly. "Liar. Just because you want it gone, doesn't mean it is. You can't forget. I see it in your eyes. There's something there that makes you keep anyone from getting too close to you. You've turned protecting yourself against your past into an art."

"I've overcome my past," he countered as he scraped uneaten noodles into the garbage disposal. "There's a difference."

"You said your father beat you. You said you saw someone shot to death."

His lips pressed into a thin line. "That doesn't come into play here."

"How do you know? You come from a violent world. Maybe its tentacles are reaching out to you."

He jerked his chin at her. "What about you?"

"What about me?"

"All this trouble started the day you walked into my office. Maybe someone's after you, not me."

"The threatening letters arrived before I did." A twinge of guilt pinched her conscience. She should tell him of her suspicions regarding Julie. But not now. That would add a layer of cloudiness to a point she had to make. "What are you covering up?"

His expression turned to rock. "My father is dead. He can't hurt anyone anymore. Looking there would be a waste of time."

"What you can't put aside follows you. It breeds in the dark corners of your mind. It chokes off a part of you until—"

"Until what?"

She raked in a long, hard breath, reeling in her near-collision with her own past. "Until you look at it and it loses its power."

He crossed his arms, cinching opposite biceps with tight fists. "I can't imagine anyone hating me so much they'd want to destroy me."

"Anger breeds hatred. And anger takes time to fester."

He shook his head. "I left it all behind—the anger, the hatred, the violence."

"Maybe it followed you...." Her voice trailed as more guilt gnawed at her. Her grandfather had followed Peter's every move. In retrospect, that much was clear. Their six months in California. The year they spent in New York, at the same time Peter was there. Then finally, the cottage on the beach in Old Lyme and the business headquarters in New Haven once she'd grown up. Close enough to keep an eye on the object of his revenge.

Peter seemed to choose his words carefully, modulate them, giving his speech an unyielding quality. "I purged it all out of my system. Exercise, hard work, healthy food. A vision." His whole body shook from his mirthless laugh. "I even took an anger-management class."

That he'd chosen to learn to tame his savage instincts told a world about his determination to sever his ties from his violent legacy. And that admirable determination had left him isolated. If he let anyone close, then he would have to admit to his tainted past. And that past shamed him.

Had he ever known any softness? Did nightmares disturb his sleep? Did memories haunt him? The sudden desire to wrap her arms around him, comfort him, tell him that all of this wasn't his fault, itched her skin. Instead, she crossed her arms, firmly pushed away this growing respect for all he'd overcome and watched him attack the sink full of dishes.

"Someone once told me a story about crabs," she said. "Fishermen'll tell you that when crabs are put in a bucket, some will try to escape. They'll claw their way to the top. And just as they're about to climb out into freedom, their fellow crabs will pull them back down."

His eyes, when his gaze met hers, were full of roiling darkness. Conflict churned just below the surface. The fierce need to protect himself from his past warred with the fear of what seedy thread he could discover tucked in the folds of his childhood. His jaw firmed, giving his voice a sandpaper roughness. "Then let's go fishing for crabs."

Although her grandfather's voice seemed to have deserted her, his last bit of advice still rang in her ear. Look closer.

Julie.

Adria still couldn't believe Julie would have betrayed them all. *Don't dwell on that. Look for the facts.*

She was sick of the game. Of not knowing who was after them and why. Of having to spend her time on the defensive rather than the offensive. Of not being able to trust anyone. She attacked her computer as if it were a punching bag, willing it to admit defeat and give up something that would help them avoid another strike. The keys clicked under her fingers. The sites and pages scrolled by. No one was safe from her prying fingers. Surely, somewhere, something had to give. Some bit of information had to burst the puzzle apart. A cup of green tea appeared hot and steaming, then disappeared once she'd drunk it.

That Peter refused to share his background galled her to no end. She'd thought they'd arrived at a certain amount of trust. Instead, he surfed the Net on his own computer, his expression stone, his exterior betraying none of the resentment that surely churned inside him.

Every hour, she took a break and walked a patrol. The exercise served to unwind the knots knitting the muscles along her spine and clear her head. Sometime after midnight, Peter fell asleep on the couch in the living room. He looked mellower in sleep, less hard, less intimidating. His feet hung over the end of the couch. The afghan barely covered his torso. He couldn't possibly be comfortable like that.

During a sweep of the upstairs, she snagged a comforter from one of the bedrooms. As she covered him with the comforter, one rolled-up sleeve of the sweater she'd borrowed from him flopped onto her hand. Shaking her head, she hiked the sleeve back in place.

She kept meaning to change out of Peter's sweater, but the cashmere kept her warm and the looseness of the garment kept her movements free.

She pulled her gaze away from him with effort and silently berated herself. Warmth. Comfort. Peter was definitely the wrong place to look for them. Not with so much history between them.

Yet she'd seen the lengths he'd gone through to protect his employees. Loyalty was a rare quality these days. She'd also seen how most of his employees offered their devotion to Peter. Both Daphne's and Romy's reports had shown the same thing in spades. She'd seen the effort he'd poured into his desire to help people with his presentation, how he'd simplified his method to make financial independence almost painless. The threats against him had forced him to delve into a world he thought he'd left behind. The memories had to eat at him as they were eating at her. But he'd put his pride aside and gamely plunged into excavating the ruins of his past. She hoped he'd soon trust her with his finds.

Adria slipped outside to patrol the grounds. She'd lost her lust for revenge. Peter wasn't like his father. Avenging the father's sins through the son wouldn't take away her loneliness and loss.

But how could she forgive him for what his father had done? How could she forget? That elephant would always stand between them, a gray and wrinkled reminder of the blood that tied them.

Determined to get to the key that would end this torture of an assignment, she went back into the house sat down again at the computer. She was smart. She was logical. She understood that the empathy welling up in her was caused by the stress of the circumstance. Human nature. When life turned into a hurricane, looking for a lifeline to hang on to was only normal. She had to remember to be careful. She couldn't let him get the best of her. Even if she could no longer hear her grandfather's voice, she had to remember the rules. Now wasn't the time to get mired in mental quicksand. Those guidelines were walls of safety—then and now.

"Today Mystic Pleasure Crafts Corporation, operating out of Mystic, Connecticut, announced that they have developed a new type of hull paint for their line of pleasure boats," the CNN reporter stated. He stood at a marina, framed by tossing gray water on one side and a weaving navy blue hull on the other. The stiff sea breeze insisted on reparting his hair from the left to the right, making his brown hair look like a rebel breaker. Beside him stood a balding, ruddy-faced man. "This new paint would release fifty percent less copper into the aquatic environment than their previous product while still retaining its ability to limit the growth of algae, barnacles and teredo.

"Last year Mystic Pleasure Crafts Corporation was fined $100,000 by the Environmental Protection Agency for the nonpoint source pollution linked to the chemicals used in the production and maintenance of their line of boats. A University of Connecticut study two years ago showed that the chemicals released into the water have led to deformities in area fish."

The interviewer turned to the man next to him. "Mr. Hatch, when do you foresee the changeover to the new paint happening?"

Hatch cleared his throat and rolled forward on his toes. "Just yesterday we were awarded a grant from the Dragon Foundation to finance this project—"

"Russell!" Peter snapped the remote at the small television screen hanging from the bottom of a cupboard in the kitchen. He stabbed at the buttons of his cell phone and paced the floor between the stove and the refrigerator like a caged lion with a need to tear into bloody meat. "Answer, damn you!"

"Don't use that phone!" Adria sprang off the chair in the dining room, raced into the kitchen and rounded the breakfast bar.

Peter ignored her, choosing instead to bark at his brother. "What the hell is going on? Why am I seeing the Dragon Foundation's name mentioned in the same breath as Mystic Pleasure Crafts on the morning news?"

"Peter, turn off the phone!"

He rolled his shoulders, angled his back at her and kept yelling at Russell. "I trusted you! I don't care about potential. I told you I didn't want to get involved with them. How could you go behind my back—"

Adria yanked the phone out of Peter's hands and pressed the End button. "No phone."

Peter's cheeks were flushed red, his voice braced with steel. "I trusted him. He waited until I was gone and went behind my back." The tendons of his neck stood out like guy wires. "My own brother. After everything."

Peter spun away from her and jerked open the pantry. He jettisoned a canister of pancake mix onto the counter. He was turning to his regular coping mechanism. When things start to sting, cook. Better than fists or weapons.

How deep did Russell's betrayal go?

"Tell me about Russell." She kept her voice neutral, both to calm him and to deny that his display of temper had rattled her.

"Russ is like a mosquito bite. You don't want to scratch it because it makes the itch worse, but you can't quite forget it, either." Peter banged a waffle iron onto the counter. "The thing is that he was a happy kid. You could always count on Russell for a laugh."

His voice was taut and his throat worked to regain control, but he was talking.

"Until…" she pressed.

Peter adjusted his glasses and concentrated on the instructions on the pancake mix. Was he seeing any of the fine print? "Until our father died, when he was fourteen. His death hit him hard. Russell got himself into a boatload of trouble after."

The silence in the kitchen had a pulse and a weight, emphasizing the complicated emotions that underlined the brothers' relationship. Was Russell the favored child? Had he not puked at the sight of death? Was his father training him to take his place and was Russell now trying to usurp Peter's place?

"What kind of trouble?" Adria asked.

Peter shrugged, slapped a saucepan onto the stove and poured frozen raspberries into it. "Regular kid stuff."

"Like what? Drinking, drugs?"

He measured water into the plastic pancake mix container. You'd think the water was some sort of biological weapon he couldn't spill with the care he was giving the measurement.

"Trouble with the law?" Adria pushed.

He shook the pancake mix so rigorously that lumps had no chance of survival.

"What kind of trouble, Peter?"

"Cons."

"Extortion?"

Peter shrugged and turned away. "He reimbursed all of his marks. It was a long time ago."

"But he's angry."

Angry enough to hate? The realization seemed to gut-punch Peter. He slammed the pancake container onto the counter and scraped a hand through his hair. "He couldn't wait for me to get out of town." Bitterness saturated Peter's voice. "He wanted me to leave the office." Peter snorted at his own gullibility. "And I just handed him what he wanted." His eyes blazed with a fire so cold she shivered. "He signed in my name."

Jeopardizing the reputation and sullying the solid-gold name Peter had worked so hard to build. "You couldn't know."

"I should have."

She'd thought breaking down Peter would require destroying his empire. She was wrong. He'd just take it in stride and rebuild, bigger and better. In truth, his brother's betrayal was cutting him deeper than she ever could.

The light vanished from Peter's eyes. His shoulders drooped as if suddenly the load of baggage carried long and hard was too much. "What if Russell did this?"

Adria understood his pain. Betrayal was like acid, but they were running out of time. He was still her principal and she still had an obligation to keep him safe. "Russell may be partially responsible for the situation, but he isn't acting alone. For one, there's Victor—whoever he is. By calling Russell, you gave away our location and gave him the means to find us."

Peter rubbed his temples as if he was trying to squeeze out a headache. "How? It's a cell phone."

She tossed the unit at him. "A cell phone with a GPS chip."

He caught it with a deft hand and swore. "What do we do now? I've left him in charge of my company."

Adria reached for his cell phone. "We're going to beat him at his own game."

Chapter 13

"How much farther?" Peter asked, watching her with a piercing gaze that seemed to see through too many layers of her crumbling armor. Could he sense her reluctance to get to where they were heading?

"Not long." Adria's foot eased off the accelerator a little more, slowing the car to barely thirty. Because of the thickening fog. Because she was on duty. Because she couldn't afford an accident. Her growing apprehension had nothing to do with Osprey Island. No, the prickly anxiety had to do with the pieces of Peter's puzzle that weren't falling into place.

Liar, liar. Pants on fire. She shooed away the annoying juvenile voice, tightened her fists on the steering wheel and scowled at the road. The swish of wipers worked like white noise, but couldn't quite keep the dark thoughts at bay.

Her grandfather's cottage was the last place she

wanted to take Peter, but she'd run out of options. This was their last chance to hide out and stay put until they caught his aggressor. Any way she weighed the pros and cons, the pros won.

Julie didn't know the cottage existed; she wasn't one of her grandfather's girls. When Adria had turned eighteen, her grandfather had stopped fostering lost girls and opened his business in New Haven. He'd taken her on as partner and also offered a position to the girls who wanted to put their training to use as executive protectors.

If Daphne or Romy or Sam or the twins guessed at her location, they wouldn't reveal it. The island sanctuary was as sacred to them as it was to her.

Adria told Peter her suspicions about Julie. She couldn't prove anything, but just in case, to keep Julie guessing, she'd made three reservations to three different hotels under three aliases Julie would recognize. And if Julie wasn't involved, then whoever intercepted the calls would have three wrong turns to check out. That should buy them some time.

Even if Julie conducted a search of real-estate holdings, she wouldn't find a record. Her grandfather had bought the land under one of his aliases. Then he'd promptly donated it to the nearby wildlife refuge as conservation land with the stipulation that he and his descendants could live in the cottage. When her branch of the family died out, the house would revert to the wildlife trust. A search of real-estate holdings wouldn't yield a trace back to her. They should be safe there to mount an offensive strike, if needed.

Peter had already taken away Russell's signatory ability and his security clearance. When Russell next tried to enter the Dragon, Inc. building, security would turn him away. For good measure, Peter had asked the private investigator he kept on retainer to do background checks on prospective companies desiring foundation grants to tail Russell and report his activities. Maybe Russell would lead the P.I. straight to the heart of this nightmare.

Peter's cell phone was on its way west in a car with Illinois plates.

She'd checked on Sam and the twins and all were recovering nicely. That eased her guilt, but didn't remove it.

Going to Osprey Island was the best thing to do. Still, sharing her most precious place with Peter was like baring her soul to him. *It's just a house.* But somehow, she couldn't quite buy that lie.

The day was raw and damp. Fog hugged the shoreline, softening the edges of the landscape, blurring the horizon and washing all the colors to gray. As she turned the borrowed Lexus from Peter's friend onto the bridge connecting the island to the mainland, the low clouds helped veil their arrival.

She entered a code at the gate. The metal barrier swung open with an ear-grating squeal. She drove up the dirt driveway and stopped the car in the spot by the house where her grandfather used to park his Jeep. The bottle-green vehicle no longer stood there, but sat in a garage stall leased by Caskey & Caskey. Her grandfather was in New Haven when he'd become sick, negotiating a contract that would have employed five full-time executive protectors for a year.

Cloaked in mist, the pale blue house seemed forlorn. The white shutters gave a drooping look to the blank eyes of windows masked by shades. On the crest of waves rode the phantom echo of teenage girls laughing. In the thickness of the fog, the silhouette of their ghosts raced through the sand.

A trickle of dread oozed like sweat from her pores. She didn't want to go in. She didn't want the empty arms of the house to wrap around her. She didn't want to admit the hole in her heart was still bleeding. If she went inside, could she hold herself together?

This was home. This was the only place she could be herself. The only place she'd ever belonged. The only place she'd ever felt safe. Here she'd learned to don the skin of a protector and it was like slipping into someone else's body. Someone who was strong and sure and secure.

Peter cupped a hand on the round of her shoulder, shocking her back to the here and now. "Are you all right?"

She nodded, the knot in her throat making sound impossible. The crack of the car door opening resounded like a gunshot. As she walked, the sand tugged at each of her steps. At the front door, facing the Sound, she hesitated. Her throat was dry. Her palms were clammy. Her heart thundered like the sea crashing against the shore.

"Where's your key?" Peter asked, palming his hand at her.

She shook her head. "Code."

With a finger, she pushed aside the antiqued brass panel on the lock assembly and slowly punched in the security code: 5-0 for Hawaii, 1-2 for her age when they'd found this haven; 2-1 for her grandfather's age when he'd married his beloved Kalani. The codes were changed at random. This was the last one, thought up only a week before he'd died. Had he sensed his death? Was that why he'd chosen those numbers? The door creaked open. Holding her breath, she stepped inside.

A stir of welcome fluttered beneath the dust and neglect. The phantom smell of Grandpa's lime-and-spice aftershave, of the peppermint candy he sucked on after dinner, of the strong ginseng green tea he drank by the potful all clung to the air as if he were still there.

Any second, he would peek out of his office and spot her. His burnished face would crack with the hugeness of his smile. The corners of it would wrap around her even before his arms did. He would walk her to the porch where they'd sit on the swing and rock to the rhythm of the sea. And all of her worries, all of her fears would just drift away on the caress of the breeze and the song of his voice as his strong arms held her close.

She rubbed a fist at the ache in her heart. A sigh of melancholy filled all the corners of her body with bleakness.

"Adria?" Worry clouded Peter's voice. She was still his protector. He should bear no doubt she could guard him efficiently.

"Take any bed upstairs," she said, her voice thick. "The safe room is the upstairs bathroom." Shielding herself from the memories that assaulted her like machine-gun fire took all of her concentration. "I need to secure the cottage."

Walking through the empty cottage left her as raw as if she'd run through a grater. A dull ache had resided inside her chest since her grandfather's death, but coming home intensified it, raised it to the surface, laid it bare. She fought off the tears. *You have to hold yourself together.*

And she did—until nightfall.

She thrived on routine. Reveled in it. Rules, procedures, tactics. They shored up her mind, gave her spine steel. She sat through the lunch of egg salad sandwiches and carrot sticks that Peter made. She helped Peter set up his computer so he could finish his presentation and continue digging into his family's past. She pored through her notes, keeping her brain too busy to feel.

But once Peter had settled down for the night, once darkness quilted around her as she sat alone in the kitchen, once the storm's fury picked up, battering the cottage with its watery fists and blustering breath, a bolt of fear came out of nowhere. It lodged in her chest and prickled down her spine, speeding her pulse into a jagged race.

She rummaged through the storage basket in the living room and found knitting needles, but no wool. She sat in her grandfather's recliner as if a mere object could replace his arms. She paced the hallway as her grandfather used to after dinner. None of her efforts could shake the sense of electric anxiety crazing through her.

She turned in a helpless circle, not knowing what exactly she sought.

Her grandfather was there. In every inch of the house. In every grain of sand on this beach. His smile formed out of memory, becoming a constellation in her grief. His patience, his kindness, his never-ending belief in her had given her strength over the years. Every thought of him made the hole in her heart expand.

He was there, but he was gone. And the missing broke over her like a tidal wave and swept her toward a dark and dangerous place.

In that kind of mood, she couldn't trust herself. She couldn't let Peter see her so weak.

She bolted outside, into the dark of the night, into the thunder and lightning. The icy rain stung her face, pelting her cheeks with the tears she couldn't shed. The cold air filled her lungs, holding back the keen of her sorrow. The wet sand sucked at her feet and she couldn't run fast enough to leave the pain behind.

An hour later Adria's gaze locked with the horizon. She concentrated on the whitecaps riding the black waves. A meditation, her grandfather had called this standing in the rain. Time passed and grew slow. Every whip of wind bit into her flesh. Every drop of rain burned like a tear on broken flesh. Every grain of sand slipping back to sea built an island under her feet. And in the space between her heartbeats, she did find a measure of peace.

She sensed him before she heard him. In her heightened state, the crackle of his aura tingled against hers. Three feet from her, Peter hesitated, standing there as if on the edge of battle, unsure as to whether she posed a threat to him or not.

"It's raining," he said.

"I know."

"You're wet."

"I know."

"I'll walk you back home."

"I'm fine."

He didn't leave.

"I don't know what to do anymore," she said without turning around. She shivered as much from the cold as from her uncertainty. "What to think. What to believe. Everything was always so straightforward. Here's the good guy. Here's the bad guy. Protect the good guy against the bad guy. But now..." Her voice drifted as her shoulders hiked up to her ears and she shook her head. "Now I don't know anything."

This raw violation was his fault. For a moment, she took pleasure in deflecting the blame. But the euphoria didn't last long. The state of her emotions had nothing to do with him and everything to do with that one night twenty-one years ago when their fates had collided.

He was a victim, too.

Peter moved into her line of sight. She searched his rain-shadowed face, looking for that nameless thing that would free her. He had such compelling eyes, sea-storm green. Right now, they reflected the roil of Sound, the chaos tossing inside her. Was he remembering another stormy night on another beach? The things he'd seen plagued him and bound them. She hadn't wanted to like him. Had needed to hate him. Yet there she was comforted by his mere presence. His fingers curled around the base of her neck and kneaded the stiff muscles along her spine. His hands were warm. His palms were rough against her skin, solid and reassuring. She dropped her head on his shoulder and sighed.

"What is this place to you?" he asked. "It seems to draw out grief."

How could she explain the collision of all that was good with all that was bad? Her throat became the logjam where all those emotions met and she couldn't speak.

His hands kept kneading at the rigid column of her neck. "Is this where you lived with your grandfather?"

She nodded stiffly. With her grandfather and her sisters of the heart.

"We can go elsewhere if this place holds too many painful memories."

"I'm fine."

"Liar." He jostled her head off his shoulder so he could look into her eyes. "I'm worried about you."

Trying to control her mind, she mashed her fingers into fists and concentrated on the push and pull of the sea at her feet. The salt of tears stung her eyes. His breath was soothing against her cheek, a pulse of life in the midst of bleak memories of death.

As if his fingers were releasing the grief she'd tied into knots in her muscles, an unspeakable sadness lapped over her. She was breathing too hard, but still couldn't manage to squeeze enough air into her lungs. She tried to escape from his grasp.

"Shh," he whispered, hot and soft into her ear, refusing to let go.

Don't cry. Don't let him see you cry. She closed her eyes and willed him away.

"It's all right to cry, Adria."

"I'm not crying. Crying doesn't help. The grief stays anyway."

"I know."

Like on another stormy night by the sea. She hurt. She hurt so damn much. Pain grabbed her throat and dragged her down, but his arms held her up. They wrapped around her like a protective shawl. "Let go, Adria. It's okay."

And then the pain shattered and spiked through her like the fall of a thousand scissors, sharp and cutting. The tears she wasn't able to shed when her grandfather died flowed in a torrent. She slapped at the flood, hating her weakness, her neediness, her inability to stand alone. Too many nightmares. Not enough sleep. The stress was splintering cracks into all of her grandfather's training—a training that was so ingrained, she was never supposed to forget. If he could see her, he would be ashamed of her weakness.

Time slipped backward and she couldn't stop it. Thunder and lightning swirled around her. Riding in on curling waves, dragons spit fire and roared. She was six again, scared in the dark and the rain.

But not alone.

This time, she wasn't alone.

In that simple truth, she grasped hold of her strength.

There was a vital quality to Peter's energy. Something inside her was sparked by it like dry kindling, flared into the intensity of a brushfire and spread a vibrant heat deep into the cold corners of her body.

"You should be resting," she said, her voice hoarse from her tears. He tightened his arms around her shoulders and pressed his forehead against hers.

"I should be, but I can't."

"You don't like storms?"

"I don't like how they wash away—" He caught himself as if the wind had eaten his words. His throat bobbed, then he said, "I don't like their destructive nature."

"I'm not scared of death." Living after someone she loved died was what got her every time. "I don't go looking for it, but I'm not scared of it."

She should tell him about that night. She should let him know about the bond tying them together. She should explain that she didn't blame him for his father's cruelty. That her grandfather had left her an honor-bound duty to perform. That she wasn't sure he'd tasked her with the right target.

That her heart was torn between devotion to her grandfather and recognition of the man of honor Peter had molded himself into.

"Adria." Her name fell from his lips in a choked breath. "I care about you." He pressed a tender kiss into the crook of her neck. The sweetness of it quivered all the way down to her soles.

Her head tilted back slightly in surprise.

He tangled his fingers in the thick mane of her hair. His whole body tensed with desire. "Come back inside with me."

She could pretend to misunderstand, but she didn't want to. That small kiss had left her breathless and alive and she wanted him to breathe more of his intense fire into her.

In all the years she'd served as an executive protector, she'd never once let herself fall for the advances of a principal—even when she was tempted. She had an obligation to him and that wasn't the way to fulfill it.

"I can't, Peter. This is unprofessional. Dishonorable."

But everything she'd been taught to trust—rules, codes, procedures, ethics, discipline—no longer existed. How could they when sister betrayed sister? When the enemy was the victim?

This was her last assignment. She'd proved to herself she couldn't run her grandfather's business. What did it matter if she found release from the crushing stress in Peter's arms?

He stroked the side of her face, erasing the trail of her tears with his thumb. "You're afraid. Of me?"

She shook her head. Her fingers grazed the stubble of beard along his jaw. No, not afraid, but needy. "I have a responsibility toward you."

He wrapped her arms around his neck. "Then hold me. I need someone to hold me."

She let him draw her deeper into his arms. Let his mouth cover hers.

Dragon fire.

She didn't even care about the devastation wrought by the fiery beast's conquests. If he left nothing but ashes, so much the better because then nothing would be left of her soul-eating pain.

Her answering kiss exposed her hunger.

"Adria?" The pulse at his neck jackhammered beneath her fingertips. His aura glowed in a multitude of soft pastels that surrounded them in a cocoon that drove out the storm. Light chased away darkness. Their mingled warmth conquered the cold and rain of the night.

"I'm not who you think I am," she whispered in his ear, not sure why it was suddenly important he knew.

He kissed the hollow at the base of her throat and seemed to drink in her essence. "No one is."

"I think—"

"Too much."

"Yes. Too much." There was no future with him. Nothing to fear. Only a man and a woman needing to reassert that life went on even after a killing storm.

They moved into the shelter of the porch and she opened herself to all he was. Smooth muscles. Solid body. Soft hair. Texture. Warmth. Pleasure. He was real in a world that had become all too unreal.

Her heart jumped under its rib-cage housing, trying to set itself free. He smelled good, like fine leather and exotic spice. She inhaled his scent deep into her lungs. He tasted rich, like dark honey and aged brandy. She savored his intoxicating flavor.

On this dark and storm-filled night, while lightning sparked and thunder boomed, his warmth poured into her.

She had crossed all boundaries. Professional. Personal. Emotional. What did it matter if it dulled the edge of pain? She stopped thinking and let herself fall into this world of pure sensation. She sampled his mouth, the prickly soft stubble of his beard, the hard leanness of his muscles beneath his warm skin. His lips, his arms, his body moved in perfect rhythm to hers. Aroused and fed by his touch, she whispered his name.

Don't let go, she wanted to say, but couldn't find the words. As if he'd heard the whispers of her need, he held on to her tighter. He took her to the brink of control, then higher and higher still, until the world seemed to shatter in an explosion of light and she was in that weightless island of bliss where there was only the here and now.

Later, inside the house, warm and dry in his bed, she stared at Peter. Her skin was flushed with his heat. Her lips swollen from their shared kisses. Her loose hair was a tornado around her face. But the sheen of their lovemaking was starting to wear off and the loneliness in the pit of her soul was returning with a more biting vengeance than when she'd sought an easy answer to a deeper problem.

All she'd wanted was comfort. Release. She hadn't wanted to feel anything at all for him. In the possessive circle of his arms, her heart swelled with tenderness for the scared little boy who'd grown into such a decent man.

A swimming sensation sang out of her heart before she could trap it. A wave of panic rippled through her. Everyone she cared for... She shook her head. *Don't go there, Adria. Peter isn't the one for you.* Not with the past they shared. This was just escape.

Survival, that most primal of instincts, rose up in a

cold rush. It barricaded her heart and cleared her mind. She needed a new life, free from pain. She stared at Peter's face, peaceful in sleep, and the emptiness inside her howled.

As dawn lifted the edge of night, reality stepped back into their night of reprieve. The gate alarm beeped. Adria scrambled out of Peter's bed and stepped into her still-damp clothes.

"What's wrong?" Peter asked, stretching. There was nothing subtle about the confidence that shone around him. Feeding off that was tempting.

"Someone's here," she said. "Go to the safe room."

He bolted upright and reached for his own clothes. "How could anyone have found us so soon? You checked every inch of our luggage for tracking devices."

"It may be nothing." Heart pounding, she raced down to the command center and scanned the three CCT screens. "Swell."

"Who is it?" Peter asked, pulling a sweatshirt over his bare torso. Of course, why should he bother listening to her? Hadn't her grandfather warned her of the consequences of sleeping with a principal? It altered the balance between protector and protectee, brought out the male instinct to defend what he now saw as his.

She forced her gaze back to the screen. "Caleb. He's letting himself in, so that means my grandfather must have given him the code."

"Does he know we're here?"

"I don't think so. He and my grandfather were working on a book."

Suspicion instantly reared its ugly head. Caleb had been close to her grandfather, especially in the months before his death. Her grandfather's death had hit him almost as hard as it had hit her. Had her grandfather told Caleb who Peter was? Did Caleb want revenge in his friend's name? Had he left the poisoned cheese for Peter, knowing she was safe from its effects because she wouldn't eat any?

Against the promise of blue skies, the aging brown Chevy crept past the gate. Norm's grinning head hung out the passenger's side window, his tongue flapping like a flag.

Adria fought the heat of anger that rushed to the surface, forcing an artificial calm in its place. She would have to toe a tentative line between exploring Caleb's reasons for driving out to Osprey Island and preserving Peter's security. And if Caleb was there for revenge, she would have to disabuse her old friend of that notion.

This time, her grandfather was wrong.

Chapter 14

From the space used as a combination mudroom and laundry room on the left side of the door, Adria had a clear view of the Chevy's arrival. Peter stood behind her, his aura crackling against hers. Her rebel mind conjured up the memory of last night's lovemaking and her body warmed in response. *Stay on task, Adria. Don't let him distract you from your duty.* That could lead to danger for both of them.

Caleb opened the car door. Norm charged past his owner, looking none the worse for his encounter with bacteria-spiked cheese. The golden retriever thundered onto the porch where he pawed at the door, tail wagging wildly as if a friend waited on the other side.

"What's wrong with you?" Caleb asked, catching up to Norm. "Nolan isn't here, old friend. You know that."

When the door opened without his having to key in the code, Caleb stumbled back a few steps, hand on heart as if it to keep it in his chest. "Adria? You scared the devil out of me. What are you doing here?"

"I could ask the same thing." For one night, she'd kidded herself that this place was safe. But Caleb's unexpected and too-coincidental arrival reminded her that no place was completely safe.

Caleb frowned and cranked his head from side to side as if he suddenly realized he was the highest object in the middle of a lightning storm. He leaned at the hip and, hand cupped to his mouth, he whispered, "I didn't know you were hiding here. I came for Nolan's files. No one followed me, if that's what you're afraid of."

Not that Caleb's brain could stay plugged into anything that wasn't work-related long enough to realize he was being followed. Warily, she stepped back, keeping herself between Caleb and Peter. "Come on in."

As soon as Adria started to move aside, Norm squeezed in and launched himself at Peter.

"I'm glad you're here actually. No one would tell me where you were. Julie's quite upset, you know. She can't figure out what she's done to earn your wrath. She was carrying on like a madwoman."

What she's done is betray me. Are you working with her, Caleb? Is that why you've appeared here without any warning? Other than the girls, you're the only one who knows about this place. A lucky guess? Or a calculated conjecture because he knew she'd run out of options?

Caleb took her hand and nearly dragged her into the large front room whose picture window gave the impression of being outside. Weak morning sunlight puddled on the multicolored rag carpet and caught on the corners of the well-loved Arts and Crafts coffee table.

He sat on the faded blue couch and pulled her down beside him. His eyes glittered with the enthusiasm he couldn't disguise. "I found some interesting information in the box of notes your grandfather gave me before he died."

His gaze strayed to Peter, who was paying attention to them while patting Norm, then quickly darted back to Adria. "Perhaps we could take a walk on the beach."

"I can't leave Peter." Not when she wasn't sure why Caleb was there or if she could trust him. For all she knew, he could have a cohort paddling his way to the island right now and his part in the covert action was to separate protector from protectee.

"Yes, yes. Of course." Caleb bent over and whispered, "It's personal."

If Caleb pulled a weapon, she could easily disarm him. She mulled over her options, then looked at Peter. "Could you make us a pot of tea?"

Caleb twisted to face Peter and lifted his index finger. "Uh, make that coffee for me."

Peter's gaze ground through her, his questions as loud as if he'd shouted them. She didn't like the new possessive edge to his manner, but chose to ignore it for now. She shook her head slightly and shrugged, indicating she had no idea what this was all about. He nodded as he rose and grudgingly stepped into the hallway. Norm scrambled to his feet and dogged Peter's heels.

Caleb resumed his perched-bird-about-to-take-off pose and tripped over his own words in his rush to spill his contained excitement. "You knew, didn't you?"

"Knew what?"

"About Peter. That's why you took the job as secretary. Does he know yet?"

"Know what?"

Caleb licked his lips as if the words were so juicy he wanted to savor them. "About the project."

"What project?" She was growing testier by the second, but knew Caleb well enough to contain her impatience. Caleb's mind didn't work in a straight line, it worked in an annoying zigzag that not even the strongest of magnet could straighten. Was the absentminded professor demeanor supposed to relax her guard?

"The Dragon project." He reached for her hand and patted it. Adria removed her hand from Caleb's grasp, working hard at not shrinking from his clammy touch.

"What's the Dragon project?"

Caleb straightened and his bushy eyebrows met in the middle of his forehead. "You had to know. Why else would have applied for the job and asked me to drive you there? You said you had to get it."

The newspaper ad detailing the secretarial position at Dragon, Inc. had appeared on her desk. At the time she'd thought it a fortuitous coincidence. But was it just another piece in a design she couldn't see? Could she have been duped so easily?

Because someone—Julie? Victor? Caleb?—caught you at a vulnerable time—and worse, that someone knew it. "Caleb, what exactly are you talking about?"

"The book. *A Warrior's Life.* Your grandfather was writing it to tell the story. I found his notes for the chapter on honor."

"What does the autobiography of his life as an executive protector have to do with Peter?"

"Not just Peter. You, too." Caleb's grizzled mustache spread along with his smile as he squeezed her hand. "He'd be so proud that you took over where he left off."

"Took over what?"

"Protecting Peter, of course."

Caleb had it wrong as usual. Her grandfather hadn't asked her to protect Peter, but to dismantle his empire. But Adria refrained from correcting him. *Give him rope; let him hang himself with it.* "It's a job, Caleb."

He shook his head and the loose skin beneath his neck flapped. "No, it's a continuation of his honor-bound duty."

He jumped up and ran out the front door. Adria stood to keep an eye on him. In the kitchen, the coffee grinder whirred and Peter mumbled something to Norm she couldn't make out.

Caleb raced back from his car with a thick file folder. He plunked back down on the couch and started flipping through the loose pages trapped in the file. "Here it is."

Half the contents of the file promptly slid off his knees as he leaned forward to hand her a section of pages. "See? Honor. Duty. It's all there."

In the typed pages, she read the lessons her grandfather had ingrained in her over the years, of honor and duty, of a philosophy that was neither eastern nor western but a universal truth. None of it was news. Why was Caleb making such a big fuss over it?

Then with Caleb's eagerness prodding her on, her gaze slid down the page and fastened on paragraphs that fluttered her heart like a caged bird.

"Life is a series of connections and breaks," her grandfather had written. "The death of my daughter and son-in-law was a painful break, yet in that break came an opportunity to exhaust an old force and create a new one. I took advantage of the break, and like pulling silk, allowed the well of regeneration to fill the hole of destruction.

"The boy's silence allowed my granddaughter to live, connecting me to him just as surely as to her. These children could rise or sink with circumstance. Only by being well rooted in the feet could they become centered. That was my task. They are yin and yang, fated to aid each other, to create positive energy out of negative intent.

"I nurtured without harm. I supported. I showed them that mind came first, then body. That the softest became the strongest. That when the spirit is firm there is nothing it can't accomplish."

Horror skittered down her spine. How could she have gotten everything so wrong? Her grandfather hadn't wanted Peter harmed, not when he'd raised him from afar like a son. Tears blurred the print. Gripping the pages with both hands, she blinked and resumed reading.

Though he couldn't reveal himself for fear harm would come to her or Peter, her grandfather had protected them both. He followed Peter's every move, making things easier for him. Everything from the new identity papers for Peter and Russell to the business thrown his way in the early days to the advance warnings of sticky situations—all done through intermediaries.

Peter had never known he'd had a secret benefactor. And Adria had never realized that her grandfather felt indebted to the ten-year-old boy who'd saved his six-year-old granddaughter's life with his silence all those years ago.

He'd been the constant in both their lives, even if Peter hadn't known he existed. How could her grandfather have kept something so important from her? All those years, how could he not have said anything?

She wanted to hit something, to hear the satisfying crack of wood splintering, to feel the bloody sting of bruised knuckles. But her grandfather's training prevailed and, even with this cyclone twisting inside her, she remained outwardly calm.

And in the center of that calm a burden seemed to lift from her heavy heart. Her grandfather hadn't expected her to ruin Peter, but to protect him—just as he had.

The backbeat of waves washing on the beach matched the tide of her pulse, pushing in relief, pulling out turmoil. Had this been a test of some sort? Had she, in her zeal to repay her grandfather's love, almost blown the true duty he'd charged her with? If yes, then she'd failed miserably and, in the process, caused a friend to betray her, allowed three members of her team to get hurt and almost destroyed an innocent man.

"That's why I'm here," Caleb said.

Adria shook her head, trying to separate herself from the folds of confusion and anger. Her wariness returned. Was Caleb telling her all this now because he hoped her love for her grandfather would become a weakness he could exploit? "What?"

"The safety box. It holds the proof."

"What safety box? What proof?" Was he truly the family friend he posed as? Or did he have an ulterior agenda? She kept an eye on his hands, ready to react. In the kitchen, the kettle whistled. Peter would soon reappear.

Caleb rummaged through the fallen pages he'd gathered until he found the one he wanted. "Your grandfather mentioned a safety box and important papers."

"His?"

"No. Rudy Hauxwell's."

Her nerves twanged with alarm. Why was Caleb so anxious to get his hands on papers belonging to Peter's father? "Why would my grandfather have anything that belonged to Rudy Hauxwell?"

"Because these papers could have put Peter's inheritance in jeopardy. Your grandfather couldn't let that happen. Of the three, only Peter would do right by the blood money."

She frowned. "Three what?"

"Three sons."

She shook her head. "No, there are only two sons."

Caleb shuffled through the scattered pages once more. "No, see, here. There was a son before Peter. Ruben Puluke. Rudy was never married to the woman. She and her son disappeared soon after the birth, which took place on the day Rudy married Clara, Peter's mother. Clara had social standing. Ruben's mother didn't. He had to make his indiscretion disappear."

Her blood drained to her feet and seemed to forget to climb back up. Had this third brother now come to claim what he thought was his? Was he using Caleb to gather the proof? "Did Grandpa try to find this Ruben?"

Caleb pointed at some handwritten scribbles on one of the pages she held. "It says he thought that Ruben and his mother might both be dead. He found no trace that they ever left Hawaii. It doesn't look as if they've popped up anywhere else, either. My guess is that Rudy had them killed."

But what if they weren't? What if they'd done exactly what they were supposed to do and disappeared? A third brother would go a long way to explain the threats against Peter. A lifetime of forced hiding was certainly long enough to build a boatload of resentment. But if he was still alive, why wait so long after Rudy's death to place his claim? "The statute of limitations for contesting Hauxwell's will is long past. What good would it do this brother, if he does exist, to get his hands on these papers now?"

Caleb's caterpillar brows disappeared beneath his shaggy blond bangs. "That I won't know until I read them."

If Ruben was alive, if Ruben wanted to claim his inheritance, then the personal bent to the assaults, the determination to toy with Peter, all made sense. The papers' existence could also explain why Peter was still alive. Whoever was pursuing them needed proof.

Bringing her and Peter together, forcing them to excavate the ruins of their pasts, would eventually lead to that proof.

Her throat closed and breathing became painful. Once the proof was found, she and Peter would have outlived their usefulness.

"Do you know where the box is?" Caleb asked, practically drooling.

Still staring at her grandfather's handwriting, willing the truth from it, she shook her head. Why was Caleb so eager to expose a secret her grandfather had hidden for so long? She chased the rungs of possibilities and ended up right where she started. Trust no one. "I don't know. I've never heard my grandfather mention a safety box."

Caleb pointed toward the end of the hall. "His office? Can I look?"

"Why don't you take Norm out for a walk first, then I'll help you look?" She needed to talk to Peter. She'd tried to tell him the truth of what she knew last night, but even she hadn't known how deeply they were linked. Now she could no longer put it off.

The click of Norm's nails on the hardwood floor pulled her gaze down the hall. Peter stood at the doorway to the kitchen with a mug in each hand. His expression could have given a polar bear frostbite. As Caleb called Norm, then made his way outside to the beach, her heart plunged to her feet. How much had Peter heard?

When Peter spoke, his words were calm, but their bite was chilling. "You lied to me."

Gone was last night's careful lover, this morning's possessive gentleman. In his place stood a man used to absolute authority. Against the cream walls of the hall, red lightning razored his aura. Abandoning both mugs on the kitchen counter, he jerked his chin toward the front door. He wedged his fists in his jeans pockets as if he couldn't trust himself to touch her without strangling her or the small space to contain the fullness of his anger.

Out on the porch a soft breeze caressed the wind chime hanging on the far end of the overhang. The notes tinkled brightly in stark contrast to Peter's dark mood. He pointed to a lone white folding cottage chair. She opted for the swing where she sat with one foot tucked under her. He dragged the folding chair in front of the swing. He sat down and stared at her. His eyes were savage storms. His fists, one holding the other between his knees, were white with tension.

"A week ago, when you practically begged me to give you this job, you asked about my background before Dragon, Inc."

To keep calm, she set the swing in motion with the toe of her sneaker. Because she partially deserved his wrath, she choked back the excuses on the tip of her tongue ready to pepper him. She *had* tried to tell him. He *hadn't* wanted to listen. "It's part of the protocol of taking on a new client."

With hands braced on both sides of her knees, he halted the swing's motion. "Two days ago, you insisted I dig into my past."

She said nothing. The thread between them was steel tempered by her grandfather's care, but the strand was thin and walking along it precarious business.

"I've asked you twice before and twice you've lied to me. I want the truth this time. Who are you?"

"I'm Adria Caskey. I'm an executive protection specialist."

He stood abruptly, knocking the chair out from under him. It clattered down the three steps and landed in a crooked heap in the sand. "Cut the crap. You knew. From the first day, you knew."

"From day one, I was protecting you."

"Stop it, Adria. Just stop it. You betrayed my trust."

And that, she suddenly understood, was the greatest sin she could have committed. Never mind the rest, withholding that one piece of information now put her in the same category of sinner as his father.

Gritting her teeth, she worked at keeping her tone even. "I tried to tell you last night. But even then I didn't know as much as I thought."

Gaze firmly cemented on hers, voice as cold as winter and as calm as summer, he said, "Go on."

"I did some background research before applying as your secretary. Before that, all I knew about you was what I remembered seeing twenty-one years ago." She swallowed hard. "The night my father and mother were killed."

Pain knifed his features into tight lines. He came to-

ward her and looked down at her just as he had that
night. His hands trapped her jaw. He raked her hair
away from her face and tipped it back until her hair
brushed against the dead remnants of last summer's
hanging flower planter. His thumbs grazed the contours
of her cheekbones as if he were blind and reading
Braille. He studied every inch of her face as if he were
a laser that would need to recreate the data it had cap-
tured. "You were there that night. Outside in the rain.
In the bushes. I never knew your first name. But your
last name was Kaholo then."

"Kaholo is my father's name. I took on my grandfather's when we moved to the mainland. Yours was
Hauxwell. We both had to hide from that horrible
night."

His hands ripped away from her face as if she'd
slapped him, and he backed away until the rail caught
his thigh. As if he were checking up on Norm, he looked
toward the west end of the beach. But a barrier was
going up around him, tight and strong. "I am not my father."

"I know," she said, heart beating fast and hard in her
chest as if the truth was now a race she had to win before he shut her out completely. "My father sold insurance for a living. He had an office in a small strip mall.
He believed in hard work and ethics and truth. Mostly
he believed in people, in helping them and standing up
for them. My grandfather told me that your father had
my parents killed because my father refused to pay for
his protection and led the other merchants on the strip
into withholding payments."

"And you're doing this for payback? My father is
dead, so get your vengeance on his son. Is that it?"

"No."

His glare became a weight that pushed against her, so she pushed back. "Did you know you have an older brother?"

His whole body stilled.

"His name is Ruben Puluke. Does that ring a bell?"

"There's only Russell."

"You have a brother who can't afford to reveal himself until he has some papers that are in my grandfather's possession." A ghost brother, an unclaimed brother.

"Why did your grandfather have those papers? How did he get them?"

"I don't know how he got them. All I know is that he was trying to protect you."

"From what?"

They are yin and yang, fated to aid each other, to create positive energy out of negative intent. "From your father's legacy of violence."

Peter crossed his arms against his chest. "Why would he care what happened to me?"

"He wanted my parents not to have died in vain. If you didn't follow in your father's footsteps, then their deaths weren't a total loss."

He swiped a hand through his hair and clamped it at his nape while he shook his head. There was a battle inside him that mirrored her own.

"This brother," she said, trying to reach through the barrier Peter had erected, "he could be **the** one who's after you. Maybe he wants a share of **the** inheritance he feels he was denied." And who had made sure this brother was disowned? Her grandfather.

The thought almost sent her reeling back to that pit of dark grief. That her grandfather was killed because he'd protected Peter's interests now seemed a certainty.

"And maybe you're painting this nice little disaster scenario for your own end. If I fail, then you win."

"No, it's not like that."

"You're fired."

"I can understand your anger." She reached for his hand. He wrenched it out of her grasp.

"Can you? I trusted you. You betrayed me."

Too much was at stake to leave things as they stood. She rose from her seat and faced him eye to eye. The chains on the swing rattled. "So that's it? You're going to go back to your office? You're going to put the people you say you want protected in danger? Do you think you'll be helping anyone if you're dead? My grandfather understood your vision. He did everything he could to help you make it a reality. Sending me to protect you was his last gift."

His jaw worked as if he were chewing on iron nails.

"Someone sent you a letter bomb. Someone broke into a secured house to get to you. Someone tried to poison you. *You* are in danger. *I* can keep you alive. Nothing's changed." But everything had changed and they both knew it. She was aware of his shame and he couldn't stand for her to know the weakness he'd spent a lifetime hiding.

They were at a critical point now. She had to keep him on her side or their division of trust could become another weakness used against them. "Are you going to let him win, Peter? Are you going to let him destroy everything you've worked so hard to build?"

His jaw worked, but his gaze didn't relent.

"You saved my life, Peter. I'm trying to repay the favor."

"Your debt is paid." He spun on his heel and stalked down the steps. On the beach, Norm canted an anxious look in Caleb's direction before he trotted toward Peter.

She let Peter go, knowing she could keep an eye on him and that he'd soon come back. Once he calmed down, he would see this through because there was no other choice.

And so would she, because she had no choice, either. She'd made a promise to her grandfather and, now that she knew his true desire, she would fulfill the debt of honor.

Chapter 15

When Peter returned, he stormed past her, his expression forbidding any communication. Keeping an ear out for him as he banged pots and pans in the kitchen, she helped Caleb search through her grandfather's files for the answer to the location of the safety box and the mysterious papers.

As she tracked each of Caleb's movements, a gentle nagging turned into a more insistent cold spider crawling up her spine. Her fingers stilled on the bank records and her eyes started to well up. Her grandfather was the kindest man she knew. He'd seen her through the shadows, given her confidence, helped her grow into a strong woman. Could Caleb or Julie really have killed a man who considered them a friend?

"Caleb?" Her gaze caught the collage of photos tacked on a corkboard on the wall in front of her grandfather's desk. A rainbow of a dozen girls whose light could have dimmed permanently had her grandfather not taught them they deserved to shine.

"Hmm?" Caleb sat cross-legged on the floor, looking through a cardboard file box labeled "Misc."

Her gaze scanned the photographs. The fast blinking of her stinging eyes acted like the lens of a camera, snapping scenes of her past. The fifteen-year-old twins, huddled together on the beach, a world unto themselves. Sixteen-year-old Sam hobbling on crutches, trying to keep up with everyone. Innocent-looking, thirteen-year-old Daphne pickpocketing candy from Adria's plastic pumpkin at Halloween. Twelve-year-old, hard-edged Romy with her take-no-shit expression. Fifteen-year-old Adria, one arm around Grandpa's waist, the other holding a wooden treasure chest. "Where were you when Grandpa died?"

"February?" Caleb stared up at the ceiling. "Home, I suppose."

She twisted the office chair around until she could study every shift of light and line on Caleb's face. Could appendicitis be induced? What if food poisoning had taken a bad turn? "When was the last time you and he shared a meal?"

He pinched his lips in concentration. "Lunch a few days before. Why?"

"No reason."

He looked up then and his gaze searched her face. "I'm sorry that I'm bringing back that pain for you. That wasn't the intent of my visit."

"I know."

That Caleb would spend a decade cultivating her grandfather's friendship just to kill him when he was finally getting a publishing payoff he'd pursued for years made no sense. Her grandfather and his treasure trove of wisdom were worth more to Caleb alive than dead—at least until the book was published.

Treasure trove. Treasure chest. The words seemed to spark a memory, but the flash soon faded. She rose and pretended interest in the supply closet to try to jog that glimpse of memory again. Then hazy images crept back. The games, of course. How could she have forgotten the hide-and-seek games?

Her grandfather had given Caleb the code for the gate and the door, but he hadn't told him about the games or the location of the papers. How far had his trust extended? Maybe he had doubts toward the end? Or had he simply died before he could tell all of his secrets? One hand cradled the eel of nausea sliding through her stomach.

The key to the mystery wasn't in the files and boxes, but somewhere else on the island. She itched to get Caleb on his way, but didn't rush him. Peter was still rattling bowls in the kitchen, and Caleb needed to know he'd searched well and found nothing so that he wouldn't return.

"I can't find anything here." Caleb sighed and pushed away the last of the boxes. "Will you give me the code to the office in New Haven?"

"No, it's important you stay away from the office for now." She needed to keep Julie and Caleb apart until she could figure out how they fit in with the missing brother. "Can you wait until Monday?"

Peter's presentation would be over by then.

Caleb's whole face drooped with disappointment. "His apartment, then. Will you allow me to search there?"

Adria tossed him a bone to mollify him. "Tell you what. I'll give you the key to his storage unit. He might have filed something there."

The storage unit was away from both the office and the apartment. Her grandfather wouldn't have kept anything of value there—too unsecured. Caleb would find only old coded business files, but it would keep him busy for a few days. She reached into the top drawer of the desk and picked out a key from the organizer there. On a piece of paper, she wrote down the storage unit's address and handed both paper and key to Caleb. "Here you go."

Caleb beamed. "Thank you."

He had a hard time disengaging Norm from the kitchen that smelled of buttery rolls and grilled beef. Norm agreed to leave only after Peter packed away a slice of the sirloin in a foil packet and Caleb used the foil-wrapped meat to lure the golden retriever into the car.

Adria made sure Caleb closed the gate and left the island before she returned to the kitchen. She leaned against the doorjamb, taking in the scene of intense concentration. Peter's wide shoulders were stiff as he scrubbed a mound of new red potatoes and dumped them in a pot of boiling water. His lean body seemed braced for a fight he wouldn't allow. Anger—he'd done everything in his power to leave it in the past, but it still flowed in his veins.

"Peter?"

"Can't you see I'm in the middle of something?" He plopped the last potato into the pan and reached for the colander of green beans in the sink.

"We need to go for a walk."

Knife in hand, he turned and the coldness of his gaze sent an icy wash down her spine. "I'm not going anywhere with you."

"Fine. I'll lock the doors and arm the alarm to keep you safe." She turned toward the command center. She didn't like manipulating him, but he wasn't the only one who'd taken a blow to the ego today. "I just thought you might like to be there when I find proof of your brother's existence."

Peter stopped his mad trimming of green beans. His left hand snaked out and his fingers dug painfully into her biceps. In this light, his eyes were steel-gray and just as hard. "Don't."

She met his gaze and held it firm. "Then stop being an ass. If we're going to find whoever wants you dead in time for you to make your presentation, then we don't have time to play power games. I know you don't believe it, but I understand how you feel."

His fingers continued to press into her flesh in a way that managed to telegraph both intimacy and physical threat. "You have no idea what I'm feeling."

"Fair enough. You have a right to whatever you're feeling. But you're working out of your depth." She flicked her wrist against his forearm and freed her arm. Not rubbing at the bruises he'd left behind made her fingers twitch at her sides. "If whoever's after you was able to kill my grandfather, what makes you think you have any chance to survive on your own? And since protecting you cost my grandfather his life, you're stuck with me until he's caught."

Color drained from his cheeks, then rose in a red rash that surely spiked his blood pressure into unhealthy territory. "I thought you said your grandfather died of appendicitis."

"I'm thinking poisoning." She softened her voice. "Whether you like it or not, I am the key to your past and your future. And the key to my grandfather's death is in your past. We need each other. So deal with it and let's get on with the job."

His throat worked as if keeping a cap on his building anger required all of his strength. To speak now would tip that fragile balance and his stiff stance said he was afraid of the power of that detonation.

This scares him, makes him feel out of control. It makes him feel just like his father. And that was the thing he feared most—being like his father.

And on top of everything, she was asking him to turn away from his anger-defusing mechanism and trust her again.

He cranked all the burners on the stove to the Off position, scraped all the food into one bowl and shoved the bowl into the refrigerator. Then he stalked down the hall toward the front door. Once there, he yanked the door open and scowled at her. "What are you waiting for?"

"What are you doing?" Peter asked.

"Trying to remember."

He stood on the rocky bluff where the Connecticut River met Long Island Sound, facing the saltwater marsh farther north on the island. Behind him Sound met sky seamlessly. The breeze, blowing in from the water, teased her nostrils with its briny scent. Its playful fingers ruffled Peter's hair and sculpted dragon scales on his sun-darkened silhouette. Overhead an osprey shrieked and dove feetfirst into the water to capture a fish.

These were the sights, scents and sounds of her young adulthood. There amid the varied landscape, her grandfather had not only served as parent, but as mentor. The lessons were ingrained through play and repetition. They were still there. All she had to do was feel them.

"Remember what?"

"The steps of hide-and-seek."

Peter swore. "Why are we wasting our time like this? Didn't you say you could find proof I had another brother?"

She gazed past the marsh grass to the three osprey nesting platforms. "Because of what he did, my grandfather learned to trust with care. He also knew that anything you entrusted to someone else could be compromised. If you want something to stay out of sight, the best thing is to hide it. You couldn't just look him up in the phone book. All of his business came from word of mouth. Nothing is listed in his name."

"So he's hidden this supposed proof out here somewhere."

"Right." Adria ignored Peter's snigger of incredulity. "He made a game out of it. I thought nothing of it at the time, but he told me that one day remembering these steps could save my life."

He planted the shovel at his side as if he were staking a claim. "What if you can't remember?"

"I will."

From the rocks, she led them to the middle osprey nesting platform where a faded paint mark on the post pointed the way. She headed upland to an old oak tree that seemed to guard the woods. Her fingers sought the mark carved into the trunk. She oriented herself, backbone square against it. From there it was just a hop, skip and a jump to the site where her grandfather had buried the first clue. A domed rock, splotched by moss that made it look like a toadstool, marked the spot. She lifted the rock and asked Peter to dig.

In the unearthed coffee can, they found a pewter dragon that resembled the one in Peter's office.

As he held the offending object in his palm, Peter's face darkened. "Is this some sort of joke?"

She shook her head, dislodging the bubbles of memories jockeying for attention.

"It's a clue."

Peter ground his teeth, but his voice still shot daggers. "What now?"

"We go back to the cottage." She placed the dragon back in the can and the can back in its hole.

"That's it?"

As she piled dirt back over the can, she let her sigh dissipate her own growing irritation. "No, that's step one."

"If all we're doing is going back to the starting point, why did we have to waste all this time traipsing all over this blasted island?"

"Because he could have hidden anything in there. And this spot was always the starting point. The object in the can was the clue and the clue leads us back to the house."

"How does it lead us back there?" He banged the back of the shovel against the already-level pile of dirt.

She rolled the toadstool rock back in its protective position. "Dragons equal stories. Stories are in books. Books are on the bookshelf in one of the upstairs bedrooms."

"This better lead to something."

She was thinking the same thing.

They made their way back to the cottage. Upstairs in the small bedroom her grandfather had partitioned off so each girl could have privacy, she went straight to the white shelf unit built into the wall. She removed the books on the fifth shelf up from the floor. A smile tempered with sadness curved her mouth as she remembered her grandfather's singsong instructions. She knocked three times on the side and a spring-loaded door opened. Inside the nook, she found a metal box and a doll-size teacup. Inside the box was a bound diary with a reproduction of Gauguin's Tahitian women on the cover. The inside page told her that the book belonged to Vera Puluke.

"Does the name Vera Puluke mean anything to you?" she asked Peter.

"No." He took the diary from her and flipped through the pages. "All the dates are before my parents got married."

Peter sat in the white wicker rocker next to the bookshelf and started reading. She perched on the edge of the woodrose Hawaiian quilt her mother had made for her and stared at Peter, trying all the while not to let memories of her mother crowd her mind.

"The teacup," he said five minutes later, gaze still on the page. "What does it mean?"

"The next clue is in the front room."

He slanted her a questioning look.

"Teacup. Toy. Playroom."

"Ah."

She thrust her chin in the diary's direction, unable to curb her curiosity any longer. "What does it say?"

"Vera was a maid in my grandfather's household." His voice was businesslike, as if he were reading a document to which he had no emotional attachment. "It seems my father seduced her, got her pregnant and had my grandfather fire her. His marriage to my mother was a business arrangement and my grandfather didn't want anything to jeopardize it. He paid off Vera and threatened her and her child if she didn't disappear. On my parents' wedding day, she showed up at the chapel.

My grandfather's goons turned her back, roughly, from what I can gather. She went into labor and bore Ruben a month early." As he flipped through the last empty pages, she thought she noticed a small shake of his hands. "Then nothing."

Another human being used and tossed away like garbage. How many ghosts had Peter's father and grandfather created to feed their greed?

Peter chucked the diary back into the metal box. Elbows propped on the rockers' arms, he tented his fingers against his mouth. "If this diary is so important for this Ruben to prove his parentage, then why didn't your grandfather simply burn it?"

She contemplated the diary's cover with its simple scene of warm colors. Her grandfather had kept it for the same reason Vera had saved it. "Insurance."

"Against what?"

She cocked her head to one side and sought his gaze. She was going to pierce his weakest point, but now more than ever, truth needed to surface. "My guess? Against your character."

"My character?" He scowled, taking offense. After all, he'd spent half a lifetime building a sterling reputation based on his ethical character. "What kind of crap is that?"

"If you proved unworthy of my grandfather's protection, he wanted a way to take away what he'd given you." She should have realized that her grandfather wouldn't use her as an instrument of destruction. Everything he'd done was to protect her, keep her safe, make her strong.

Peter shot up from the rocker, setting it in mad motion, and paced the tiny room like a dog in a cage that was too small. "I don't care who he was or that his in-

tentions started out as noble. Your grandfather had no
right to play God."

"I don't know the right answer, Peter. I just know
that we have to finish what was started and put an end
to it."

A sudden lethargy weighed her limbs. Yes, when it
was done, when Peter was safe, the debt would be paid
off. He would return to his world. And she…she would
have to redefine hers.

She stowed both the metal box with the diary and
the teacup back in its cubbyhole, closed the spring-
loaded door and returned the books to the shelf, all the
while careful not to bump into Peter in the small space
he all but dominated.

Silently, they made their way to the front room
where Caleb had dropped his bombshell about the third
brother. One, two, buckle my shoe. Three, four, shut
the door. Five, six, pick up sticks. She headed toward
the organizer against the wall closest to the front door.
The bottom shelf was meant to house shoes, but contained instead a stack of board games. The wooden
pegs on the left-hand side held Sam's floppy sunhat,
the Peruvian knit cap Romy had worn for two years
straight, an assortment of gimme caps in all sizes and
colors and her grandfather's lure-spiked canvas fishing
hat. And inside the door of the armoire section on the
right hung a collection of her grandfather's walking
sticks.

She chose the bamboo one and pulled on the rubber stopper at the end. With her knife, she peeled away
the protective wax seal. A metal key dropped into her
hand. With a finger, she prodded the inside of the cane
and drew out some papers. She set aside the walking
stick and unrolled the papers. Two birth certificates.

The first one named Vera Puluke and Rudy Hauxwell as Ruben Puluke Hauxwell's parents. The second one showed only Vera Puluke as the mother. The father was listed as unknown. And Ruben was demoted to simply Puluke. Had Peter's grandfather arranged to have history rewritten? She passed the certificates on to Peter.

Staring at the key, she turned the old-fashioned brass over and over in her hand. A flag was etched into the scrolled head. The flag of Great Britain to honor a friendship and eight stripes to represent the eight main islands.

"Where does it lead?" Peter asked. He let the certificates roll back into themselves and choked them in one hand.

She looked up and handed him the last answer he wanted. "Hawaii."

Hands on hips, he turned his back to her and stared out to sea. Still, remote, cold. The one place he probably thought he'd put behind him forever kept calling him back.

The Face had learned the art of capitalizing on one's strength from Father. From Mother came the craft of pain without bruising. She hadn't been able to stand up to the one person who'd turned her life into hell, but she'd taken her repressed rage out on those smaller than she. At least until adolescence had made them equals.

On the outside, she'd appeared meek and mild-mannered. She'd played her roles as suffering mother, PTA slave and kowtowing drudge with such convincing efficiency that no one would have believed the child if it had told of the horrors suffered at her hands. Such a gifted actress. The one attempt to escape her clutches had resulted in a paddling from the elementary school principal for telling lies. Where she'd learned such skills was a mystery, but each painful practice was now part of The Face's repertoire.

At the office, there was a key to the storage unit used by Caskey & Caskey. All the office's paperwork found a final resting place there. Amazing, really, what one could learn from listening to those desperate for attention.

As the dying afternoon bled red, The Face spied an old Chevy parked in front of the unit and a smile fluxed. The golden retriever inside the car barked.

"Quiet, Norm! I'm almost done."

All it took was a sleeping-pill-laced snack cake to silence the mutt. Insomnia had its advantages after all.

A step inside was made to look like a casual encounter. "Hey, Professor!"

The professor looked up from his crumpled stance over a cardboard file box. He shaded his eyes against the last of the sun eking into the unit. "What can I do for you?"

"I was walking by and saw you. Spring cleaning, you know how it is. Can't seem to part with anything, so I store it." Letting a smile grow, The Face crossed the few feet separating them. The Face squatted next to the prey and wrapped a hand around the professor's shoulder as if he were an old friend. An almost imperceptible shift of finger located the network of nerves that was sought and applied pressure. "I want you to please tell me where the Dragon and his guard are."

The professor's eyes went wide. His face drained of all blood. He tried to scramble away from the source of his pain, but all that did was render it more excruciating. "I—I don't know."

"I asked nicely. Please tell me where they are."

The professor's mouth worked, but he couldn't quite manage to spill his lie while agony pulsed in a wave.

Increased pressure popped the professor's aging bones. Grating the freshly broken end of bone against the bundle of raw nerves yielded a satisfying sound of pain. "Now, do you want to tell me what I want to know or shall I continue?"

The professor told him everything. He blubbered the enemy's location. He shared the cottage's layout. He spilled the code to get through the gate and the door and the one to silence the alarm once inside.

For his good behavior. The Face rewarded the professor with a jab on the chest at just the right spot on the midline, stopping the old man's heart instantly.

Searching the unit didn't yield what was expected. The Face placed the professor inside the Chevy and drove him and his dog home. When the professor was found, it would look as if he'd suffered a heart attack and fallen down the stairs. A study of forensics allowed for just the right placement of body. As an added touch of realism, the drugged dog was placed on his plaid bed in the living room. The car keys tossed on the telephone table in the hall continued to set the proper scene. So did the typed note tucked in the professor's hand.

Once all the prints were wiped, there was nothing to do but leave. A short walk to the beach. A taxi ride. Then the next domino could be set in motion.

Chapter 16

The house was burning. This wasn't happening. Her grandfather's house wasn't burning. It was tough and strong just like he was. And he'd filled it with bells and whistles to protect it. Grandpa's house was safe. Just a nightmare. *No, wake up!* She was going to die. She was going to blaze like a torch all alone in the night. As these needles of thought penetrated the layers of sleep, Adria scrambled to her feet, heart racing.

Fire. The room was on fire. She had to get out. Peter. He was upstairs. She had to get to him.

The smoke was already thick. Choking, she dropped to the floor. The fire drills were ingrained. Stay below the smoke. Fire ladders. Rendezvous point. Except this time, she wasn't the kid; she was the protector. And this wasn't a drill. The urge to scream bubbled in her chest. But it would be a waste of breath. Peter wouldn't hear her and she'd inhale toxic fumes.

She couldn't see, but crawled toward the door. The flames bit through the house's wood siding with a roar. She couldn't hear anything else. Like a mask, heat smothered. The hot wood floor burned her knees and palms as she tried to escape the room that was fast becoming a hellish tomb. As she traveled across the floor, her muscles responded with uncharacteristic sluggishness.

Layer upon layer of shadows twisted and writhed so that she couldn't make anything out of the smoky gloom. Her grandfather had taught her to hear the sound of a striking match, the feet of crickets, the trail of evil intent. How had this happened? Why wasn't the smoke alarm shrilling a warning? How could a fire have gotten so big without her noticing?

But she knew the answer already. Peter. She was the worst kind of fool. Even in sleep, her mind had tossed with the chaos his mulishness was causing. Her resentful concern had drowned out everything else, especially instinct.

For the past two days he'd used his silence as a weapon, keeping their conversations to clipped exchanges, and then, only when absolutely necessary. He'd refused to follow the trail to Hawaii—not with his presentation only three days away. He believed that whatever damage was done twenty-one years ago could wait another few days for a resolution.

So she'd left the brass key out on the kitchen counter as a reminder of the consequences of things left undone. He'd spent all day ensconced in one of the bedrooms putting the final touches on his presentation. And she'd stalked the house and its perimeter with the skin of her neck bristling. Someone was watching them. Someone who held his breath with anticipation.

And she hadn't heeded that nagging small voice of intuition.

Peter was wrong, of course. Hadn't she told him that three days might be two too many? Now, because of his stubbornness, they were being smoked out like vermin.

On her hands and knees, she crawled along the floorboards. Where was Peter? Still upstairs where she'd left him? Or had he managed to find his way outside?

No, he wasn't outside. As much as he hated her right now, he wouldn't have left her to die.

She reached the door, touched it. Still cool. She cracked it open and the smoke from the room escaped in a whoosh into the untouched part of the house. Like a funnel cloud it smothered what oxygen was left in the room, leaving her choking and her lungs desperate. She aimed herself at the stairs.

Right now, she hated her grandfather, hated the skills he'd given her, the responsibility he'd left her. Why had he put her in that position? Protecting an enemy? Making it personal?

The smoke smarted her eyes. The acrid smell irritated her nose and pinched at her lungs until they hurt. A sense of urgency drove her on, allowing her to leave behind the early prickles of panic.

"Peter!" She ran up the stairs to the landing of the second floor. There a fresh wall of black smoke blasted her face with heat and forced her to drop and crawl on tender knees down the hall to the room Peter slept in. Red light throbbed at the end of the hall. *Close your mouth. Breathe shallow.* She lifted the neck of her T-shirt over her nose and mouth.

"Peter!" she yelled, then choked on the backwash of smoky air. How could he not have felt the heat, heard the roar or gagged on the smoke? Unless it was already too late. Unless the smoke had already stolen all of his oxygen and he was lying there asphyxiated.

With a growl, she muscled open the door to his room. Although she'd seen him go up the stairs just shy of midnight, although she'd heard the shower and flush of water as he'd gone through his bedtime routine, although the steady creaks of his pacing had acted as a lullaby, the bed was undisturbed and flat and no one was in the room. As if riding on a fast-falling roller-coaster car, her stomach fell.

The blasted presentation, of course. As if something as trivial as words on a page was worth risking his stubborn hide. He was almost done, eager to finish. If sleep hadn't come, he would have sought solace in work. Because it was easier to face graphs and charts than his own feelings.

She backed out of the room and nearly retched as a new slap of smoke filled her airway. "Peter!"

Out of the corner of her eye, something caught her attention. Swiveling her head toward the oddity, she spotted a shape at once too big and too small to be Peter. She heightened her awareness and sensed a punch of rage searching for Peter. The intruder raised an arm as if to swing a hammer.

She rose and bolted toward the room Peter used as an office, tried to warn him, but a gluey mass of phlegm lodged in her throat and all that came out was a gurgle. Arms raking his presentation materials into a box, Peter turned his head toward her.

"Fire!" He coughed. "Get out of here." Then he noticed the black shape of the intruder bearing down on them. He dropped the box and reached out for her as if to keep her out of harm's way.

"No!" The croak ripped through her throat as he blocked access to the advancing black mass.

Relax, float the bones, concentrate. She pressed her focused energy into her skeleton and directed it outward.

With one fluid motion, she pushed Peter out of the way and deflected the object thrown by the attacking shape.

Peter crashed against the wall, but managed to keep himself upright. The palm-size container of thin glass shattered inches from his head with eerie crackling pings. Steam rose from the wallpaper, snaking out in Medusa-like wisps that folded into the thickening smoke. Acid. Why bother when the fire would have eaten all of Peter's flesh anyway?

With a roar that would rival a rabid ogre, the shape plowed toward her. His footsteps shook the floor beneath them and rippled through her bare soles. She couldn't let him reach his intended target. *Relax. Focus.*

In a split second, she jerked her hands up to her chest to gather energy. Leaning back, she thrust her leg out into the advancing black blob's stomach, exploding the gathered force. The arrow of loosed power drove him back as if he'd run into a battering ram. Unbalanced, the shape backpedaled, windmilled its arms, then fell backward into the void that was the stairs.

The thumps of flesh against wood, the crack of bone and the scared cat screams betrayed his human incarnation.

Fire lapped greedily at the walls. Chunks of burning wood dropped from the ceiling onto the first floor.

"Get out!" Peter croaked in her ear.

Their attacker deserved to burn in hell. But he was still alive. No matter how much she wanted to, she couldn't leave a live man to burn. "There's a fire ladder in each of the bedrooms," she rasped. "Use it."

"What about you?"

"I can't leave him."

After a heartbeat of silence, Peter nodded, but instead of obeying her order, he followed her down the stairs.

Her throat was raw and tasted like blood. Her nose was so filled with smoke that she couldn't breathe through the swollen tissues. The cant of the man at the bottom of the stairs reminded her of the rag doll on the dresser the night her mother had died. Peter grabbed the man's shoulders; Adria his feet. They bumped and coughed their way down the hallway and out the front door. As soon as they'd reached a safe distance, Peter let go of the man and turned back toward the house.

She dropped the man's feet and chased after Peter. "Where are you going?"

He was gulping in air as if it was a rare supply that would soon shut off. "Presentation."

Lungs hurting, she held him back and sputtered out a caution. "It's not worth your life."

Gasping in air, he broke free. "Then he wins."

"No!"

The sleeve of his T-shirt ripped under her fist, unbalancing her. Lungs still trying to suck in fresh air, she staggered after him and had barely reached the door when he came out again, carrying his box of materials.

"You're a protector's worst nightmare," she said between coughs.

She couldn't assume the man in the sand was the one who'd lit the fuse. They were on dead ground, perfect targets, and needed to get some protection around them. Whoever had set this fire would stick around to see it. "Stay alert. We're sitting ducks out in the open like this."

"What about him?" Peter's chin jerked toward the gasping black shape on the ground.

"He's hurt. We need to call for help." The fire's teeth gnashed at the house like a giant beast on a feeding frenzy. The push of Sound lapped at the sand, too far to do any good. Nothing would save the house. But the man was still alive.

Moving with cautious haste, she and Peter carried the man away from the open beach to the side of the house where the borrowed Lexus stood, alee of the wind. The pulse of heat still belted them.

Peter raced back for his box, then stuffed it in the trunk. She reached for the twelve-pack of bottled water that was there, handed Peter a bottle and gulped down a full sixteen ounces. It tasted like soot and burned going down, but was also a balm to the raw flesh. Sweat sheathed her, gluing hair to scalp and clothes to skin. She opened the driver's door, grabbed the cell phone plugged into the console and handed it to Peter. "Call an ambulance."

A hum of tension drummed along her nerves. Armed with a bottle of water and the first-aid kit stowed in the trunk, she made her way back to the man lying in the sand.

Leaning forward, hands braced against her knees, she looked down at the mound of man who only minutes ago had sought to obliterate her and Peter. The man's lungs had suffered as much as theirs and each breath wheezed through thickened trachea and bronchi.

Peter came up behind her. "Ambulance and fire are on their way."

Moonlight spilled its light on the shape at their feet.

It gleamed on the slickness of wet blood pouring from his scalp and seemed to glow on the flecks of white skin showing from beneath the soot smears. Adria crouched and ran her hands over their attacker's body, searching for both concealed weapons and the state of his injuries. His face contorted with pain and he bellowed like a dying walrus. In the blur of movement, the features came together.

Her breath logjammed in her throat, then came with machine-gun bursts. Anxiety gnawed at her skin. A sickening feeling wormed its way through her gut. Slowly she turned toward Peter, holding her breath even though her lungs were still desperate for air.

Cheeks striped with soot, Peter stood there like an ancient warrior. His face was stone, his exterior chillingly calm. Then an eerie sound, a cross between a rip of pain and a bite of rage escaped him. "Russell."

Russell sputtered and wheezed, floundering like a small whale out of water. Holding his right arm with his left, he howled like a tortured dog.

Adria stood like a wall between the brothers. Peter's calm was a poor mask that could barely contain the ripeness of his anger. She didn't want him lashing out, then torturing himself with regret. "Take the car and go open the gate for the emergency crews."

She gave him the code, tossed him the keys and turned away, giving him no chance to argue.

"You are one sorry bastard," Adria said as she knelt beside Russell and assessed his condition. Soot lined his nose and mouth. His chubby cheeks were swollen. Heavy-lidded eyes hung at half-mast, as if lifting them up all the way was too arduous a task. The air straining through his fully opened mouth sounded like a prank heavy breather. His right arm puffed out the elastic cuff of his black windbreaker. He reminded her of a circus clown who didn't know he wasn't funny. "How did you get here, Russell? How did you know where to find us?"

"The professor." Russell coughed, rounding into himself like a fat lawn grub, then collapsing again. "He told—" Another spasm of cough jerked through his body.

Caleb had talked to Russell? How had they even known the other existed? "Why did you set fire to the house? Don't you realize you could have killed your brother?"

The scuffing thunder of Peter's footsteps announced his return. He dropped to his knees beside his brother, wrapped his fists around Russell's black windbreaker and pried him off the ground until they were nose to nose. "Answer her question. Why do you want me dead? Didn't I help you out of all your scrapes? Didn't I give you everything you needed?"

Russell reached for Peter's shoulder with his left hand and hung on to it with what looked like desperation. "I'm sorry. So sorry."

"Answer the damned question!"

"I tried to stop it." Russell's voice was three-packs-a-day smoker hoarse. "I tried—"

"You tried to kill me."

"No." Russell coughed again as if the words were too big and hung on thorns in his throat. "I wanted…I wanted …" Russell shook his head. "To show you. Then maybe…"

Tears streamed from Russell's eyes, causing crooked rivulets on his soot-smeared face. Fresh blood flowed from the wound at the back of his head. And for the first time, Adria noticed the burned flesh blistering down his neck.

"Maybe what?" Peter ground out between clenched teeth.

"I wasn't good enough. I wasn't perfect enough." His words were choppy, his breathing shallow and rapid. "So, in your eyes, I just wasn't."

"That's not true and you know it."

Russell's eyes looked wild with their red-veined whites. "Know it? How could I know anything when you shut me out."

"I gave you the run of the foundation."

"You don't listen." His voice spasmed. "You never listen."

"For that you tried to destroy my company and kill me?"

"No!" The shout was nothing more than a whisper. "I knew the letter bomb wouldn't hurt you. It was just supposed to wake you up and give me a chance."

Peter's lips compressed into a bloodless line. "And when I gave you the chance you wanted, you went behind my back and betrayed me."

"Peter," Adria said, willing the ambulance to hurry and bring this macabre theater of brotherly rivalry to an end. "Take it easy. His condition is deteriorating."

Peter let go of his brother as if he were ridding himself of slime.

Adria lowered Russell back to the ground. She lifted Russell's head and pressed gauze against the bleeding wound. "Stay calm. Help is on its way."

"It wasn't like that, Pete." Russell ignored her. Wincing, he grasped Peter's forearm and held on as if, if he let go, the big brother he so wanted to impress would disappear forever. "I could've made something. I just needed the chance to prove it."

"You tried to poison me."

Russell shook his head. "Bad cheese. Julie said so."

"Julie?" Adria asked. Foreboding crackled as loud as the fire. Had Julie involved Russell as well as Caleb in her scheme? "How do you know Julie?"

"She was looking for you." Russell's breathing sounded like a watery gurgle. He turned his red, swollen face back to Peter. "I swear, Pete, I didn't try to kill you."

"You set fire to the house."

"Mistake." He coughed and black mucus spotted his lips. "Too late."

"You threw acid in my face."

Russell's face wrenched with pain. "You think I'm like him, so for a minute, I was him. Pete, please, you have to believe me. I missed on purpose. I'm not him. I wanted to scare you. I was going to save you."

Their father's violence had become a knife used to cut the last tie between them. The realization seemed to hit Russell with a punch. Spirit and body both caved.

"Dizzy." Russell's grip loosened. "Feel strange." His breathing rattled and raled. His face was turning blue. "Pete," he whispered, "please, you've gotta believe…"

Russell passed out, becoming limp in Adria's arms.

The screams of the ambulance and fire truck sirens managed to cut through the roar of feasting flames and the pounding of the surf. The firemen did a surround-and-drown drill, arcing water from hoses through any opening they could find, but the building was beyond their help. Two EMTs worked on Russell and attached an oxygen mask to his face.

Peter stood aside, a block of ice. Yet Adria had the impression he would pounce on the EMT if he thought anyone was causing his brother harm. As paramedics stuffed the gurney onto the ambulance, Russell reached out for Peter with feeble fingers and failed to hold on to the slickness of Peter's sweaty skin. His eyes were downcast, filled with sorrow. "Pete…"

Peter turned his back on his brother and barked at the EMT. "Where are you taking him?"

More gently, Adria added, "We'll follow in the car."

The EMT addressed her. "To Backus in Norwich. He's got burns and it's a Level II trauma center."

Peter stalked to the car. Once seated, his gaze centered on the back end of the ambulance. He couldn't let go of the past any more than it could let go of him.

At the car door, Adria hesitated. Over the water, smoke tatted a hazy veil over the far away purple of night, the glitter of stars and the gleam of a fat moon.

The structure that was once a home was nothing more than a pyre. The marsh glowed like an orange sunset. Heat waves distorted everything, giving the scene a surreal feel. By daylight, nothing would remain but a tattered frame and bed of coals.

The phantom girls with their laughter so free no longer danced in the haze. Her grandfather's face no longer smiled on the porch. Her mother's quilt, the books of dragons to conquer her fears, the albums of photographs that helped her remember her mother and father were all gone.

Loss caught her in the center of the chest, knocking the wind out of her. *Don't think. Don't feel.* But of course, she couldn't stop the beating of her heart or its all-encompassing peal of desolation. All she had left of her grandfather now were memories.

Something jacked her gaze up past the blazing remnants of her home toward the marsh. The piercing drill
of unseen eyes bored into her. In the mirage of pulsing
heat and smoke haze she thought she saw movement.
A man standing like a pirate surveying a prize, his
head thrown back laughing. Along with the crackle of
fire, the breeze seemed to carry shreds of that laugh and
scraped down her spine.

She shook her head and the illusion was gone. Probably just a firefighter.

The one thing she knew for sure was that this
wasn't over.

The Face loved fires. The cleansing power of it. The
fierce hunger of it. That first time, when a match had
fallen on the mattress, had been an accident. The others were reminders of power at the fingertips—just
like Father's. Practice, really, for when results counted.

When the guard and the Dragon had gone out to re-
plenish supplies earlier that day, The Face had used the
codes the professor had so kindly shared to enter the
house. Setting up the fire triangle of heat, fuel and oxygen had taken a bit of imagination. Against the screen
of closed eyes, the map of the flames' course appeared.
Vivid imagination showed the fingering of accelerant
catch. The slow burn under the bed that would smoke
the guard, turn her cyanotic and steal her breath before
she could wake. Patting the smoke alarms' pilfered
back-up batteries in the pocket of the windbreaker,
The Face moaned at the pictured sweet burst of
flashover vaulting from her room to ignite the rest of
the house.

When smoke curled against the night sky, making
imagination real, when the glow of fuel betrayed its vo-

racious hunger, The Face sniffed in the cold air and, on the taint of smoke, could imagine the crisp aroma of burning flesh. Nothing could get in its way—not even the idiot in there pretending he was a lion when really he was nothing more than a chicken.

Turning over the brass key in the pocket gave a moment of pleasure as the picturesque tableau so carefully painted came fully to life. The creation was as beautiful as any of the art postcards Mother had collected in a photo box.

The Face had the key—the treasure needed for these past five years. The thought of going home, of using that key, of finally proving lost heritage, was enough to make the heart pound.

Figures, shadow puppets in the firelight, staggered out of the house. *No, you're supposed to die!* A burst of anger exploded. Then the brass teeth of the key bit into the soft flesh of palm—a reminder of success already won.

Somehow they'd managed to get out. Guard and Dragon worked furiously on the chicken's carcass. Not that it mattered. The Face understood what fed her just as well as how to feed a fire. And just as the flames were turning her childhood home into a memory, The Face would make sure that guilt at her principal's death would eat at her soul.

She would never again rest in peace.

One down and dying. One to go. Peter would look into The Face's eyes when he died and he would know who truly was the father's child.

Chapter 17

At the hospital in Norwich, a technician X-rayed Russell's chest and arm. His head went through an MRI. A nurse drew blood that was counted and analyzed for pH changes, renal function, oxygen shortage and various other things Adria couldn't remember. He had a bronchoscopy. A team of nurses tended to his head laceration, his burns and his broken ulna. On the upside, he didn't have carbon monoxide poisoning. On the downside, his head injury was more serious than first suspected. The skull had cracked and his brain was swelling. The doctors were keeping him in a drug-induced coma in an effort to help the injury heal.

She'd answered questions by both police and fire personnel about the arson that had leveled her home. But her statements didn't answer the series of questions parading in her mind. How had Russell gotten into the house? How had he gotten the codes? From Caleb?

How had she missed the fact that the smoke detectors had been tampered with during her daily reconnaissance?

She'd insisted that a doctor check Peter's condition. Naturally, he balked. He complied only when she agreed to also submit to an exam. A nurse bandaged her feet. Her throat was sore and her eyes still prickly, but otherwise, she was fine. A dull ache throbbed all through her body. Nothing a good night's sleep wouldn't cure. Of course, that wasn't apt to happen anytime soon. Was there really someone out there in the night, watching her grandfather's house burn? Her heart hitched and she knuckled her sternum. That house represented her happiest years and someone had taken it from her. Caleb? Julie? Victor? Ruben? She wanted answers.

An orderly had loaned them scrubs until they could purchase a new set of clothes. His were green. Hers were purple. *That's it. Think of facts. Don't let emotions seep through now.* The urge to move Peter to a safer location ticked inside her like a bomb. But another move was easier said than done; she'd exhausted all of her resources. She didn't want to involve anyone new for fear she would lead them into harm.

Tiredness was making her brain foggy. As much as she hated doing it, she fed coins into a vending machine and got two cups of coffee. The caffeine would keep her going—for a while anyway.

Back in Russell's room, she handed a cup of coffee to Peter, who mumbled his thanks.

"He'll be all right," she said, watching as Peter paced the private room like a restless dragon that was left with no prey but had a deep hunger to sate.

"I hope he dies." Guilt and shame wove like twin

serpents in his eye, poisoning his clear vision. A man, even a good man—maybe especially a good man—was allowed a few destructive thoughts. He would come around. His character wouldn't let him do otherwise.

A small smile touched her lips. "That's why you asked for the best pulmonologist, neurologist and burn specialist around."

"He tried to kill me!" He slammed the disposable cup of coffee onto the window ledge, then raked both hands through his hair and held on to his nape as if somehow that would consolidate his warring thoughts. "He threw acid at my face."

And for some reason that seemed to hurt him more than the fact he was almost burned alive. At the window, gray sky framed his body, accentuating the shadows under his eyes.

"Did you know that ruining a face with acid was one of my father's favorite pranks?" In his voice, she heard a man haunted.

She shook her head.

"I can still hear his laughter echoing through the house. He thought it was funny, making people look like creatures that belong in a museum of horrors." Peter drew in a ragged breath. His face became all sharp edges.

With one step, he ate the ground separating him from the small television set in the corner. He flicked on the remote to turn it on and pretended rapt attention at the news, effectively tuning out all other conversation.

A few minutes later, still staring at the screen he said, "I'm taking him home."

"No." The coffee went down crooked.

"It's over, Adria." He shook his head. "I thought

knowing the answer would feel different, but it's just more of the same."

"There's still someone out—"

"Russell confessed. He was behind this. Not some unknown brother, not Terry Atwell, not the People for Resource Parity, not Mystic Pleasure Crafts. Russell. The only way I can fight the past is by doing what I've been doing for the past twenty years. Standing my ground."

"You can stand your ground after we find out who Russell was working with. He breached the house's security. He had to have known the codes. But Russell can't talk right now. He can't tell us who else is involved."

"You don't get it, do you?"

"I get that you're still in danger and going home right now is not the wisest choice."

"Nothing I do will make a difference." He glanced at Russell and the octopus of tubes that attached him to the machines monitoring his condition. "I can't escape my DNA. Violence is encoded there. My grandfather. My father. My brother. Me. I fight it every day."

"And you win."

"Only because I refuse to act like a raging bull shoving his weight around."

His gaze sought Russell and sadness seemed to climb on his shoulders and weigh him down. "Look at him. He couldn't get what he wanted so he tried to take it by force. It nearly killed him. My grandfather was murdered. My father was murdered." His gaze connected with hers and the gleaming light in his eyes frightened her. "You die the way you live."

"They took and it was taken from them."

He nodded. The unspoken *I give* hung between them.

"Someone still wants what you have, Peter. And that someone is willing to kill you for it. You have two hundred people coming to hear your wisdom on Saturday. Keep fighting for them."

But he was deep in his own soup of guilt and didn't hear her. "It's my fault. I didn't hear him. After…" His Adam's apple bobbed in his throat. "After our father died, Russell got in a lot of trouble. He wanted the attention he'd gotten from our father. But I couldn't give it to him. I was too focused on getting away." His body straightened, but the burden was still there in the strained lines of his face. "It's time to go home."

"Peter—"

"My seminar is in two days. I'm going home." He strode out of the room.

He was too grief-stricken over Russell's betrayal to think clearly. His stubbornness left her no choice. Reluctantly, she followed him out into the hall. If they were going to head back into a kill zone, she had to be prepared. She wouldn't let any evil touch him.

Caleb Stuart had died of a heart attack in his home a few days ago, Daphne had informed Adria the next day after she and Peter had returned to the house in Darien.

After hearing Norm howl, a neighbor found Caleb at the bottom of the stairs, a letter to Russell clamped in his hand. According to Daphne, the letter spelled out the plan to burn the cottage and free Russell from his tyrannical big brother. For his part in the scheme, Caleb would receive a foundation grant to finish his study of the sociology of ancient arts of defense.

Peter had taken this as more evidence that the threat to him was gone and fueled his drive to go on with his plans. Despite the shock, a small voice in Adria's solar plexus insisted that all was not well. Julie was still out there. So was Ruben Puluke, the brother with more than enough motivation to want Peter dead.

"Caleb, how could you?" Adria shook her head as she dumped coffee grounds into a filter. How could he have used her grandfather? How could he have used her? His involvement in this scheme made no sense. Not that it mattered. He was dead. Maybe Peter was right. Maybe you did die the way you lived. That didn't make for a promising outcome to the situation.

Still that nagging voice inside her insisted that Caleb wouldn't have written a letter. Why would he write his plans down on paper when he could have picked up the phone more easily and more anonymously? This stank of a setup. But who? Russell was still in the hospital in Norwich. Julie? Ruben? Victor? The mysterious Mr. Poole? But Julie wasn't strong enough to kill a man, was she? No one knew for sure if Ruben was alive or exterminated by his own father years ago. Henry Poole was probably nothing more than an alias. And where was Victor?

Swallowing a growl, she flipped the switch to the coffeemaker and leaned against the counter. Coffee dripped into a pot like a Chinese water torture, brewing a fresh batch of caffeine to help keep her awake. The television at the corner of the breakfast bar was on to break the depth of the silence brooding over the dark house. Waiting for the pot to fill, she watched the eleven o'clock news with half her attention.

Romy's report had shown little progress on deciphering Henry Poole and Hank Waters's identities. The aliases showed nothing going further back than five years. And their ties to People for Resource Parity were probably nothing more than a smoke screen. She was still hunting for connections.

Terry Atwell and Peter's secretary were finishing up their vacation in Mexico. The authorities would be waiting for the Atwells upon their return to the U.S., ready to question Terry about his embezzlement of Dragon, Inc. funds.

Adria was pouring a cup when something on the television caught her attention. She turned to the set and a marina filled the screen. With a flick of the wrist, she turned up the volume.

"Hank Waters, representing Mystic Pleasure Crafts, announced that a suit was filed today against the Dragon Foundation for breach of contract...."

Everything led back to the foundation and its funding. Was Ruben bent on amassing the fortune he'd felt cheated out of? If so, they were after the same objective.

A mind switch clicked on. The foundation. Its funding. Where did the funding come from? She'd focused her revenge on Peter's company, but what if that was truly his own?

They are yin and yang, fated to aid each other, to create positive energy out of negative intent.

What if Peter had done exactly that with her grandfather's guidance?

She raced up the stairs and entered Peter's office without knocking. "Peter?"

He was bent over his work. "I'm busy."

"The money you inherited from your father—what did you do with it?"

Frowning, he tapped at keys of his computer as if she were a mosquito he was trying to ignore. "I set up the Dragon Foundation."

"Why?"

"So that good could come out of bad."

He'd known. On a soul level, he'd known he couldn't taint his own vision with his father's blood money. A warm glow radiated inside her. *He was worthy, Grandpa.*

"Why the question?" Peter's chair creaked as he turned to face her.

"Where did you get the idea for a foundation?"

He tented his hands over his lap. "A business advisor."

"Do you remember his name?"

"Where is this going?"

"Curiosity."

"Glenn Parr. Why?"

Uncle Glenn. Not a real uncle, of course, but a trusted friend of her grandfather's. They'd learned their craft together and often traded favors. He was the one who'd taught her to fly and skydive.

Her grandfather had guided Peter through intermediaries like Uncle Glenn. Spreading warmth melted some of the tension straining her muscles. Grandpa had seen that his daughter's death would yield to good. "Get some sleep. You want to be fresh for your presentation in the morning."

"Glenn has nothing to do with Russell's betrayal."

"I know."

"I haven't heard from him in over a decade." Then a thought seemed to jolt through his body. "You know Glenn."

"An associate of my grandfather's."

"How many did he send my way over the years?"

"Enough to guide you. Enough to keep you safe."

He grumbled an answer and swiveled his chair back to his computer.

If Ruben Puluke or Julie or whoever else was caught in this viper's nest of greed got their hands on foundation money, they'd use it for personal gain rather than the positive use her grandfather and Peter intended.

She wouldn't let that happen. She wouldn't let anyone use the money for ill. Her grandfather had sacrificed too much to see good come out of evil.

The situation had to end.

She scratched at her arms, willing the creep of unease to leave. It would end. One way or another, it would all end tomorrow.

Adria felt almost impotent to protect Peter. Even with Daphne's security-controlled entrance into the seminar room, Romy's electronic surveillance and the assistance of hotel security, how could she track every single person in the audience and still appear as nothing more than a bystander?

Under ideal circumstances, she would have a whole team of security personnel on duty, both armed and unarmed. But her team was mowed down one by one. Sam was released from the hospital, but her arm still gave her a world of pain. The twins had recovered from their food poisoning, but both were still weakened from their ordeal.

Peter was convinced the threat was gone and saw no reason to turn his presentation into a circus. "Russell is in a hospital room in a coma. Caleb is dead. Your Julie can't carry on the plot by herself. Everyone will be safe."

He buried himself in last-minute preparations, doing his best to avoid her.

The seminar was slated to start at nine and would go on until four with a one-hour break for lunch, provided by the hotel in the room next to the presentation hall. She and Peter had arrived at the hotel at five that morning. He'd gone on to set up his seminar materials with the help of the conference coordinator and her staff.

Adria had checked the site, set up a command post from where Romy monitored the electronic equipment Daphne had installed. Daphne had set up a magneto-meter at all three entry points of the room in which Peter would speak. The metal detectors should catch any concealed weapons. She'd arranged seating so that there would be a gap between the speaker platform and the audience. Peter had the cordon taken down, saying it distanced him from the people he was trying to get close to. So much for the psychological barrier that would give his protectors half a chance to react to an attack.

Naturally, Peter wanted no one else on stage with him, making him a bull's-eye target for anyone with vengeful intent.

Adria shivered again as a sense of evil pried its cold fingers between her shoulder blades.

He was there. He couldn't miss such a public retri-bution. She scanned the room. *Where are you, Ruben? Show yourself!*

Relax, she reminded herself when her tense muscles caused a crick in her neck. Flexibility was the key. *You'll find him.* Heightening her senses, she continued her reconnaissance.

By seven o'clock, a beehive of hotel staff worked in and around the room. Time for one last perimeter walk, then she'd have to concentrate on the seminar hall and the arriving guests.

Moving as naturally as possible, she assessed her

surroundings, all the while alert to everything and everyone. The hair on the back of her neck twitched like antennae—her protective instinct revved into high gear. Every detail around her appeared in sharp focus.

She'd studied the hotel plans and mapped out her reconnaissance path. Not only did she have to worry about personal attacks that could include anything from firearms to bombs, even if the crowd was friendly she had to protect Peter against being trapped or trampled by his fans. In that unstable condition before and after his presentation, someone with ill intent could find an opportunity to aim and kill.

Every event so far had a personal focus. This attack, when it came, would happen close in. He needed to see Peter die.

Keeping in mind that evasion always came before confrontation, she studied escape routes. There were too many security hazards in the hotel. The big birdbath of a flower arrangement in the middle of the lobby, the cushy sofas scattered here and there for possible networking conversations, the decorative knickknacks meant to lend an air of hominess to a big impersonal space, all presented a determined murderer with places to create mayhem. Then there was the balcony one floor up that gave a clear view of the entrance and a possible angle of attack. Each step she took seemed to make a new hiding spot pop up. The minutes were ticking by with winter molasses slowness. She punched the stairwell door open.

She gave the basement room below where Peter would present his seminar particular care. With a long, slow look, she scanned the entire room, observing its layout, listening for any sounds out of place. It was a repository for chairs with red-cushioned seats and stages. Two platforms were piled against the wall. One was folded in half and sitting on a dolly. Another was set up as if someone would give a presentation to the dust and cobwebs at any minute. She did a waist-to-floor inspection, then a waist-to-ceiling one, using a chair to see every inch of space. She looked behind fixtures, gaudy reproductions of oil paintings and ornate sconces. She checked the red carpet for unseemly bumps and the folds of gold curtains.

She approached the set stage with caution. Her intuition buzzed as she examined the raised rectangle from all sides before pulling away the black pleated skirt that hid the metal legs.

A box sat beneath the plywood covered with red carpet. The label on the box belonged to the printer that had delivered the photocopied handouts for Peter's presentation. Except that this box was stained with greasy marks on the sides.

Then she heard it, the muffled tick-tick like a clock.

She reached for the radio at her belt. "Romy, come in."

"What's up, princess?"

"Alert hotel security and have them evacuate the hotel. Call the police and have them send the bomb squad. There's a possible bomb in the storage area beneath the room where Peter is doing his presentation."

"I'm right on it."

"I'll be waiting here for the police. Get Daphne to cover Peter."

"Roger."

The bomb squad and its explosive ordnance disposal personnel arrived within fifteen minutes. She pointed out the device to them and was then told to evacuate. They would handle it from there. She was more than glad to let them defuse the bomb.

She went in search of Peter and found him across the street in the lobby of the Dragon, Inc. building along with his growing crowd of seminar guests. Daphne, with her long strawberry-blond hair, stood on one side and Romy, with her spiked brown hair, on the other, protecting him in her stead. On the positive side, each guest had to go through the near-invisible gauntlet of security Daphne had set up at Dragon, Inc., and Dragon, Inc. security officers were on duty monitoring the equipment. She scanned the lobby for someone who didn't belong.

When Peter saw her striding toward him, he met her halfway. "What's going on?"

"Someone planted a bomb in the room below where you were going to present your seminar. The bomb squad is there now, defusing it." *Still think no one's after you, Peter?*

His face blanched and his jaw flinched, but he kept his voice as calm as if she'd announced a rain delay instead of a possible plot to end his life. "Caleb's dead and Russell's in the hospital. Couldn't they have planted the bomb a few days ago?"

"I'm not willing to bet your life on it."

His gaze swept across the street to the hotel. "How long will it take?"

"As long as it takes. They're not going to allow anyone in there until it's safe."

He glanced at the growing crowd milling like picnic ants behind him. "My guests have already started arriving."

"Cancel your seminar and reschedule for another day."

"I can't. If I do, he wins."

"And if you're dead, he still wins."

His jaw worked in tight circles that seemed to match the grinding of gears in his mind. "Okay, then we'll hold the seminar, here, in the conference room on the tenth floor. It's a tight squeeze, but the crowd falls within the fire department code."

"No, Peter. We haven't had the chance to secure the building."

"Whoever set the bomb won't expect the move, so we'll be safe even if there is someone else to worry about. Daphne's installed a top-of-the-line security system. She monitors that thing like it's an expectant mother." He wrested a rough smile. "For once, the good guy wins."

Before she could elaborate on all the reasons why this was all wrong, he nabbed the conference coordinator. Within minutes the coordinator's mink-sleek French braid flew from side to side as she barked out orders. Peter disappeared up the elevator to set his plan in motion, leaving her to play catch-up.

Daphne and Romy performed like the aces they were, directing the flow of security and making the process as painless as possible.

The seminar started half an hour late, but somehow everyone had a seat, a pad of paper and a pen. The coordinator would shuttle the handout booklets to the Dragon, Inc. building once the hotel was cleared. The hotel manager, with his slicked hair and proper penguin suit, agreed to let them know when the lunch was ready and the guests would simply walk across the street. The news did nothing to calm her nerves.

The oily sensation of something wrong still nagged at her, even though she, Daphne and Romy had cleared the building. The entrances to the building were all locked. No one could come in without Romy noticing.

Adria studied every face and set of hands in the room. Less than an hour to go before the lunch break. Daphne sat in the first row, right in front of Peter, ready to spring to his aid.

Adria scanned the room again, letting her intuitive antenna seek out the thread of evil. *Where are you?*

Every person in the room seemed captivated by Peter, hanging on to his every word as if it were gold. She had to admit, he was a changed man. Definitely a gentle eastern dragon in this mode. When he spoke, he glowed—there was no other word for it. Why couldn't he let this side of him shine through all the time?

Seeing him like this brought back the night they'd spent together and ignited a soul-deep longing.

Keep your attention on the job, Adria. He's here. You know he's here. Find him. If she were a crazed brother bent on revenge, and if there were a last-minute change of plan, what would she do?

"Miss?" The conference coordinator was frowning at her. "Excuse me. There's a phone call for you."

"Take a message. I'll call back later."

"It's the hotel manager. His staff can't get in the building with the box lunches."

"No, the guests are going to the hotel."

"We thought this would be easier for you, security-wise."

That Peter had thought to make her job easier caught her by surprise. She sighed. "Okay, tell him I'll meet him down there in five minutes."

As she stepped off the elevator and into the lobby, something hit the back of her skull and everything went black.

* * *

When a hard hand slapped her face, she woke up with a start. The shadowy darkness made her think she'd gone blind. Her body was precariously perched on a rubber-threaded utility stool. A gag stretched her mouth tight. Her ankles throbbed against their rope bindings. Her wrists stung from the cut of rope that tied them behind her back to the pipes on the janitor's sink.

"Don't worry. I'm not going to kill you. Not now anyway."

The face looking down at her was the last she had expected.

"You can't stop me now." His smile spread like a leak. "How will you deal with the guilt, Adria?"

Chapter 18

The closing of the janitor's closet door pitched the small room into total darkness. Her head pounded like a steel hammer against the cold anvil of her galloping pulse. Her feet and hands felt as if they weren't quite hers. Her stiff leg and arm muscles shook from their cramped positions. Peter. She had to get to him. She had to warn him.

She fought the bindings at her wrists and ankles, but only managed to more deeply abrade her skin. *Breathe, Adria.* Panicking wouldn't get her anywhere. She forced air through her nose and was rewarded with a nauseating mix of floor wax and disinfectant. *Think. This is a setback, but not a complete disaster. You're still alive.* And Daphne and Romy were guarding Peter. They knew the drill. He wasn't alone. Except— Her heart knocked hard once. *Except nothing.* Whatever feelings she had for him were tied with this mess.

He was depending on her and she wasn't going to let him down. Because it was her duty as his protector. That was her job. It was her promise. Nothing else.

She wouldn't let his own brother kill him. She wouldn't let scum like that win. Not after everyone he'd hurt to get what he wanted.

Who would have thought his brother had been there all along? But then, why not? Infiltrating your enemy's camp was a wise tactic. Make yourself useful. Gain his trust. Hadn't that been her own plan for Peter? And she'd thought, just as this brother did, that she was entitled to her revenge. She'd been wrong about so many things. His brother's identity was just one more. She had to get free.

First, assess.

The ropes around her wrists were hard nylon. Easy enough to rip apart with something sharp. She ran her bound wrists up and down the sink's pipe. The pipe was smooth with no burr or sharp edge. She rubbed her calves together and realized that her attacker had missed her knife. Not that it did her any good with her hands tied back behind her around a sink pipe. Using her more mobile legs, she explored the contents of the janitor closet.

Her feet knocked over a forest of brooms and mops. They clattered over and around her, clanking against the sink and floor, snapping against the top of her head, her arms and her legs. She slipped off the stool and landed hard on her rear, yanking her arms painfully in the process. Bristles, no matter how hard, weren't going to work and the cotton wigs of mop heads weren't going to serve much good, either. She managed to kick most of the mess away, then returned to her search. Her feet banged against a pail on wheels that sloshed with water.

Water, on hard nylon rope like this, could work like grease. Her first attempt at drawing the bucket closer sent it skittering away. Stretched out as much as she could, arms practically tearing out of their sockets, she edged the toe of her shoes under the wheeled cart's edge. Carefully, she drew the bucket closer. When it was as close as she could get it, she tried to curl her body around it and squeeze it toward her hands. That only sent the wheeled contraption squirting out of her hold.

Mumbling an oath against the gag, she stretched the toe of her shoes to the bucket lip once more. She cajoled the rolling pail closer. Then she lifted her bound legs and, using them as a hockey stick, shot the bucket toward her hands. It landed with a thud against her shoulders and toppled, spilling its load of water. Adria gasped as the cold, slimy water soaked her jacket and pants, but missed her hands.

She squirmed her upper body closer to the floor, hoping to catch the puddle before it spread too thin. She dipped the rope and her wrists. The open skin at her wrists burned from whatever chemical the bucket contained.

Slowly, painfully, she worked one hand free and reached for her knife. Within seconds, she was free.

Ignoring the pain at her wrists, she inched the closet door open. She blinked at the sudden shot of light spilling in. The hall was empty. Hugging the wall, she made her way to the receptionist's desk and placed a call to the police and another to Romy in the control room. Romy would get word to Daphne.

Not wanting to risk another bad surprise at the other end of the elevator and wanting to take her attacker by surprise, she used the stairs. Her shoes scuffed against the concrete. Her heartbeat seemed to echo in the stairwell. At the steel door on the tenth floor, she hesitated. Forcing her mind to relax, she placed an ear against the metal and listened. Peter's strong voice reverberated through the steel, calming her. She cracked open the door. It moved in a smooth, oiled glide. The hallway was empty. Attuned to everything around her, she made her way to the conference room where the door was ajar.

She slipped into the room and made herself part of the wall.

Peter stood at the head of the room, a trio of whiteboards behind him. Power surrounded him as he showed them how giving up the equivalent of a doughnut a day could lead to thousands of dollars of savings to invest in their dreams. The attendees' faces lit up with hope and something more: belief. Belief that they, too, could take control of their own destinies.

Daphne was where she should be—in front of Peter. Romy was probably manning the computer that monitored the crowd through electronic eyes.

Adria scoured the crowd for the face she knew was there. But he was good at blending, too. Had done it for years, laying the groundwork for revenge. And he was patient. Why he'd needed all that time was a mystery she would have to solve after she apprehended him.

Peter wound down the first half of the seminar. "We're going to take a half-hour lunch break. That'll get us back on track. Then we'll tackle building your security basket."

A roar of applause filled the room. Adria scanned the room as the crowd got to its feet and started toward the front of the room. Would he strike now when a bit of chaos was natural?

Peter's gaze found hers across the room. Pride gleamed in his eyes at his success.

She lifted her bloody wrists for him to see and mouthed, "Danger."

But the crowd pushed in around him before he could register her warning. They wanted to see him, touch him, tell him how much his advice would change their lives.

Alarm skittered down her spine as she lost sight of him in the crush. She battled forward, toward him, looking at every face, reminding herself to look at hands. People everywhere. Too many people, too tightly bunched. A solid wall of flesh and anticipation. Their voices rose in a pulsing roar. She caught a glimpse of Peter's dark head for a fraction of a second, then he was swallowed up again.

No, no, no! Stay where I can see you!

Then she saw him—the shaggy hair, the watery smile, the big lumbering body that seemed to coil into itself. Except now the turtle was out of its shell, back straight, aim true, goal straight ahead.

Her breath caught in her throat. *You're not going to get Peter. Not today. Not ever.* She moved to intercept. *You'll have to go through me, you bastard.*

Her heart slammed against her rib cage as Ruben/Ben, the mailman, reached inside his windbreaker and pulled out a revolver.

"Two o'clock!" Adria yelled. "Man with gun, twelve feet!" A surge of adrenaline numbed her hands and feet and for a second, she couldn't move. Her stomach was a fist. Then training took over and electricity rocketed along her nerves, propelling her into action.

A hush fell over the crowd, stilling them like ice sculptures. The silence, brief and utterly dense, had a terrifying pulse. Then it exploded into a fountain of screams. Daphne attempted to shield Peter. He broke free of her hold.

People rushed toward the two exit doors, knocking over chairs, bumping into each other like pinball marbles. Peter was suddenly exposed.

In slow motion Ben swept his weapon and locked it on target.

Half-sick with the presentiment of death, she dared not look at Peter now. She kept her attention firmly focused on Ben and the old Colt revolver in his hands. He was closing in on point-blank range. She stretched her gait. *Move, move, move! You can't fail. You can't let him die.*

"Adria!"

She didn't let Peter's fear-filled warning distract her from her target. Daphne's voice vaguely registered as she ordered him to stop fighting her and get down.

Ben's finger started to squeeze the trigger.

Dread grew into a weight that made her legs seem as if they were moving through wet cement. She was too far. She wouldn't get to Ben in time.

"No!" *Please, no. Not Peter.* She'd lost too much; she couldn't lose him, too.

In that instant a mob of sensations swarmed her— the fullness of her heart, the peace she'd felt in his arms, the loneliness only he could fill because of their shared past—then nothing.

Her mind grew still. Her body took over. She launched herself at the gunman. *Relax. Float the bones.* The energy loosed by her hand came into contact with Ben's wrist at the same instant the hammer hit the cartridge's primer. The bullet was on its way down the barrel before her body could tackle his to the ground. Smoke spun like gray cotton candy out of the muzzle. The concussion spanked her eardrums, filling her whole body with its noise. Ben twisted away from her. She caught his legs anyway and brought him down in a crash of chairs. The impact of bullet tearing through flesh, of someone grunting, penetrated her explosive-deafened ears.

Peter!

Out of the corner of her eyes, she saw him sag. His right hand held his left biceps. Red oozed from between his fingers. Oh, God, he was hurt.

"Get him out, Daph!"

Before she could neutralize Ben, he shoved the still-hot muzzle of his weapon against her temple.

"Up," Ben said, and dragged her by the tight knob of hair made by her chignon.

Somehow his left arm snaked around her chest, pinning her arms to her side. He squeezed at her chest like a boa. Even his strength was deceptive. She struggled for breath. Red dots danced in her vision. She reared her head back into his face to crush his nose. He swore, but didn't release her—instead he squeezed harder. Her strength ebbing, she stomped on the outside edge of his foot, but he wore steel-toed boots. She kicked his shin. That only made him laugh like someone on the south side of sane.

"There's no need for this." Peter. Her stomach sank even as her vision blackened.

"It's your choice, Peter. She can take the bullet for you or you can be a man and take it for her."

"Ben is Ruben, Peter. Get out!" Adria croaked in a thin and thready voice, unable to quite see them through her diminishing vision. "Daph, get him out of here!"

"I'm trying!"

"We can talk this through," Peter said, and his voice sounded closer.

"I tried, Peter," Ben said, squeezing harder at her chest. No air was eking through. Her lungs were burning. "I tried, but you didn't listen. I didn't even want all of it. Just my share. But even that seemed too much to ask."

She bent forward as if she were passing out. Instinctively, he followed and before he jerked her back up, she used what strength was left in her numbed hands to grab the knife strapped to her calf. Breathing in energy from the small gap he gave her, she turned the knife's blade inward and stabbed at his hands. Screaming, he released his hold. She sucked in air, clearing her vision. Then hit him with a backward kick to the stomach and a hand thrust to the face.

Peter rushed toward her. "Adria!"

Daphne tried to block his path. Ben fired the revolver. Peter stopped where he was, mouth open, expression stunned. He looked down at the red stain spreading over his white shirt, his face turned ghastly gray. He grunted as all air seemed to escape his lungs. Then he fell, splayed on his back like a corpse. Daphne covered his body with hers.

No! Adria had to get to him. Now. She had to tell him he was more than just a job. She had to tell him she understood. She had to tell him....

Blood boiling, she snapped the gun out of Ben's hand. Energy gathered in her center. She let it fly and thrust the gun's butt into Ben's face. He crumpled, going down, holding his face with both hands and crying in a thin, high voice like a schoolgirl.

"Not so tough now, are you?" Going against everything she was ever taught, she used the butt of the gun and the butt of the knife to beat at him, taking perverse pleasure in the thwacks of metal connecting against flesh, in his screams of pain, in the bloody destruction of the face that, without disguise, looked too much like Peter's. He had no right to those features. He had no right to anything that was Peter's. He was nothing like Peter. He was lower than dirt. He was—

Daphne pulled her away. "You got him, Adria. He's out. You take care of Peter. He needs you. I'll secure this scum."

Outside, below on the street, sirens wailed. "Cops are on their way," Romy announced from the door, holding back the evacuated crowd who'd now grown curious. "Ambulance, too."

Panting like a madwoman, Adria dropped to her knees beside Peter's still body. The gun and knife fell from her hands. Too much blood. Too much... *Peter, no.* She ripped his shirtsleeves and stuffed the material against the exit wound in the back of his shoulder.

Pillowing his head in her lap, she held him tight. Cold. She was cold, so cold. Her teeth chattered. She couldn't feel her fingers. "You're going to be fine."

Her voice sounded as if it were coming from a long metallic tunnel. "You hear me?"

Her vision blurred. She was all alone in the dark. "I've never lost a principal and I'm not about to start now. Not for you."

Her chest was cracking with pain. "Do you understand? Peter?"

His chest heaved, lifting up the hand she held on top of the entry wound. Then the balloon of his lungs collapsed. Helplessly, she wished it to refill. His skin took on a blue cast. "Peter! Please. Stay with me."

The spirit is the commander and the body is subordinate. It is over now, keiki. *He was worthy.*

A cry ratcheted up her throat, bleeding it raw as it exploded in a thunder of denial.

The last of the ghosts tying her to her past was gone.

Adria lost track of the hours she'd paced the hospital waiting room before a doctor told her that Peter had made it through the surgery and would live. Then she'd hounded a friend of her grandfather's on the police force until she had the answers she needed.

Watching Peter now, so pale and still, in the weak night light of the hospital room disturbed Adria to no end. The risky jobs had always before given her purpose—a barrier to climb, an obstacle to overcome, a way to transcend the constant wash of terror just beneath her skin. Protecting others had made her feel strong and secure. This case had cut too close to all that she cherished, to all that haunted her. This time, she hadn't been able to remain detached. And chaos had come of it.

The click of her knitting needles matched the speed of her thoughts, but did nothing to calm them. Pink wool wound from the bag at her feet and spooled onto her needles, becoming another blanket for Project Linus. As long as she placed her fulfillment of security outside herself, she'd always find it taken away from her. Not even the fiercest of martial arts could protect her from her own demons.

So where did that leave her?

With the whole world at your feet, keiki.

She could almost feel the warmth of her grandfather's smile, looking down on her. She missed him so much. *I could really use a little guidance, Grandpa.*

Listen to your heart. It knows all the answers.

The ache at her sternum deepened and she rubbed it with the heel of her hand. Her heart didn't seem to know its mind at all.

Her gaze drifted to Peter and the even up-and-down movement of his chest. The first bullet had grazed the fleshy part of his upper arm. The second one had collapsed a lung, yet somehow avoided damaging any other vital organ. A bandage covered his arm and another wound around his chest. Nasal prongs hissed a stream of extra oxygen into his lungs. An IV pumped him full of painkillers to allow for easier breathing. He would have to rest for the next few weeks and watch out for infections. She felt sorry for whoever would have to take care of him. A wounded dragon wouldn't make for an easy patient.

But he would live. He would continue to make good out of evil.

He no longer needed her. The thought saddened her more than she cared to admit. She stuck the knitting needles back in her bag. It was time to move on to the next adventure.

"Adria." The call of her name was nothing more than a broken whisper. His eyes were closed and, for a second, she wondered if she'd imagined his voice.

"I'm here," she said. The clutch of fatigue plagued her bones and the bruises covering her body made her feel like a punching bag without stuffing. She didn't have the strength to deal with the emotional maelstrom that Peter had become for her. She needed time alone to find herself.

Now that all Peter's ghosts were exposed, he could

finally settle for the life he'd deprived himself of, believing that nature was stronger than nurture.

His hand stretched out.

She reached through the bed rails and curled her fingers into his. "I'm sorry I…"

Peter gave a small, lung-clearing cough. "I told you before I wasn't expecting you or anyone to take a bullet for me."

"Daphne tried."

"I'm in her debt."

Adria attempted a smile, but failed. "She'll love that."

He licked his dry lips. "I still can't believe Ruben was working for me for almost five years. I never saw the resemblance."

"He made sure no one did. He used theatrical makeup and prostheses"

"Still. I should have seen it."

With the threat of an extended prison sentence, Ruben had sung his rotten little heart out. "Do you want the scoop from the cops who arrested him?"

Peter opened his eyes and turned his head toward her. "Yes."

Adria fished a small notebook from her knitting bag and turned to the notes she'd made. "He lived in California until five years ago when his mother died. That's when he found out who his father was. He felt cheated because his childhood was nothing more than a hand-to-mouth existence. That never improved much. He was trying to make it as an actor, but got nothing more than bit parts. Hardly enough to make a decent living. And there you and Russell were with all your money."

Peter coughed again, using his hurt arm to brace his torso.

"Should I call a nurse?"

He shook his head. "Go on."

"Resentment grew until Ruben had to do something about it or explode. But to get his hands on the money, he had to prove to a court that what his mother had told him was true. He got that information from Hank Waters, his lawyer who, interestingly enough, reinvented himself from Henry Poole after being disbarred. The authorities are looking into him, especially his business practices with Mystic Pleasure Crafts."

"Like attracts like."

"His mother told Ruben about her diaries, about the original birth certificate she'd hung on to even after your grandfather bribed his way to a new one. She also mentioned a letter written by your father, acknowledging Ruben as his son."

"They burned with the house."

"But he didn't know that. He thought since he had the key, he had the treasure."

Peter nodded and closed his eyes, listening as if she were reading him a bedtime story.

"Vera sent all these items to my grandfather."

Peter frowned. "Why?"

"Ruben didn't know, and I certainly don't." She'd thought of her grandfather as such an open man—at least with her. But it turned out that he shared the inner workings of his mind with no one.

"You should've heard the things Ruben called his mother," she said, wishing hers was still there with her. "She slaved as a housekeeper and seamstress to support him and, in his eyes, she was nothing more than a cockroach. I wouldn't be surprised if it turns out he killed her. He thought of her as weak and blamed her for their situation. If she'd been stronger, then he wouldn't have had to fight for what was his."

"Just like my father, he couldn't take responsibility for his actions." Peter reached for her hand again and rubbed the bandage at her wrist with his thumb, as if he were trying to erase the wound beneath. "How is Russell mixed up in all of this?"

Distracted by his touch, she concentrated on her notes. "While masquerading as Ben, it didn't take Ruben long to figure out that Russell wasn't a happy camper. They became friends and once those bonds were forged, he used the friendship to talk Russell into giving him and Hank Waters foundation funds. But you had so many checks on Russell that that venue fell through twice."

"So Ruben and Russell came up with the letter bomb."

"Right. That forced you out and gave control to Russell. Except that you still managed to foil his plans."

"And Julie—she was innocent?"

"I feel so bad about misjudging her. She was just another victim. She was dating Ruben, only he was calling himself Luke Peel." Adria hadn't trusted her own instincts when it came to her friend. The rift between them was wide and might never be repaired. The damage Ruben had caused traveled deep, but she was determined to do everything in her power to fix it. "He saw that she didn't quite fit in with the rest of Grandpa's girls and used her loneliness and her desire to be one of us to get information about our movements. She had nothing to do with the cheese, by the way. But

Ruben did get a lot of information from her without her realizing it. He even found the storage unit after one of his chats with Julie. That's where he killed Caleb. The scene at the house was staged." Adria swallowed hard. "And I sent Caleb right into his clutches."

"You couldn't know."

That didn't stop Adria from blaming herself. Caleb had loved her grandfather. He'd truly admired her grandfather's work. And he was dead because she'd doubted him.

"Where's Norm?" Peter asked.

"He's with Caleb's neighbor until they can find a home for him."

"I'll take him."

Why hadn't she thought of that solution? Norm would live out a pampered life in Peter's care. Peter would have someone to care for who adored him. They would be good for each other. "I'll make the arrangements."

"Your grandfather," Peter asked. "Did Ruben kill him?"

The threat of tears tightened her chest. She still missed him dearly. "I don't think it was intentional because once he died, the location of the documents Ruben needed was lost. He was only supposed to get sick and weak, so Ruben, disguised as a nurse could pry the location out of him. Using different stage makeup he was Victor, by the way. When my grandfather died, Ruben had to turn to me."

"The secretarial job?"

She shrugged and turned her gaze to the night-darkened window, suddenly unable to look into Peter's earnest eyes. "Indirectly. I'd thought my grandfather had asked me to avenge my parents' deaths by destroying your financial empire. The job was my way into your intimate business secrets. But almost from the beginning, it felt wrong."

He let out a rough laugh that creased his cheek. "It's the dimples. My mother always told me that they charmed women."

A reluctant smile curved her mouth. "Yeah, that's it."

Adria cleared her throat. "There's one more thing. The Colt Ruben used was your father's."

"My father's? That's impossible. It's locked in a safe in my house."

"A house that didn't have a security system until a few days ago."

He flashed her his winning dimples. "I didn't think there was anything of value to take."

"Except the one skeleton in your safe."

He attempted a laugh, but stopped short and braced his ribs. "So, what now?"

"Now you go home and rest. Get better and continue your work."

His gaze locked with hers and wouldn't let go. "What about you?"

"Me? I'm not sure."

"Another executive protection job?"

"No. I need a change. I want—" She shrugged. She didn't know what she wanted, but she wouldn't find it living out of her office between jobs.

"Your skills are a treasure, Adria."

And not using them felt a bit like betraying her grandfather who'd spent so much time teaching them to her. "Maybe I'll teach people how to protect themselves so they won't need someone like me."

Peter perked up. "That's an excellent idea. Write up a proposal and put it in for a foundation grant."

"Peter—"

"No, I'm serious. You're right. People should know these skills. They should be able to protect themselves."

The idea sank to her solar plexus and shimmered. She could teach others as her grandfather had taught her. His legacy would go on. "Think I have a chance at a grant?"

"I have an in with the boss." He tugged on her hand and brought her closer, but the bed rail separated them. "Come here."

She pulled her hand out of his. "Peter, I'm not sure this is a good idea."

"It's the best medicine going." At her hesitation, he added, "I'm figuring it out, too, Adria. I know that when I thought Ruben was going to kill you, I realized I cared for you. I know I'm not ready to let you go. I know that I don't want to put off caring anymore because I'm afraid of getting hurt. Let's take it one day at a time and see where it leads."

His aura glowed in a rainbow around his head—yellow, gold and pink, alternating with clear green and pale blue, a touch of violet. His eyes reflected his inner turmoil, but a smile burgeoned on his lips in invitation.

He'd lost a lot, too. He understood her hesitation to throw her heart on the line, but he was also ready to take a chance on something that scared him more than a million-dollar deal. Her.

The smile on her face bloomed to match his. A slow exploration of possibilities. She could deal with that.

Silently, she moved the rail out of the way and let him

draw her into the circle of his good arm. Maybe something positive could come from this situation caused by evil.

Holding her like a treasure, he drifted off to sleep. And there, beside him, with lightning crazing the night sky outside the window and the thunder of Peter's heart against her palm, she was at peace.

* * * * *

If you enjoyed what you just read,
then we've got an offer you can't resist!

Take 2 bestselling
love stories FREE!
Plus get a FREE surprise gift!

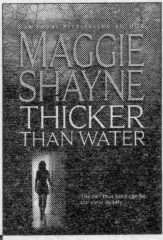

INTIMATE MOMENTS™

Explosive action,
explosive passion
from

CINDY DEES!

Charlie Squad

**No mission is too dangerous for these
modern-day warriors when lives—
and love—are on the line.**

She was his enemy's daughter. But Julia Ferrare had
called *him*—soldier Jim "Dutch" Dutcher—for help
in escaping from her father. She was beautiful,
fragile, kind...and most likely setting him up for
a con. Ten years ago, she'd stolen his family, his
memories, his heart. He'd be a fool to trust her
again. But sometimes even a hardened soldier
could be a fool...for love.

Her Secret Agent Man
by Cindy Dees

Silhouette Intimate Moments #1353

On sale March 2005!

Only from Silhouette Books!

Silhouette® BOMBSHELL™

BRINGS YOU THE THIRD POWERFUL NOVEL IN

LINDSAY McKENNA's

SERIES

Sisters of the Ark:

Driven by a dream of legendary powers, these Native American women have sworn to protect all that their people hold dear.

WILD WOMAN

by *USA TODAY* bestselling author
Lindsay McKenna

Available April 2005
Silhouette Bombshell #37

Available at your favorite retail outlet.

COMING NEXT MONTH

#33 SILENT WEAPON by Debra Webb
Her entire life changed when an infection rendered her deaf. But Merri Walters used her disability to her advantage—by becoming an expert lip reader and working for the police. Now, her special skill was needed for an extremely dangerous undercover assignment—one that put her at odds with the detective in charge…and in the sights of an enemy.

#34 PAYBACK by Harper Allen
Athena Force

Dawn O'Shaughnessy was playing a dangerous game—pretending to work for the immoral scientist who'd made her a nearly indestructible assassin, while secretly aligning herself with the Athena Force women who had vowed to take him down. But when she discovered that only the man who'd raised her to be a monster could save her from imminent death, she had to choose between the new sisters she'd come to know and trust, and payback….

#35 THE ORCHID HUNTER by Sandra K. Moore
She was more hunter than botanist, and Dr. Jessie Robards knew she could find the legendary orchid that could cure her uncle's illness—Brazil's pet vipers, jaguars, natives and bioterrorists be damned. But the Amazonian jungle, filled with passion and betrayal, was darker and more dangerous than she'd ever imagined. This time it would change her, heart and soul…*if* she made it out alive.

#36 CALCULATED RISK by Stephanie Doyle
Genius Sabrina Masters had been the CIA's favorite protégée—until betrayal ended her career. Now she'd been called back into duty—to play traitor and lure a deadly terrorist out of hiding. Only she had the brains to decode the terrorist's encrypted data, which was vital to national security. But when the agent who'd betrayed her became her handler, the mission became more complicated than even Sabrina could calculate….

SBCNM0205